Dearly DEPARTED

HY CONRAD

KENSINGTON BOOKS
http://www.kensingtonbooks.com

KENSINGTON BOOKS are published by

Kensington Publishing Corp.
119 West 40th Street
New York, NY 10018

All Kensington titles, imprints and distributed lines are available at special quantity discounts for bulk purchases for sales promotion, premiums, fund-raising, educational, or institutional use. Special book excerpts or customized printings can also be created to fit specific needs. For details, write or phone the office of the Kensington Special Sales Manager: Kensington Publishing Corp., 119 West 40th Street, New York, NY 10018 Attn. Special Sales Department.. Phone: 1-800-221-2647.

Kensington and the K logo Reg. U.S. Pat. & TM Off.

ISBN-13: 978-1-61773-684-1
ISBN-10: 1-61773-684-8
First Kensington Hardcover Edition: February 2016
First Kensington Mass Market Edition: January 2017

eISBN-13: 978-1-61773-683-4
eISBN-10: 1-61773-683-X
First Kensington Electronic Edition: February 2016

10 9 8 7 6 5 4 3 2 1

Printed in the United States of America

Praise for the Amy's Travel Mysteries

Dearly Departed

"Credible characters enhance a fast-paced plot and vivid travel descriptions."
—*Publishers Weekly*

Toured to Death

"*Toured to Death* is a deftly constructed puzzle—fast-paced, entertaining, and a mystery-lover's treat. Conrad's signature wit and talent for complex, three-dimensional characters shines through in this clever mystery within a mystery."
—John Clement, co-author of the Dixie Hemingway series

"What could go wrong on an international mystery tour where the game of murder turns deadly? How about . . . everything. Fasten your seat belts and prepare to be entertained!"
—Maddy Hunter, author of the Passport to Peril series

"An absolutely wonderful mystery, served just the way I like—with heart and humor."
—Tony Shalhoub, star of TV's *Monk*

"Fast-paced with an appealing international flair . . . Characters with plenty of flaws offer enough red herrings to keep the ending a surprise, even for seasoned mystery fans. A delightful new series."
—*Booklist*, starred review

"Smart, snappy dialog and fun, likable characters keep this series debut moving right along."
—*Library Journal*, starred review

Books by Hy Conrad

Toured to Death

Dearly Departed

Death on the Patagonian Express

Published by Kensington Publishing Corp.

To the real Evan and Barbara Corns, who bear little or no resemblance . . .

PROLOGUE

Peter Borg was pissed.
Under normal circumstances, he enjoyed visiting clients. It got him out of the office and into some phenomenal homes. It also, in the case of new clients, gave him some sense of their taste and history. For example, if he walked into a living room filled with dark, intricately carved teak, he would know (a) these people had an affinity for Southeast Asia and (b) they'd already done the Cambodia/Thailand/Vietnam circuit. Much better to push the more exotic Micronesian islands, preferably on a leased private jet.

Peter's assistant had set up this particular visit. Eleven a.m. at 142 Sutton Place. Penthouse 2. It wasn't until he was on the street, approaching the polished chrome entrance and the Burberry-clad doorman, that he even checked the name. Miss Paisley MacGregor. Otherwise known as MacGregor. Otherwise known as his ex-maid.

Peter Borg was very pissed.

MacGregor had been glowingly recommended

by Maury and Laila Steinberg. The couple had just
sold their business and were moving to Maui. They
seemed devastated by the upcoming separation from
their full-time maid, much more than by the separation from the two grown children from Laila's first
marriage. As he listened and pretended to sympa-
thize, Peter grew intrigued by the notion of employing
a maid. It was an extravagance he felt he deserved.

At first, he'd been thrilled with his decision. Mac-
Gregor was large and warm and capable, with hair
the color of lemon Jell-O and the texture of Brillo.
He'd estimated her age at around forty-five, but she
had probably looked the same since twenty and
would remain basically the same until sixty.

Every morning MacGregor had been there, a
human alarm clock who pulled back the curtains at
exactly seven, to the smell of coffee and sizzling
bacon drifting in from the kitchen. Granted, it had
been a bit odd that she was actually in his bedroom,
pulling back the curtains. Perhaps that should have
been a warning.

For a moment, Peter had thought about
canceling—texting his assistant with a few abbrevi-
ated profanities and having her phone in some
excuse. But he was already here. And MacGregor
had obviously transferred her affections onto someone else, someone with a posher address.

The thick white door opened into a startlingly
white oval foyer with bunches of ghost lilies posing
on a tabletop. Peter girded himself with a fake
smile, ready to kiss MacGregor on both cheeks and
say how happy he was to see her and how he'd been
meaning to get in touch, but wasn't that just how it
went?

Instead, he found himself staring at a middle-aged, patrician face that stared back with mild curiosity. His irritation grew. "So sorry. I don't mean to intrude. I'm here to see . . . This is awkward. I came to visit your maid. Why she asked me to come to your home . . ."

"Quite all right," the aristocratic woman replied with a Boston Brahmin accent and the hint of a smile. "Please come in." Peter was relieved by how accommodating she was, considering the situation. *Just another example,* he thought, *of how MacGregor could insinuate herself into your life.* "Can I take your coat?" she asked.

Peter refused the offer, then followed her through the all-white leather and plush living room.

"Miss MacGregor." She knocked on a bedroom door and called softly, "There's someone to see you."

It was at this point that Peter pushed aside all speculation, his mind growing numb.

MacGregor was sitting up in bed, framed in a spectacular view of the Fifty-Ninth Street Bridge. Like everything else, the bed was white and large and luxurious. The linens were smooth and crisp and served to accentuate the wrinkled head in the middle, propped up on a goose-down pillow, with wispy lemon hair framing it flatly. She had shrunken considerably since the last time he'd seen her—not aged so much as grown unmistakably ill. *Perhaps this explains it,* he thought, his mind unfreezing. Her employer had taken pity on a sick maid and was taking care . . .

"You can go, Archer," MacGregor said with a wave. The woman left the room, and Peter's mind froze again.

Paisley MacGregor's laugh was soft and affectionate. "Yes, Petey, dear. She's the maid."

"Did you win the lottery?" It was the only possibility he could think of.

"Inheritance." And, of course, that made sense. MacGregor must have had half a dozen employers during her years of service. All of them except one or two, maybe just one, must have considered her a treasured part of the family. Someone was bound to leave her something. "It came around six years ago."

"Six years?" Another brain freeze, but this one he powered his way through. "So . . . when you were working for me . . ."

"I was already rich. This place is more than I need, but I'm renting it from some friends."

"Did you have a maid when you worked as a maid?"

"Yes. And I pay her more than you paid me." She seemed to be enjoying his befuddlement. "I loved my work, Petey. I got to be part of all your fascinating lives, all your dreams, your worries."

Peter flashed back to the time he came home and found that she had taken it upon herself to rearrange the personal files in his study. Her system was actually much better than his, but that wasn't the point, as he tried to explain. Peter had never stopped to analyze exactly what was so unsettling about MacGregor. She was totally supportive of her clients, even loving. But she could also be quietly judgmental, like a nanny you were deathly afraid of disappointing.

"Why would I give up my life?" she said, following the statement with a slight shiver.

"Are you very sick?" He reached out to touch a spidery hand. He had never been completely immune to her homey charms.

"I'm dying, Petey."

"No, no," he said instinctively. "You'll get better. You should be in a hospital."

"I was in a hospital."

"I didn't know."

"All my families expect me to live forever. But I didn't ask you here to talk about my health." Her bluntness served to smooth over the awkward moment. "I need your professional services."

"You want to take one last trip?" he guessed. Peter had done deathbed trips before. They were difficult, yes, but given the right planning and the right money . . .

"No," she said with a wag of the head. "I'm much too ill. But I used to dust so many photographs on mantels and piano tops. Families posing by the pyramids or on the Great Wall. I would look at them for hours, imagining myself there, instead of staying home alone, feeding their goldfish and walking their dogs." Her eyes strayed to another part of the room, and Peter's eyes followed.

"A Steinway grand?" he blurted out. "In your bedroom?" Yes, there it was, by the flowing white gauze of the balcony curtains. A concert grand, barely taking up a corner of the room. Every inch of the lacquered white top was covered in framed photographs—wealthy, happy travelers, all shiny and neat and smiling directly into the lens.

"I had to special order it," MacGregor explained. "I don't play. But I like the way they look on a white piano."

Peter's mind went from one improbability to the next. "And people gave you their travel photos?" he deduced. "Why would they give—"

"I asked them. They were all tickled by the idea,

made special prints, threw in expensive frames. Except you, Petey. Yours I had to borrow and make a copy. Actually, Archer made a copy. Isn't it lovely to be able to indulge in a little staff?"

Peter crossed to the Steinway and quickly found it, a small print in a silver frame, near the back. He had the original sitting on his own secondhand spinet. It had been taken in Belize, on a jungle-side beach, with Amy Abel nestled in the crook of his arm, her face framed by her signature eyeglasses. His eyes were half shut and his face was peeling red, but Amy looked great.

His face remained expressionless as he returned to Paisley MacGregor's bedside. He had been tempted to react to this new invasion of privacy but didn't want to give her the satisfaction. Besides, she was dying. "How can I help?"

"It's all written out," said the ex-maid, her voice a little cottony.

Peter handed her the glass of water from the nightstand. *Baccarat crystal.*

"Thank you." She handed back the glass. "I want to be cremated. And I want the ashes to be strewn around the world."

"Literally?" Peter was already envisioning some kind of NASA mission or perhaps a high-altitude jet releasing several pounds of MacGregor powder into the stratosphere of an unsuspecting earth.

"Yes, literally," MacGregor answered. "I want all my families to fly around the world and to hold these little wakes along the way. I want them to dance and drink and tell stories and spread little bits of me around. Take loads of pictures. Then fly off to the next. All first class and all on me. All the spots I've dreamed of but will never go to—until then, of course. Then I'll be there forever. Isn't that nice?"

"Oh," said Peter, relieved, and then it hit him. "Oh!" Maybe it wasn't as bad as a NASA trip, but it still had the makings of a logistical nightmare. "Will they all want to do this? It'll take a week or two."

"There aren't that many. And yes, they'll want to." A practiced, slightly hurt expression wrinkled her eyes and mouth. "You want to, don't you, dear? A last tribute to your old MacGregor?"

"Of course." Hey, it was a job, probably with an unlimited budget. "But let's hope that's years away."

Ten minutes later, Peter was walking back out through the white marble foyer, with the contact information for the lawyers and bankers and ex-employers. *Would they really do this?* he wondered. *Circle the globe with the ashes of their maid?* And then there was the matter of transporting human remains through half a dozen countries—some with tight security and drug-sniffing dogs, some with unstable governments.

"What did you think of him?" Paisley MacGregor asked her own maid after the thick white door had closed and they were alone. The interview had taken a lot out of her. She was just a few nods away from a nap, but she wanted Archer's opinion.

"He's pretty much how you described him." Over the years, Archer had found that this was always a safe response.

"Yes." MacGregor chuckled, and her eyes wandered over toward the grand piano. She'd had the building's handyman and his brother move it in here from the living room just so she could lie in bed and look at the photos. Even from a distance, with her fading eyesight, she recognized every face and pose and familiar monument. Why, there was young Nicole, straining every muscle as she propped up the Leaning Tower of Pisa. There were Evan and Barbara Corns, grinning on either side of a Buddhist monk, solemn faced in his saffron robes. There was one of her favorite families, posing in front of . . .

MacGregor's face wrinkled itself more than usual as she tried to recall. She remembered their names, of course. That was easy. But there was some drama involved with this one family, wasn't there? Some secret. Some responsibility that someone had given to her, MacGregor, the trusted maid. That was the trouble with pain and medication and the cancer eating through her insides. Facts and memories came and went.

"Is there something wrong, ma'am?" Archer asked.

Damn. It had been on the tip of her mind. "No, dear," she whispered. It was important, whatever it was. It was something that she had fretted about during the past few years, as she routinely checked her mail and her e-mail and the newspapers and Facebook and the obituaries. Something with life and death importance. Something that would never get taken care of now . . .

If only she could remember.

PART ONE

THE WAKE

CHAPTER 1

At the sound of the electronic buzz, Amy Abel glanced up and let out a little moan. This wasn't her usual reaction to the sight of two smiling people bouncing into her travel agency and waving a check, but she couldn't help herself.

"We're so excited," said Donna Petronia. "Aren't you excited?"

Amy stood to greet them, stretching to her full height of five feet ten, then slipping off her heels, an almost unconscious reaction when people shorter than her walked into the office. She picked up her favorite red Lafonts from the desk, and the couple came more clearly into focus.

"The second annual mystery road rally," Donna chirped.

"I know you can't guarantee us a real murder this time," said Daryl.

Donna slapped his arm playfully. "He doesn't mean that. It must have been perfectly awful for you. And those poor people."

"I was just being naughty," Daryl apologized.

"Still . . . seeing someone actually killed while you're playing a mystery game . . . That must have been a once-in-a-lifetime thing."

"For the victim, yes." Amy tried not to sound judgmental. After all, Daryl and Donna were just a couple of bored, rich New Yorkers looking for a thrill. "And you should be careful what you wish for."

Donna laughed. "Oh, we really don't want a murder, especially not one of us."

"No one wants to kill us," said Daryl with a kind of false modesty. "It's just the possibility that's so fascinating, isn't it? The feeling of danger."

"Donna and Daryl, about the tour . . ." There was no easy way for her to say this. "I know I told you . . ."

"It's not fully booked?" Daryl's smile dimmed by several watts. "Because we would've paid earlier. I offered to put a deposit down. On more than one occasion." He pushed the check across the desk.

"I know." Amy's eyes drifted past the shedding ficus toward the bathroom in the corner. Her mother had disappeared in there right before the couple arrived. Amy figured she had anywhere from another minute to ten. "Look." She spoke quickly now. "I'm not sure this is going to work out." She tried pushing the check back.

"What do you mean, not work out?" Donna pushed it back again. "Is this tour happening or not?"

"Um . . . it's not." Amy hadn't firmly decided, not until the moment she said it. "It's probably not in the best of taste for me to organize another murder mystery, considering what happened." She tried pushing again, but now three hands were on the check, and it was two against one. She hadn't seen such fighting over a check since the last time her uncles were in a restaurant.

"But it's such a hot ticket," Daryl argued. "That write-up in the *Times* . . ."

"I know," Amy said. "All the calls and the press. But I don't think I can do it again."

"Don't do this to yourself," Donna murmured, trying her best to look motherly. "For your own good, dear. You have to get back up on the horse. . . ."

"On the dead horse," Daryl interjected. "Isn't that the expression?"

"No," Donna said, turning on her husband. "You beat a dead horse. You get back up on a live one."

"We're not doing anything with horses, alive or dead." It was a fourth voice, and for a moment Amy couldn't tell whose side it was on. Fanny Abel had stepped around the ficus, pasting on a smile that was broad, artificial and, to Amy at least, frightening. She was nearly a foot shorter than her daughter and weighed perhaps a few pounds less. "Sorry to interrupt—Donna and Daryl, hello—but it's probably easier, sweetie, to tell them the truth." She paused now, running her fingers dramatically through her auburn pageboy. "We are being sued."

"Sued?" All three of them said it at once, although Amy tried to hide her surprise.

"Yes." Fanny adjusted her smile to look apologetic. "I'm afraid the victim's family has slapped an injunction on all future mystery tours. Cease and desist. Something to do with intellectual property and how another tour would do irrevocable harm to the victim's reputation."

Donna's fleshy face contorted. "That doesn't make sense. First off, being killed has nothing to do with your reputation. Plus, Amy has every right to do another mystery. Otherwise, there wouldn't be any mystery games at all."

Fanny held up a red polished fingernail. "Then there's the suit from the accused's lawyers, saying how another mystery tour would be prejudicial to their defense case, since the real-life case mirrored a mystery game in which their client was involved. Did I say one cease and desist order? I meant two."

"But that makes even less sense," Daryl said.

"Well, don't look at me," Fanny shot back. "I'm not a lawyer."

Amy allowed herself a crooked smile. She was in safe hands. Fanny, bless her, was definitely on her side. And that gave Amy an advantage of about 1,000 percent. No one could beat her mother in a fight like this, especially when she only half understood the argument and was making things up as she went.

By the end of five more minutes, the Petronias had beat a confused, ignominious retreat, and the check lay torn in the bottom of a rattan wastebasket. Fanny had even had an extra minute at the end to fill the electric teapot and bring out the Earl Grey.

"I'll take care of the other cancellations," Fanny said. "To tell you the truth, I kind of enjoy it, except for the money part."

"I don't know what got into me," Amy said as she watched her mother push aside her keyboard and arrange the bone china she kept stored in the bottom right of the file cabinet. "I know we need the money."

"I'm the one who should apologize." The words sounded strange coming from Fanny's lips, unexpected and foreign, as if she had learned them phonetically. "I shouldn't have pushed you to do another mystery rally. But that's all my readers on TrippyGirl wanted to talk about."

TrippyGirl was the blog Fanny had started shortly after her daughter's European escapades, a combination of a little fact and a lot of fiction that followed a girl nicknamed Trippy, loosely based on Amy, and her adventures around the world.

"I thought I could do it," said the real Amy. "I did. But the idea of getting up every day and facing vultures like Donna and Daryl and treating death as some form of entertainment, which it is, of course—between books and TV and the news . . ."

"But you've had to face the real thing, dear, more than once. You know what? I think you should forget about murders. Don't even read those cozies you're so fond of. It's not good." The tea bags were in the cups; the pot was whistling. Amy watched, the calmness growing inside her, as Fanny Abel eased the hot water over the bags.

Amy's Travel was the name on the door. Her first impulse had been to name it Amy and Eddie's Travel, except that people would always ask who Eddie was, and she didn't think she could bear that.

Travel had been their shared passion. Amy loved the exotic and the history of it, like the Edwardian splendor of the Victoria Falls Hotel in the heart of Africa, where they'd been given the honeymoon suite, even though he had just proposed. Eddie had enjoyed all this, plus the thrill of bungee jumping from the staggering height of a bridge just downriver from the falls.

"How many times will you get to do something

like this?" he'd asked as a pair of sketchy-looking entrepreneurs tied the frayed bungee rope around his feet and nudged him out onto the platform.

"You mean jumping off a bridge on the border between two third world countries, over the friggin' Victoria Falls?"

"Exactly." Eddie laughed. Then, without another thought, he turned and whooped and dove out over the rapids. A world-embracing swan dive. "Whoooo!"

On that afternoon, he jumped the falls twice and talked her into doing it once. She was sick for the next four hours. No one had told her there would be so much bouncing and spinning involved, and that wasn't even counting the free fall and the snap. But it would become one of her proudest moments and fondest memories.

The memories all changed one month later, when Eddie was killed by muggers just a few blocks from their Greenwich Village apartment.

Nearly two years after the mind-numbing horror of that night, after retrenching completely from life and moving back into the comfort of her childhood home, Amy finally made another daring leap and opened up shop. Eddie would have loved it.

"If we don't do this," Amy murmured, blowing steam off the rim of the dainty white cup, "are we broke? Are we going to have to close the doors?"

"Yes, we are broke," her mother replied. "I mean, a travel agency in this day and age? But we're building some momentum with TrippyGirl. Some of them are booking little trips. Of course, everyone got very excited about the next rally, which apparently is not happening."

Amy sighed. "Mother, please."

"I can't help making you feel a little guilty. It's my job."

Before Amy could retaliate, the phone rang, the actual landline reserved for business. It was an odd enough occurrence that it galvanized their focus. Fanny lifted a finger, counted silently to three, and answered. "Amy's Travel. From the ordinary to the exotic. How may I direct . . . Oh, hello, Peter." Her enthusiasm dipped. "She's not here at the moment."

Amy held out her hand for the receiver. Fanny ignored her. "Yes, I gave her your message, and she wants to call you back. But you know the travel business. Busy, busy. Yes, I'll tell her you need to speak to her. Bye-bye."

Amy watched her mother hang up, then cleared her throat. "How long has Peter been calling?"

"Two days. He says it's business and urgent, but I don't believe a thing that man says."

"Why?" Any normal woman, she thought, would be incensed that her mother was screening her calls. But that battle had been fought and lost years ago. "Has Peter ever lied to you?" Amy asked. "No. You just don't like him. Unlike some men who lie all the time and you still like them."

"There's more to honesty than telling the truth."

"Excuse me. Sorry to interrupt." It was Peter Borg himself, standing in the front doorway, tall, bland, and blond, but looking good today in a narrow-cut Marc Jacobs suit. "The door buzzed," he said, pointing behind him with one hand. In his other was his iPhone. "I guess you didn't hear."

"I told you she wasn't here," Fanny said without batting an eye.

"I know," Peter apologized. "But I was in the neighborhood."

Any normal mother, Amy thought again, would be embarrassed to be caught in a lie mere moments after telling it. Not Fanny.

"In the neighborhood?" she mocked and pointed a fat, accusing finger. "It's not bad enough that he makes me fib. No, he has to rub it in my face. If that's not dishonest, I don't know what is." And with that, she pivoted and marched off to the back office, slamming the door behind her.

Amy watched her go, then sighed. "I have no control over her. None."

"Why doesn't Fanny like me?" Peter asked. Tentatively, he sat down in a client chair, all the while keeping one eye on the back office door.

"Take it as a compliment." Amy pushed over her mother's untouched cup of Earl Grey. Peter picked it up without comment and sipped. Peter Borg was everything a normal mother could want for her daughter: handsome, hard-working and well-to-do. He was also devoted to Amy, although she'd given him very little encouragement. They had dated once or twice and been on a Caribbean tour together, for business. But there had never been that spark. For Fanny—and to a slightly lesser extent for Amy—it was all about the spark.

"I hope you're not going to do another mystery rally," he said, lowering the half-empty cup. "No matter how popular . . . it won't be good for your reputation."

"You're right." Amy hadn't thought of that angle. She knew only that she couldn't go through with it. "I know you never approved, but . . . it's not happening."

"Good." Peter scooted his chair forward, closer,

planted his elbows on her desk, and steepled his long, thin fingers. "Because I have another proposal. Less work, more interesting, and probably just as lucrative."

And with that, Peter proceeded to outline his meeting two weeks ago with Paisley MacGregor.

Amy listened, her interest growing with each odd little revelation. She vaguely recalled the large, informal woman in her formal whites serving lunch one day, when Peter had persuaded Amy to come over. She'd known Peter was just showing off the maid. MacGregor had known. Everyone had known, and everyone had played along.

"And you fired her?" That was a detail Amy had never heard.

"I made up some excuse," Peter said. "But it doesn't matter, does it? She got sick and quit working. Then she died."

"Oh." Amy was taken aback. "I'm sorry."

"Oops. I should have said that at the beginning. She died three days ago."

"I'm sorry," Amy repeated, although it wasn't a surprise, given the story that he'd just told. "Did she have family?"

"MacGregor?" It was almost a snort. "No. Just her beloved employers. So, what do you say? I checked with her lawyers. I'm also a guest, so that gives me the right to involve another tour operator. You'll be paid well and get an around-the-world trip."

Amy hesitated. "I don't know."

"I'll split my commissions with you. Fifty-fifty."

"Why would you do that?"

"I need the help. You've worked with the rich and fussy. And I need someone who isn't attached to MacGregor. Even now it's a handful, contacting everyone and getting them on board. You've always wanted to see the Taj Mahal. Right?"

She must have mentioned this dream to him at some point. "You're spreading ashes at the Taj Mahal?"

"We'll be throwing MacGregor right into it."

"Eddie and I always wanted to go."

"The Taj Mahal at dawn. Something you'll never forget. And we're going to be flying private." There was a sharp gleam in his eyes.

"I've never flown private," Amy had to admit.

"A reconfigured seven-fifty-seven. I'm leasing it from some oil sheik. It seats twenty, with a crew of six. Everyone practically has a room. Of course, with us, there'll be only eight. Nine if you come along."

Amy was prepared to hear more. But then Fanny reemerged from the inner office. She was emotionally composed now, fluffing out the ruffles on her favorite beige blouse and checking the time on her Lady Hamilton.

"Hey, Fanny," Peter said smoothly. "How is Trippy-Girl? I'm a huge fan, by the way."

Amy was surprised. "You are?"

"It's a great blog," Peter said, aiming the words at Fanny. "Although I think you may be getting some traffic from people who think it's about drugs."

"We get a bit of that," Amy admitted. "But Mom likes the name."

Fanny's eyes were still on Lady Hamilton. "Amy, dear," she said. "Don't you have to be somewhere for Marcus?"

"Damn it." Amy checked her own watch, then gathered her things—her shoulder bag from the desktop, her keys, and a newly purchased pair of

Bebe Misfits, black and tortoiseshell. "Peter, I have to get moving. It's Marcus's birthday. Marcus Alvarez?"

"I know who Marcus is. Wish him a happy birthday for me." Peter was already walking her toward the door. He stopped her in the middle of the door's electric eye, and the door started to buzz. It kept buzzing as he looked deep into her eyes. "Promise you'll think about my offer?"

"Yes, of course. Although I'm not sure—"

"Think about it."

CHAPTER 2

Amy had only a few dishes in her repertoire—squid in white wine (better than it sounded), beef cheek *barbacoa* (when beef cheek was available), guinea hen with pine nuts (hard to ruin)—all just esoteric enough to persuade her guests that (a) she was a real cook and (b) if they didn't like it, it was probably their fault. She had considered branching out tonight, but the last time you want to try out a new guest dish, she told herself, is when you're cooking for a guest. It was the perfect catch-22.

Her plan for the evening was simple. All day long she had refused to acknowledge Marcus's birthday, either on the phone or in any of their texts back and forth. But when he came home from work, he would open the door to the warm aroma of roasted guinea hens. She would be in the kitchen, wearing nothing but an apron and a smile and maybe a few spatters from the sauce, which would be totally delicious, by the way.

His apartment was on the third floor of an old brownstone. Marcus had given her a key, which Amy

considered a positive step. Struggling with the grocery bags up the uneven stairs, she half listened to
the muffled sounds filtering out from the other
apartments—a playful toddler on the first floor, a
pair of male-female voices somewhere upstairs.

It had been six months since Marcus had been
free of suspicion by the police, nearly seven since
they'd met for the first time in Monte Carlo. In the
early days, she felt things were moving too quickly.
Did he love her just because she'd believed in his innocence? Was it the excitement of the chase that
made things so electric between them? But then,
after the case was solved, after all the press and noto-
riety, then things did get slower. Predictably slower.
Annoyingly slower.

This is a good thing, she kept telling herself. He
might indeed be perfect for her, this olive-skinned,
sharp-featured man with wavy jet-black hair. But
maybe not. He could be so maddening, with his honestly dishonest behavior and his need to keep so
much of himself private.

She'd assumed they might have moved in together by now. Over six months. But Marcus's apartment was in his roommate's name, and the idea of
him moving into Amy's half of the Abel brownstone, just steps away from Fanny, his coconspirator
and new best friend . . . Well, that wasn't going to
happen.

Amy lugged the bags up another flight, and the
male-female voices grew louder. They were laughing now, sounding more than a little playful. She
wasn't paying attention to the muffled words. Her
mind was on the guinea hens and whether Marcus
might have an old onion stashed away in the back of
his crisper.

As she rounded the landing onto the third floor, she realized that the voices—the playful, sexually tinged male-female voices—were coming from his apartment. *That's funny*, she thought. *The roommate's on vacation. Marcus is at work. Supposedly at work.* Her heart began to sink.

Making as little noise as possible, Amy set the bags down on the landing, by the door, took the keys from her shoulder bag, found the right one, and gently inserted it. "What are you doing?" That was the first thought in her head and the first words out of her mouth—although it was fairly clear what Marcus was doing.

He was sitting on the brown herringbone sofa in the middle of his living room, holding the remote, and watching a rather steamy scene in a daytime drama. Alone, yes, but that wasn't the point.

"Why aren't you at work?"

"Hey, babe." He switched off the set, and the voices disappeared, along with their images. "I got home a little early."

Amy quickly took stock of the situation—Marcus's slippers, his coffee mug, a sandwich from the deli down the block. He looked so comfortable. "You didn't go into work at all," she deduced.

He shrugged and nodded. "You're right. I took the day off. It's my birthday, although some people didn't seem to remember." A boyish, lopsided grin. "Are you making me dinner?"

"I am. Happy birthday." But something still wasn't right. "When you texted me, you said you were at the office. You complained about Sandra."

"Well . . ." He shrugged again. "I didn't want to announce my birthday, not if you'd forgotten it. So I pretended it was a normal day at work."

The logic was slightly convoluted but flawless, which was the only clue Amy needed to know it was a lie. "You were fired, weren't you?"

Marcus didn't take offense or skip a beat. "No, I quit. About two weeks ago, although they're doing me a solid by saying I was laid off. This way I get unemployment."

"Fine. Whatever. I don't know which is worse."

"I think getting fired is worse. That's why I said the other."

"Which was it really? Fired or quit?"

"The job wasn't a good fit."

"So just last week, when we talked about going to look at apartments together . . ."

Marcus frowned. "I don't think we'll have the money, given your state of business and my state of unemployment."

"What?" Amy was furious. "You said you were calling up brokers, setting up appointments."

"I wanted to."

"But you already knew better. You were already unemployed."

"Amy, I think you have to put this in context. We were in the middle of a romantic evening and a few glasses of merlot. Remember?"

"Of course I remember," Amy stammered. It had been a very nice evening.

"Talking about an apartment together . . . Well, that was part of the moment, like asking, 'Do you love me?' What did you want me to say? 'Yes, I love you, but I lost my job, and we can't get a place of our own in the foreseeable future'?"

"It would have been the honest thing."

"Really?" Marcus rubbed his chin. He hadn't shaved in a couple of days, it seemed, which only made him sexier. "Then you're better than me. I was too caught in the moment to ruin it. I'm a romantic. Maybe that's my problem."

It was at that exact moment when Amy decided she would go around the world on a wake.

CHAPTER 3

Amy did not find MacGregor's penthouse to be as pristine and blindingly white as Peter had described it. She found it a cluttered combination of white and everything else. Cheap patterned throw pillows littered the sofas and chairs. Shoes and the odd piece of clothing lay scattered across the marble floors, along with a dozen glossy magazines with assorted Kardashians popping off the covers. Archer, it seemed, had made the place her own.

The maid who opened the apartment door was no longer starchly dressed. Her hair was pulled back in a loose bun, and her outfit was flowered and, from a couture standpoint, about half a step up from a housecoat. Peter wasn't good at hiding his dismay, but he glossed over it by introducing Amy.

"You wanted something with the pictures?" Archer's accent was still Bostonian, but from a different neighborhood. It seemed odd, almost a mistake, not to find gum lolling in her mouth or a cigarette dangling from her lips.

"We need to borrow a few," Amy said. "If that's all right."

"Knock yourselves out," Archer said and led the way into the bedroom. The woman really needed a dangling cigarette.

The first thing Peter noticed was the huge, empty bed—unmade, with pastel pink sheets. It was the first physical reminder he'd seen of MacGregor's death. Archer followed the line of Peter's gaze and grew defensive.

"Why not? The place is empty. I'm being paid to look after it."

"What happened here? Miss Archer!" Peter had turned from the bed and was looking across to the white Steinway. Its expansive top was barren.

"The pictures are there," Archer said, pointing to a pair of large sealed boxes under the piano. "I didn't want them staring at me," she said with a sniff. "Creeps me out." And with that, she turned around and retreated into the living room.

It had been Amy's idea. The framed photos had been part of MacGregor's life. They were the whole inspiration behind this worldwide wake. So, wouldn't it be a nice touch, she'd suggested, to enlarge a few and display them at the New York service?

"It was your idea," Peter said, keeping a lazy distance from the impending chore. Then he softened. "I'll help out. . . ."

"No," Amy said. "I like unpacking things. It's like Christmas." She found a box cutter on a windowsill and soon was on the floor by the first box, slicing through the tape, showing no concern at all for the knees of her black skinny jeans. "You can pack them back up tomorrow."

"Thanks."

Her idea had been to take the "inspirational" photos, the ones representing the five different stops around the world. But she was leaving herself open. Was MacGregor herself in any of them? Something like that would make a nice centerpiece. Amy began to unwrap each frame, laying the white tissue paper off to one side, half expecting Peter to join her and smooth the paper into a neat pile. But Peter was taking her at her word and not even pretending to help. Instead, he was at the Steinway, easing his long legs under the keyboard, then teasing out a few tentative scales. At least it wasn't "Chopsticks."

The first unwrapped frame was a marquetry herringbone showing a sunburned family of four on a pink-sand beach, probably in Bermuda. *Definitely not funeral worthy,* she thought and put it off to one side. The second frame was silver, with a happy older couple on a private grass terrace with the unmistakable peak of Machu Picchu looming close in the background. Amy recognized not only the hotel but also the room. Sanctuary Lodge, room 40. She had a similar photo on her bedside table, but of a younger couple who would never grow so old and happy together. This one went into the keeper pile, even though each glance would bring a little pang.

What was it about travel that was so potent? she wondered. People went thousands of miles to wind up with the same views as every other traveler, the same exact experiences repeated a million times. And yet within that rigid form, as you joined the millions posing in front of the same icons, everything wound up seeming unique and personal and worth the trip.

The music brought her out of her reverie. Peter, to her surprise, could play. Not just tunes, but the classics. From memory. She recognized this one as Russian, something romantic. She probably could have named it on a better day, when she wasn't on her knees, pawing through other people's lives. The familiar melody rose slowly to the upper keys. Then a few muffled notes sounded, then stopped.

"Don't stop," she said, barely aware of having said it.

"Sorry," Peter said, standing up with a frown. "There's something wrong with these strings." A few seconds later and he was propping up the lid, looking inside. "Like there's something on top . . ." He squinted and reached around with his right hand. When he removed it, he was holding a standard-size manila envelope, folded in half. He unfolded it and saw that there were a few words written in pen across the center. "Open only in case of my death." The words hung melodramatically in the air.

"What?" Amy was off her knees now, stumbling over to the piano. "Are you kidding me?" But, of course, he wasn't. There they were, in sloppy, uneven block letters.

"Open only in case of my death," Peter repeated. Then, with a lift of his eyebrows, he obeyed, inserting his hand in the envelope and rummaging around. "Nothing," he reported and handed it off to Amy.

The envelope was indeed empty, but they could see from the creases and the open tear across the top fold that it had once held something. "Is this her handwriting?" Amy asked in a whisper, glancing off toward the open door. Archer was nowhere in sight.

"Block letters? Could be anyone."

"Maybe it's not her." Amy's mind was racing around the possibilities. "Could this be a used piano?"

"Well . . ." Peter thought. "We can ask Steinway to look up the serial number. But I think she ordered it new."

"So if it's not from some previous owner . . . ," Amy thought out loud. She held the envelope at arm's length, like a dead rat.

"She wasn't murdered."

"I didn't say she was."

"You're implying it. This was cancer. She had the best doctors at Sloan Kettering working for months to keep her alive."

"Of course." But the words still stared up at her. "Peter, we need to call the police."

"Call the police? Wha . . ." Amy hated it when people laughed and spoke at the same time. It was an irritating affectation. "About what?" he continued, laughing and speaking. "An open envelope?"

"Don't you think it's suspicious?" she argued. "A woman dies, and we find a message saying, 'If I die, open this.' And it's empty."

"It could be anything," Peter reasoned. "It could have been a note saying, 'Feed my cat' or 'Here are my computer passwords' or 'I'm the one who broke your favorite vase.' "

"Someone removed the letter."

"Yes, just like she told them to. You want to ask Archer about it? Let's ask Archer."

"Yes. No. I guess so."

"Why are you reacting this way?" Something about Peter's lack of suspicion was helping to put her at ease. "People leave notes when they die. It's kind of normal. Miss Archer!" He aimed his voice in the direction of the living room. "Will you come in here a minute?"

They stood side by side as the emotionless Archer entered, stopping by the bedroom door. "Yeah?"

Peter held up the envelope and casually asked her about it. Amy saw no reaction on the woman's face, except perhaps a tinge of boredom. No, she had never seen it before. No, Miss MacGregor had never given her any envelope. No, no one had come to visit except the ambulance people. Would that be all?

Yes, that would be all.

CHAPTER 4

After several tries, Amy had decided on her old black Fendi with the scoop neck and the long-sleeved jacket. She didn't like wearing new things to funerals. It made the clothes somehow sad and hard to wear again. But this wasn't really a funeral, was it? More of a business obligation.

Marcus sat patiently behind the wheel as Amy swung her legs over to the sidewalk and eased on the three-inch heels. He was borrowing the Abel family Volvo. It was for some errand or a job search. Amy hadn't paid much attention, since the odds of him telling the exact truth were about fifty-fifty. She just needed a drop-off first.

"I'll take the subway home," she said and straightened her eyeglasses, also black Fendis, also old.

"If you feel nervous about this trip, you shouldn't go."

"No. Peter's right. It's a silly envelope. And she died naturally."

"Amy, your instincts are good. If you think there's a possibility of danger . . ." Marcus and Fanny had been trying for days to talk her out of this, both for the same reason. It wasn't because of the potential danger, but because they both liked Marcus and disliked Peter. "You shouldn't do it for the money."

"Of course I'm doing it for the money." She buckled the last strap. "We have to keep the doors open. And it's good to get away. We both need a break." Marcus didn't have a response for this, and she mentally kicked herself for wanting one. "How do I look?" she asked.

"Too good for a funeral," he said. As soon as she was out and the door closed, he put the Volvo in gear and started heading north on Madison Avenue. Amy watched him disappear, then turned and looked up at the imposing gray-brown box.

The Frank E. Campbell Funeral Chapel was an East Side institution. Everyone who was anyone, from Rudolph Valentino to Jackie O to the Notorious B.I.G., had put in a final appearance here. Campbell's was understated, expensive, and clearly stipulated in Paisley MacGregor's rather detailed instructions. Peter was waiting for Amy under the chandelier in the cream-colored lobby, and together they took the stairs. Their employer was waiting for them in one of the reposing rooms on the third floor.

The service that morning would be informal, bordering on the nonreligious. One of MacGregor's bosses had recalled that she had been raised Church of Scotland, but the best that Amy could do on short notice was a Presbyterian minister from a tiny congregation in the Theatre District. His presence would serve to give some structure to the proceedings.

Amy was glad she had gone to the trouble of

blowing up the photos and placing them around. It gave the illusion of a few more people having shown up. She was also glad about the catering. The table of wines and hors d'oeuvres provided a much-needed centerpiece, drawing focus away from the open casket and the shriveled head propped up on a powder blue pillow. *Is this what MacGregor imagined?* thought Amy as she examined the peaceful, artificial-looking features, the maid finally being the center of attention, the benefactress of an unforgettable trip.

There were perhaps two dozen mourners, and none of them seemed to be curiosity seekers. Peter, always mindful of publicity, had given the story to the *New York Times*, which had done a charming article, half a page, complete with photos, about the maid sending her former employers around the world. Amy had been wary about the funeral turning into some sort of circus, but it hadn't.

Archer was in attendance, back in her prim, pulled-together disguise, along with two other women. Amy assumed they were fellow maids, then immediately wondered why she had made such an assumption. Perhaps it was the fact that they were chatting so tightly in their little bunch—and instinctively cleaning the buffet table, disposing of the used corks and stacking the plates to one side.

A fourth woman joined them at the buffet. After a few moments, Amy realized that she wasn't subtly cleaning like the others, but subtly herding a row of mushroom tartlets into a plastic bag inside her large black purse. Her hair was ash blond; at least that's what the bottle probably said. Despite her heels, she remained petite, with features that would remain pinched even when she wasn't sneaking food. In her twenties, a little younger than Amy, the woman wore a stylish black dress, one approximately the same age as Amy's. When the woman eased an unopened bottle of Pouilly-Fuissé into the purse, Amy wasn't outraged or annoyed. She was fascinated.

"Are you Nicole Marconi?" Amy gave her a moment to recover before sidling up and introducing herself. "I'm Amy Abel. We've spoken and e-mailed a few times."

"Yes, Miss Abel. Nice to finally meet you."

Amy was taken aback by the formal tone, the kind used to address service providers. Of course, Amy was technically a service provider. But then Nicole Marconi was technically a food thief. "I'm sorry we have to meet under such circumstances." Amy mentally berated herself for sounding like an undertaker.

"No one knew she was sick," said Nicole, warming ever so slightly. "I have fond memories of Paisley. Of course, my parents adored her. More than they adored me."

Amy nodded. "I think every girl feels that way about somebody. Not that we ever had a maid."

"Oh, it wasn't Paisley's fault, but it still hurt."

Amy didn't know what to say. "Well, I'm glad you'll be able to join us in celebrating her life. It's an unusual bequest."

"To be honest, I was expecting something like this. Paisley would never let us off so easily." Nicole's pinched features grew even tighter. "You know of course that it's my money that's paying for this."

"Your money?"

"My inheritance. Or what would have been my inheritance. But that's not your concern. Your concern is to spend as much as you can, fulfilling the demented last wish of a dying maid."

"Oh. It was your parents' money. . . ." Amy knew that MacGregor's inheritance had come from one of the families, but she'd never considered the implications. Did Peter know about Nicole's situation? If so, why hadn't he warned Amy? A little information would have gone a long way.

"Yes. They left most of it to the maid. You can imagine having to deal with your parents' deaths. And, on top of that, when the lawyers told me . . ."

"Must have been horrible." Amy herself had an eccentric mother, but this would have been too much, even for Fanny.

"By the way, when is the will being read? Six years ago, when this travesty happened, MacGregor assured me that the money, what's left of it, would be returned to the Marconi family. Of course, a lot of things are said in the heat of embarrassment. And there was plenty of embarrassment."

"Um . . . there's a reading of the will set up for the last stop. Part of the grand finale."

"Not until then? Well, I guess I've starved for this long. . . ." And, as if to illustrate her point, Nicole took a final tartlet from the tray and popped it into her pinched little mouth.

After that, Amy shied away from conversations. She let Peter hand out the condolences and the small talk and wondered how soon the minister would start earning his money—Nicole's money. Amy found it relatively easy to disappear, even in a sparse crowd, to wander among the easel-mounted photos, gazing pensively at some, hiding behind others. This was always her fallback position, a reflex she usually fought against, but not this time. She could only imagine what other land mines might be buried around the room.

To her amazement, all of MacGregor's old bosses had said yes, although the travel dates had become an almost insurmountable challenge. Of the eight tour members, including Peter, six had shown up at the New York service. The Maui-based Steinbergs would be joining them in Paris to help throw the first pinches of Paisley out over the Seine. Amy thought she recognized the Corns, a fleshy, red, slightly over-size couple who always looked like they had just come out of the sun. And, of course, it was impossible not to recognize Herb Sands and David Pepper—not because they were in any way famous, but because they were standing in front of their own photo, inspecting a younger version of themselves, arms around shoulders, posing among the long morning shadows of Stonehenge.

"Eight years ago?" David asked, studying the image from a happier day. He was the younger of the two by about twenty years, although Amy would have guessed a larger gap if she hadn't seen the passports. He looked no more than thirty, at least in this soft lighting, and was incredibly handsome and tanned, with a bright white smile and wavy golden-red locks.

"More like ten," countered Herb. "Before you started dyeing your hair." Herb Sands was still an attractive man, but with the usual surrenders that men make to the advancing years—not heavyset but thick, his hair thinning and more gray than brown, features that had once been nicely proportioned now continuing to grow into a slightly saggy face.

Amy wouldn't have been so critical of his looks, except that Herb was being so critical of his perfectly beautiful partner.

"I don't dye. I highlight," David shot back. Amy had been expecting a more sarcastic retort, especially since the man was looking just as perfect as he had eight or ten years ago, while Herb . . . Of course, Herb didn't have to look good. He was the one with money.

In all their correspondence, the couple had called themselves the Pepper-Sands, Herb and David Pepper-Sands, a mouthful that stopped just short of being funny. On their passports, of course, their names were separated. The men had begun their romance while Paisley MacGregor was working for Herb, and true to the MacGregor formula, the three had become a family of sorts, until Herb Sands decided that what their town house needed was a butler—a handsome English butler, it turned out—and the perfect maid made up some excuse to quit. This was all secondhand information gleaned from Peter, who had gleaned it from MacGregor herself.

"I don't think Peter Borg highlights his hair." Herb's gaze had wandered across the reposing room, seeking out the tall, blond tour operator. Peter was leaning absently on the open casket, his elbow almost grazing MacGregor's face, as he chatted amiably with the Corns. "Of course, he's a little younger than you."

"There's always someone younger." David was making a heroic effort not to take the bait—and failing. "If you think I'm going to stand by and watch you hook up with a damned travel agent . . ."

"You were a waiter when I met you." Herb's smile grew unexpectedly warm. "The most gorgeous waiter in New York."

Amy listened and couldn't help fantasizing about the upcoming journey—Herb making up an excuse to visit Peter's room on some "tour business," David becoming a simmering pot of resentment, Peter doing his clueless best to be ingratiating to everyone. She really ought to warn him.

"Stop it. You're not throwing yourself at Peter Borg. Besides . . ." David studied Peter for a second, trying to be objective. The travel agent was indeed younger and taller and blonder, even without chemical assistance. "I think Peter thinks he likes women."

"We'll see," said Herb with a sigh and a shrug. "Around the world is a long way."

It was at this moment that Peter pushed himself up from his employer's resting place, subtly checked his watch, and gently extricated himself from his conversation. When he managed to catch the minister's eye, Peter raised an elegant finger, perhaps a little too elegant. Herb saw it and chuckled. "We'll see."

The clergyman had been trying in vain to find a mushroom tartlet, anything to help fortify him for a eulogy for yet another unknown corpse. Half the funerals he presided over seemed to be for people who'd never entered a church while alive. He poured one more half glass of the Pouilly-Fuissé—in low supply, like the tartlets—and started off in the general direction of his late hostess.

"Having fun?" Peter asked. He had been keeping Amy on his radar as she hid behind this easel or pretended to be absorbed in that one. He didn't mind that she hadn't been working the room. It would come.

"Fun?" Amy asked. "I can't tell if you're being serious or not."

"Half and half. Do you think you'll be transporting the ashes as carry-on or as luggage?"

"Luggage, definitely. Again, I can't tell . . ."

"Serious this time."

She covered her gasp with a little laugh. "Are you sure? Because it would make a funny joke."

"Serious." Peter looked serious. "With most countries and airlines, transporting ashes is more or less legal. But I'm not sure about Turkey, and I really don't want to ask. It's not one of those questions you can take back."

"Do you think many dead people are smuggled into Turkey?"

"Another thing you don't want to ask the authorities."

"And why am I the one doing this?"

"Because you're an innocent-looking woman. And you have no past history of problems with Turkish immigration."

"Again, I can't tell . . ."

"Serious. An unfortunate misunderstanding." Amy's face must have formed some equally unfortunate expression, because Peter reacted with a coy grin and a complete change of subject. "I saw you with Nicole Marconi. She seems nice."

"She's terrific." Amy wasn't in the mood to let him off lightly. "You should get her talking about MacGregor and her parents. She's got some great stories."

Peter's face brightened. "What kind of stories? Do you think she'd tell them at one of the wakes? That might be fun."

"Loads of fun." Amy tried to match his coy, reassuring grin. "And Herb and David. You should get to know them, too. I'll bet if you flirt a little with Herb, you can get them thinking about some over-the-top trip. Maybe an anniversary extravaganza?"

"You're serious?" Peter asked. "I can't tell . . ."

"Serious. You should flirt with both of them."

"Hmm. You think they'd respond to a little harmless flirting? I don't want to seem rude."

"Oh, they'll respond," Amy promised. "Absolutely."

CHAPTER 5

It was almost exactly two days later to the minute, if you took into account the six hour time difference between New York and Paris. Two days from the end of the East Side memorial to the start of the first of the wakes.

"We kept getting these horrible, ugly presents from Laila's mother, year after year. I mean, lamps covered in seashells. Atrocious paintings on velvet that she'd picked up in Mexico. Horrific stuff."

The thin middle-aged man continued to weave his anecdote as the silver yacht glided through the shadows of the Pont d'Austerlitz. "So we did the only thing we could under the circumstances. We gave them to the maid." As his voice echoed off the stone arch a few feet above their heads, Paisley MacGregor's wake floated west with the current, toward the lighted towers of Notre-Dame and the gathering sunset. "Each time we did it, we told Paisley we had picked out this crap just for her. And she'd thank us profusely in that way she always did and tell us how wonderful we were for buying such expensive things."

A good-natured groan welled up from the listeners, and everyone took another sip of champagne. The next bridge would be the Pont de Sully, which framed the eastern bank of the Île Saint-Louis, part of the ancient heart of Paris.

The air was surprisingly still, and the man barely had to raise his voice to be heard. "Come on," he said with a twisted grin. "We all give our horrible junk to the maid."

"It was Maury's idea," Laila Steinberg protested from somewhere near the front of the group. "Although I have to say, Paisley loved them. She did. She'd get the handyman from her building to come over, and they'd cart it all away."

The Steinbergs looked like a perfect match. They were both shortish, and fit, and they had allowed their hair to go gracefully gray. Their skin was flawless, Maury's as well as Laila's, and their teeth were straight and white, but not overly. Such perfection might have occurred naturally, but not in a couple of fifty-five, which was what Amy estimated their average age to be.

Their most striking attributes, to Amy's mind, were their eyeglass frames, thin and elegant, with layers of subtle color running through them, hers in red hues, his in dark brown. Amy didn't envy the rich, not much, just their frames.

"Right." Maury Steinberg's mouth tightened at his wife's interruption. He was standing at the stern, champagne flute in hand, next to a photo of MacGregor's smiling, precancerous face. "So that became our routine about twice a year. We got crappy stuff from her mother. We gave it to Paisley. Everyone's happy."

"Until my mother decided to pay us a visit."

"Uh-oh," said Herb Sands.

David laughed, as if Herb had said something clever. They were getting along fine now, Amy noted, although . . . Herb's roving eye did seem to be roving toward Peter, who responded by smiling back and giving him all the extra attention Amy had suggested.

"A visit. Exactly." Maury pressed on. "Laila's mother was coming to New York, something she never, ever did. So you can imagine, we're in this predicament. What do we say when she sees that none of her presents are anywhere in the apartment? For a while we thought of telling her there'd been a fire—"

"Maury even thought about setting a fire. Just for a second—"

"Right," Maury interrupted back. "So . . . finally the day comes. We pick her up at LaGuardia, and all the way home we say nothing and we're thinking and there's no ideas coming, none, and we don't know what she'll say. And we walk into the house—"

"And it's all there," Laila said, stealing the punch line again.

The listeners did not erupt into laughter. This time the laughs were small and knowing and affectionate. Except for Maury, who didn't laugh at all.

"It was all there," he said, trying to regain momentum. "Every tasteless lamp and Peruvian wall hanging. All of it was crowded in there with our stuff. Everything rearranged. I don't know how the hell the woman did it."

"Or how she even knew," Laila added. "Because we never told Paisley where the furnishings had come from. And we certainly never told her about our predicament, although she did know my mother was visiting." She shrugged her shoulders. "But that was dear Paisley. She knew everything."

"It actually didn't look horrible. Paisley had a good eye."

"And the upshot of it all was that my mother had a great week with us, and the second she went home, Paisley moved all the stuff out. Without ever saying a word."

The laughter grew and remained warm.

"It's true." Laila Steinberg had, perhaps unconsciously, joined her husband at the center of attention. "Paisley never, ever mentioned it. And we never mentioned it. We were way too embarrassed and grateful, and I don't know what."

"To Paisley MacGregor," Maury Steinberg said and led the final toast of the evening.

When Peter stepped forward with the urn, he didn't need to speak. The moment felt instinctual. The small silver scoops had been lined up on a white linen tabletop, and one by one the mourners came forward and silently, meditatively took scoops of their maid and cast them into the breeze above the Seine. From here the ashes would scatter and join the dust of the city and perhaps fly through some tall, laced-curtained window of some riverside apartment, to be dutifully dusted away by someone else's maid.

Amy giggled at the notion, a maid's dust being dusted by a maid, and drained her flute. It had been a great trip so far, exactly what she'd needed. Even Peter's one attempt to get romantic had been sweetly lame.

Amy had known he would try something, that

her skill as a travel agent hadn't been the only reason for his generous offer. And now that they were in Paris, thousands of miles from Amy's boyfriend—and, more crucially, her mother—it hadn't taken him long.

Their rooms were at the Hôtel de Crillon, a palatial pile on the place de la Concorde, mere steps from where French peasants had once set up a guillotine to deal with just the sort of people who could now afford to stay at the Hôtel de Crillon. On their arrival, Peter had taken the manager aside and spoken with him in French, arguing politely, probably about some misunderstood detail in the reservation. When Peter had turned and walked the fifty feet back to Amy, his expression had turned apologetic.

"They made a mistake and put us in the same room."

"Us? You and me?" Amy had done her best to look surprised. "How could that happen? I made the reservations myself."

"The good news is I managed to talk them into a suite. It's got two bedrooms and a balcony and this incredible view of the Eiffel Tower."

"Don't they have two singles?" Amy had asked. "A hotel this size?"

"Completely booked," Peter asserted. "Springtime in Paris. But the suite has two bedrooms." He raised his eyebrows and looked helpless.

"Excuse me," said Amy. Then she walked back fifty feet to the sleek, Armani-clad manager. If she had spoken to him in English, the man might have been able to maintain the ruse. But Amy's French was better than Peter's, and more importantly, she had mastered the sardonic little twist of the head, so important in any Gallic conversation. The man twisted his own head in response and quickly gave up.

"Nice try," she shouted back over her shoulder to Peter as she followed the manager back to the front desk for the new room keys. "You didn't think I'd figure it out?"

Peter trotted to keep up. "I didn't think you'd want to." Which was the perfect answer. She didn't even pretend to be mad at him.

Their guests began arriving later that afternoon. The only glitch was the Steinbergs' room. Apparently, Laila mentioned to her husband the possibility of noise drifting up from the patio bar two stories below their balcony. Maury proceeded to take this on as his mission, rejecting the manager's assurances that it wouldn't be a problem and demanding another room. "My wife is very sensitive to noise," he kept repeating like an accusation. Amy felt sorry for Laila, who just stood in the background and looked mortified.

"Don't ever interrupt one of my stories again."

The hushed, angry words brought Amy sharply back to the present. After the ceremony, while most of the guests had stayed glued to the yacht's bar area, still getting acquainted, she had wrapped herself in a pashmina shawl and had wandered up to the top deck to enjoy a private view of the City of Light's lights. She knew she was neglecting her duties, but just for a minute. No one would mind.

The argument, Amy saw, was happening directly below her, half whispered and barely audible above the thrum of the engine. Maury and Laila, of course. Their long shadows moved eerily on the lower level.

"I got carried away," Laila's shadow tried to explain.

"Is this the way it's going to be the whole trip, you sabotaging everything I say? God, I am so sick of you."

"I said I'm sorry."

"You'd think I'd be used to you by now. But it just gets worse."

"Do you want a divorce, Maury, is that it?"

"Divorce?" His laugh was soft and mean. "It should be so easy."

This was the second time today that Amy had seen Maury Steinberg go ballistic. The first outburst had been over something just as trivial, berating the hotel manager over the mere possibility of noise rising from the patio to their balcony. Poor manager. Poor Laila. Amy now realized that this incident had also been a case of Maury lashing out at his wife, but with the Hôtel de Crillon standing in as her proxy.

CHAPTER 6

"**S**hould I say I'm twenty-five or thirty?"

Marcus was forced to look up from his game of *Angry Birds* and across the living room. The woman sitting at her computer was easily in her sixties—real person sixties, not movie star sixties—and her frilly brown blouse and defiantly auburn pageboy weren't helping. She peered over the top of her reading glasses, silently demanding an answer. "Do you think you could pass for twenty-five?" he asked back.

"Of course I could pass," she said. "I'm youthful enough."

"I'm not sure a youthful person uses the word *youthful* these days."

"My question is, which is better? To be a thirty-year-old with some life experience or some know-it-all twenty-five-year-old?"

"Why does TrippyGirl have to be any age?"

"Because my followers keep asking. And I have to keep TrippyGirl real. That's the whole point of a blog, isn't it?"

"Let me think." Marcus put aside his phone and saw that his glass was empty and Fanny's only half full. It was a good excuse to grab the bottle of white from the coffee table. He liked Fanny's half of the Abel brownstone. The bottom two floors were homey and eclectic, with old rugs and dark furniture that had been built to last. Amy's half, the upper two floors, felt a little more IKEA, although Amy would insist that none of it was. But it felt that way.

"Why don't you make yourself Amy's age?" he asked as he crossed to Fanny's side and topped off her glass.

"That old?" Fanny made a face.

"She's only what? Thirty-three?"

"She is? You'd think I'd know that, being her mother. She seems older."

"And you're younger? Do your readers really believe that you're at this moment"—Marcus stopped for a second to look at her screen and skim her most recent entry—"in your bra and panties, playing backgammon with a sexy albino waiter on the Trans-Siberian Express?"

"Well, the nights are long in Siberia. We have to do something."

"Actually the nights are getting shorter."

Fanny waved him away like a fly. "Oh, that's just the kind of mistake TrippyGirl would make. It adds realism."

Marcus wasn't sure how to respond, which was just as well, since the house phone had decided to interrupt them. Fanny checked the display. She was about to pick up but changed her mind and let it ring.

"It's Amy," she said in a half whisper.

"Why are you avoiding Amy?"

"I'm not avoiding her. I'm just not here. I stepped out." Even Fanny knew this deserved more of an explanation. "I picked up a copy of Paisley MacGregor's will at the lawyer's. Amy wanted me to scan it to her, but I forgot."

Marcus understood. "We'll do it right now."

Since the brownstone was divided into two separate apartments—Amy's lone stipulation before agreeing to move back into her childhood home—they had to go out to the landing, climb up two flights, and unlock Amy's front door. An interior set of stairs led them up to her bedroom and the sunroom/office at the top-rear of the house. Marcus switched on the computer and the copier, which was on a small side table.

Fanny was less familiar with machines than Marcus, so she fed him the pages—a copy of the will itself, a few codicils, a handwritten letter from Paisley MacGregor, all notarized. There was a homey feeling to these documents, Fanny thought, a reassuring indication that there had been a real person behind all the planning and the demands. Within a minute they had a system going: from the file folder to the scanner to a neat pile on the seat of a chair. Fanny had handed off about a dozen pages—legal size, letter size, single sided, double sided—when there was a stop in the supply chain.

Marcus reached out behind him. "Is that all?" Then he turned to see. Fanny was at the desk, looking curiously at a handwritten letter. "What's up?"

"Letter from Paisley," said Fanny, looking a little somber. "She wants it read aloud in Hawaii before they dump the last of her."

"It's nothing bad, is it?"

"Basically just thanking them for making the trip, for all the years that they let her be a part of their families. A little odd," Fanny added as she scanned the page a second time. "Not that I want to criticize the dead."

"Let me see." Marcus took it. It was one page long, written in tight block letters on fine, heavy stationery. He felt slightly guilty, even though it was a document meant to be read. He, too, had to read it a second time. "She's implying a lot in this little 'thank-you.' Some of it not very nice."

"Good. I thought it was just me being sensitive."

"No, it's definitely her." Marcus set it aside, as if it might be radioactive. "I don't know these people, but even I can figure out . . . she must have known all their secrets."

"From what Amy says, they were very dependent on her."

Marcus pushed out his lips and frowned. "That must have been an odd kind of life, don't you think? Living through other people. Do you think Ms. Paisley was happy?"

"Maybe. In her own way." Fanny gave it a few seconds of serious thought. "As happy as you can be when your job includes cleaning toilets. She was a part of their lives—big houses, smart, successful people confiding in her—with very little downside. No actual family to deal with. She could always leave and move on to the next."

"But she still loved them."

"It's easy to love someone when you can leave." Fanny glanced down at the radioactive page. "I do envy her writing skill."

"You think? It feels stilted to me."

"I meant handwriting. It's very precise and tight."

Marcus nodded and continued to stare at the page. Then his brows drew closer together, and his forehead wrinkled. "I'm not sure this is Paisley Mac-Gregor's writing. Did Amy keep that envelope, the one Paisley left in the piano?"

"Amy's a mess, but she keeps everything," Fanny assured him. "The way her system works . . ." She pulled open the top center drawer of the old wooden desk. "Stuff she thinks she's going to use soon is put here . . . Hmm, it's not here." She closed that drawer and went for the top left. "Stuff she wants to throw out but can't bring herself to . . . Not here either."

"I hate to be obvious, but wouldn't she put it there?" Marcus pointed to the file cabinet.

"No. Then she would have to label and alphabet-ize, and I doubt she figured out how to categorize something like that." Fanny went for the desk's right bottom drawer. "Stuff she feels she has to keep but doesn't want to think about . . . Ah, here it is." And she pulled out the folded manila envelope. With silent fanfare, she handed it to Marcus.

Marcus put the pieces of paper side by side. "You see?" he said almost immediately. "Different hand-writing." He held the two samples under the light of the gooseneck lamp. The sloppy, bold block letters of the envelope—*Open only in case of my death*—contrasted sharply with the neat block print of the letter.

Fanny took one good look. "No, that's impossi-ble," she said, which was her standard way of agree-ing. "The letter was notarized by her lawyer." Fanny indicated the signature and the seal in the bottom left corner. "In her own hand."

"Well, then the envelope was written by someone

else," said Marcus. "Who would give MacGregor an 'if I die' envelope?"

It was the simplest of deductions. But the implications were much bigger. Fanny and Marcus stared at the writing on the letter, then at the envelope, then back again. "Oh, dear," Fanny finally mumbled.

"Must have been written by one of her people." Marcus was recapping what had just gone through their minds. "One of the people who loved her and trusted her gave her this envelope and said, 'If I die, under any circumstance, please open this and take it to the police . . .'"

"You're exaggerating."

"And now MacGregor's dead and the letter she was entrusted with is missing."

Fanny tried to laugh it off. "Are you saying one of her old employers is going to be killed now?"

"You're right. I'm probably exaggerating."

When the landline in Amy's office rang, they jumped. Fanny paused for three rings before answering. "Hello?"

"What are you doing in my apartment?" Amy asked, the first words out of her mouth.

"What are you doing calling your apartment?" Fanny countered.

"Because I thought you might be there."

"And you were right." Fanny switched the phone over to speaker and cradled the handset. "Marcus and I were just sending you the will documents. You should be getting them any second."

"Thanks. Wait a minute. What is Marcus doing there?"

"We're having an affair. I got him on the rebound when you ran off with Peter."

"Hey, Amy," Marcus said, aiming his voice at the speaker. "Miss me?"

"Yes." Amy drew out the word teasingly, well aware that Fanny was listening. "I do."

"Good," said Marcus, also teasingly. "How was the first day of the wake?"

"Going great. The weather's holding out. Customers are content. Paris is gorgeous, all the soft green shoots and buds. I forgot how everything blooms a little earlier here." She did indeed sound happy, which annoyed Marcus to no end. "All in all, I'm glad I came."

"All in all? What's wrong?"

"Is Peter being a douche?" asked Fanny. "Did he try to make you share a hotel room?"

"No, no," came Amy's voice with a laugh. There was the sound of people in the background, like in a café or a lobby. "Peter's fine. But you know. There's always someone making trouble."

"Is it Peter?" asked Fanny.

"No, no. It's this couple from Maui. I tell you, if there's a murder on this trip, it's going to be him killing his wife."

"What?" They said the word in unison.

"I'm joking," said Amy. "He's a man with some anger issues. Nothing dramatic."

"Anger directed against his wife?" Fanny raised a pencil-lined eyebrow.

"Is she afraid of him?" asked Marcus.

"Good question," Fanny agreed. "Has she maybe been afraid of him for a while now?"

"What?" Amy was taken aback by the sudden, somber-sounding barrage. "She might be a little afraid of him. Why?"

"When did Paisley MacGregor work for them?" Marcus asked. "Recently?"

"Good question," Fanny agreed again. "The envelope doesn't look old."

"It's the Steinbergs." The good humor drained out of Amy's voice. "They employed Paisley right before Peter did, maybe two years ago. Why?"

Silence filled the home office as Marcus and Fanny played sign language back and forth.

"Hello, Mom?"

Marcus wanted to tell her. Fanny wasn't so sure. "She has a right to know," Marcus signed.

"Are you guys there?"

"She's going to overreact," Fanny warned as she used the universal hand signal for *crazy*.

"Hey, what's going on?"

Her mother sighed and looked resigned. "Amy, dear," she said directly into the speaker, "are you sitting down?"

"Don't ask if she's sitting down," Marcus blurted out. "That makes it worse."

"I'm at the bar in a crowded bistro, standing up."

"Well, find a bar stool and sit down."

"The only reason I would need to sit down is if you two were really having an affair."

"Have it your way," said Fanny and turned to face Marcus. "You tell her, lover boy."

CHAPTER 7

Amy did not sit down. Instead, she took her phone out onto rue du Vertbois, away from the noise of the bistro. The air was chilly, and the narrow cobbled street glistened from what must have been a passing shower not long before.

It was well after midnight on what had already been a long day—until now a long, satisfying day. She listened more than spoke, first to Marcus, then to Fanny, then to Marcus. What they told her was both far-fetched and made a horrible kind of sense. MacGregor had always been a receptacle for her people's secrets. And now, even in death, she was holding onto one final one. With her free hand, Amy pulled her pashmina around her shoulders, imagining it as a blanket and wanting nothing more than to be snugly asleep in bed.

Back inside the bistro, behind the red checkered curtains, a few stalwarts continued to drink and laugh and trade more Paisley MacGregor stories. Peter Borg listened with mixed feelings. There was no doubt that his maid had been a colorful character. And the stories were great. But he wondered, quite seriously, why he wasn't as fond of colorful characters as other people were. Did this mean that he lacked the joie de vivre necessary to enjoy them? Or did it mean, as he preferred to think, that colorful characters were best enjoyed from a distance, preferably in someone else's stories?

"Did she have any relations?" Maury asked. They were sitting side by side at the end of the bar, with Barbara Corns just around the bend of polished mahogany, nursing a club soda. It took Peter several seconds to realize the question had been directed his way. "As far as you know from her will? No family?"

"Um, no," Peter said, pushing through the mental haze of brandy enough to recall.

"She was an only child," Barbara interjected, filling in the blanks. "No husband. No kids. Evan did some legal work for her."

Maury nodded. "So, what's happening with all her stuff?"

"You mean her inheritance?" said Peter. It seemed a rude thing to ask about your maid, even if the woman did die with millions. "We're going to be reading her will in Hawaii. That's what she wanted."

"No, I mean her stuff." Maury motioned the bartender to pour Peter another brandy. "Photos and scrapbooks and papers. Personal stuff."

"Why? Is there anything you want?"

"No, no," Maury said quickly. "There's just some things Laila and I gave her over the years. Not the stuff from Laila's mother, trust me," he laughed, then paused as the bartender slid another brandy smoothly across the bar top.

"I probably shouldn't say this," Peter said, but he was saying it, anyway. "Most of the presents we all gave her, for holidays and birthdays . . . she never opened them."

"You're kidding." Maury looked disappointed. "Really?"

"They're all crammed into a big closet, some of them still in the wrapping paper. I opened the closet one day by accident. I couldn't believe it. Who doesn't open a present?"

"I guess they weren't important to her," Maury said.

"It was the thought that counted," said Barbara. "I know that's a cliché, but I know MacGregor loved the fact that we gave her things. She did."

"I know," said Peter. "But still . . . when you search all over town to find her the right perfume at a good price, and then she never even opens it . . ."

"It makes you think about things," mused Maury.

"Like perfume?" asked Barbara.

"Not that," Maury said meditatively. "The personal stuff. All the things that make up a person's whole life—papers and letters and files and photos . . ."

"I imagine the estate will hire someone to sell it," said Peter. "I was the executor when my aunt died," he went on, dredging up the details in his foggy mind. "A houseful of junk. But the funeral home knew someone. The furniture was sold at an estate sale. And the personal stuff was just thrown out. If you're worried about a stranger reading something personal, diaries or letters . . . I don't think that will happen. People do this for a living."

"It all gets thrown out," Maury mused with a crooked grin. "That makes sense." When he glanced up at the mirror behind the bar, he was surprised to see Amy standing right behind him. She had an odd, almost stricken look. "Amy, is something wrong?" He turned to face her directly. "Your call home?" He pointed to the cell phone dangling from her hand. "Everyone good?"

"Everyone's great. You were asking about something that your wife gave to MacGregor? Was this like a letter, an envelope, something you want back?"

"Something Laila wrote? No, no. It was just a general question."

Later, after finally stumbling back to her room at the Crillon, Amy did not spend the night snugly asleep, but tossing and turning on her six-hundred-thread-count sheets. She tried not to obsess about her suspicions. *Think about something else*, she ordered herself as she wound the duvet mercilessly around her torso. Perhaps she should confide in Peter. That would be the logical thing. *Amy, stop it. Stop thinking.* But she couldn't.

Peter, if she told him, would probably be logical and say it was a coincidence. That's what Peter did. It was his strong suit, to see everything as normal, and she often admired this quality. But what if everything wasn't normal?

That's where someone like Marcus would be better, wouldn't he? Impulsive, conniving Marcus— someone who refused to just stick his head in the sand. So, should she confide in Peter, after all, or should she . . . *Augh, stop thinking.* Why couldn't she stop thinking?

CHAPTER 8

By mid-morning everything seemed fine again. It was surprising what a perfect April day in Paris, along with a little shopping, could do to a girl's mood. There were three of them sharing this excursion: Laila Steinberg, Nicole Marconi, and Amy, who had beguiled them with the promise of some exquisite little shops hidden among the steep, twisting alleys of Montmartre.

She made a single purchase that morning, an irresistible set of antique buttons, etched silver with mother-of-pearl inlays, which could just possibly renew her Lanvin silk jacket for a few more years. While the others continued to comb through every nook and cranny of the boutique, Amy accepted an espresso from the gracious owner and stood in the doorway, observing Parisian life on the street.

Just a few doors down, a woman with a shaved head and a neck tattoo was sitting on a stoop, rolling a cigarette with expert ease. Across the street, a pair of grandparents alternately laughed and panicked and did their best to chase down a three-year-old on a tricycle. Young girls in uniform skipped by arm in arm and absently played with a few handfuls of grape leaves. They were only a block or so away from Clos Montmartre, Amy seemed to recall, a tiny hillside vineyard, the last vineyard left in Paris.

"We got some real steals," Nicole whispered as she sprang through the doorway, her string bag full with half a dozen colorfully wrapped baubles.

Laila Steinberg followed with another string bag, plus two large shopping bags. "I am so ready for lunch," she laughed, gasping out the words, as if she'd just completed a marathon.

Lunch was at Le Moulin Orange, a trendy brasserie on rue Lepic. The place had been hard to track down. Laila's husband had seen a rave review in the *Times* praising its unusual blend of French and Italian, a heretical concept for a Parisian brasserie. They settled in at a window table, and Laila ordered a lamb chop, highly recommended in the same *Times* review, according to Maury. Nicole stuck to her diet with a *salade niçoise*, dressing on the side. And Amy, who never worried much about weight, ordered a traditional cassoulet, a sentimental favorite and a surprising find on a springtime menu. Paisley, of course, would be paying.

"Help me understand." Amy was sipping more than her share of the cru Beaujolais and feeling emboldened. "Why all this fuss about a maid? I know it sounds callous. She was quite wonderful, and this is a free trip. I get it. But all of you . . . most of you . . ." She avoided glancing over at Nicole. "You can afford your own first-class travel. And you have such busy lives."

"So why are we taking off eleven days to spread her ashes around the world?" Laila stared out over the rims of her narrow, enviable maroon frames. "Because she asked, I guess. It never occurred to us to say no. I can't speak for Nicole. . . ."

"The same," Nicole said with a nod. "Paisley would do anything for you, no questions, no judgments. That becomes very seductive. Inside a week this woman would be your best friend. Inside a month, you couldn't live without her, which is stupid."

"Not that she would ever betray a confidence," Laila asserted. "Or ever remind you that she knew."

"You don't realize until after she leaves and the spell is broken. . . ." Nicole pushed aside her untasted wine. "I think part of being on this trip is the therapy. Sharing all the Paisley stories. You realize how many others put themselves in that same position. Smart, well-adjusted people, like my parents, who left her nearly everything, for God's sake. I was a teenager, so I was probably less susceptible to having this kind of best friend."

"Therapy," Laila said and nodded back. "An apt way of putting it. At the time, it seemed all good, like an addiction does, I suppose."

Therapy? Addiction? Amy had been expecting a simpler, sweeter explanation, similar to the testimonials everyone had been spouting last night on the yacht. The perfect servant—from Jeeves to Hazel to Batman's Alfred—was an easy, comforting cliché. But perfection could have its dark side, she realized.

The table fell into an awkward silence as the waiter arrived with their lunches and a second bottle of Beaujolais. When he walked away, the talk resumed and became small, the usual inspection and smelling of the food and comments about the weather, over the background music of knives and forks and quiet chewing. And breathing. Someone was breathing. Loudly. *A little annoying*, Amy thought casually as she dove into yet another spoonful of white beans and meat, this time a succulent shred of duck. *Very annoy . . .*

When Amy looked up from her cassoulet, Laila had dropped her fork and was grabbing at her throat. At first, Amy didn't think, *Choking, or too much salt*. She automatically thought, *Poison*. "What's wrong?" she asked, trying to get Laila to focus. Of course, it couldn't be poison. Who would poison her here? The chef? The waiter?

Laila couldn't answer. By now she had both hands on her chest, her eyes staring down at the lamb chop and the brown stuffing as if they were terrorists.

"Allergy?" Nicole asked with surprising calm.

Laila bobbed her head.

"I thought so. Shellfish?" Nicole continued, as if in a game of Twenty Questions. "Of course not. Peanuts? Tree nuts?"

Laila bobbed again and, with a shaky hand, tried to reach down for the purse at her feet. Nicole helped her to grab it.

"It's anaphylactic shock," she said to Amy. "I've seen it before."

Amy was already pushing herself up from her chair and calling for the waiter. "Monsieur?"

He was nearby, discussing with his customers their choice of starters. Everyone at the table stopped their chatter and looked perturbed. Americans could be so pushy.

"Monsieur," she said again, the panic rising in her voice. "Ces côtelettes d'agneau. Y a-t-il des noix?"

The waiter blinked at Amy, then blinked at his

customers, a well-dressed table of six. "Bien sûr. Pâte
de marrons." Of course. Chestnut paste. The others
all murmured in agreement—"Chestnut paste in a
lamb stuffing, of course"—as if it were a ridiculous
thing to ask, and so rudely put, without even a "*Par-
don*" or an "*Excusez-moi.*"

When Amy looked back, Laila had collapsed on
the marble floor. Nicole was still going through
Laila's purse. A second later she pulled out a small
zipped pouch and out of the pouch an EpiPen.
Amy had never seen one before, but she knew what
it was.

"My niece has a nut allergy," Nicole said, still relatively calm. The device looked like a Magic Marker;
it was around the same size and shape. Nicole made
a fist around the pen, pressed it against the thigh of
Laila's silk dress, and pushed. Laila was still gasping.
Nicole held it in place for nearly twenty seconds.

Amy wasn't sure what she should expect. Nothing
as dramatic as an instant recovery, maybe. Maybe a
slow recovery of breath or a calming effect. Certainly
not a worsening of the symptoms, not like this. Laila
gasped in desperation. Her face flushed. Her eyes
widened, searching the room, begging for help,
even as they seemed to lose focus.

"It's empty," said Nicole, finally losing her calm.
She sent it scuttling across the floor, then turned
back to the purse and began rummaging for another. "Who the hell brings an empty pen?"

"No," Laila managed to say between her gasps.

"Damn. That was the only one." Nicole had emptied everything out onto the marble. Nothing looked
even remotely like an EpiPen case. "Was that your
only one?"

"No," Laila said again. Her voice was weaker now.

Amy was about to reach for her phone when she remembered it was back at the Crillon. She turned to face the rest of the room. By now the waiter and his patrons and everyone else were staring, open-mouthed. "SAMU," she shouted to everyone and no one. "Appelez le SAMU! Composez le quinze. Vite!"

A dozen phones materialized out of pockets and purses. All it would take was one call getting through to the emergency number fifteen. And after that, how long? Amy had experience with the emergency response in Rome, not in Paris. And Rome had not worked out well. She tried not to think about that.

"*Ici.*" A woman's voice cut through the concerned murmurs and the soft beeps of a dozen phones. The woman rising from her chair on the other side of the brasserie—young, under twenty—was looking straight at Amy, holding something in the air.

At first Amy thought it was another phone. *What? You want me to dial for you? You can't dial your own . . . ?* Then she realized.

The woman and Amy edged through the tables and chairs and curious diners and met halfway. "*Merci,*" Amy said, filling the word with as much meaning as she could. Then she took the stranger's EpiPen, raced back through the tables and chairs and curious diners, and handed it off like a baton. Nicole grabbed it in her fist, removed the cap, and jabbed it smartly into Laila's other thigh.

CHAPTER 9

Amy could have flown first class. No one would have said a word, except perhaps Nicole, who seemed to take each expenditure personally. No one else would have raised an eyebrow.

Amy wouldn't have minded flying coach under normal circumstances. The actual flight was comfortable, with decent KLM service and a plane that was less than half full, such a delightful rarity. No, the reason she wanted to be in first class was that Laila and Maury Steinberg were up there, without adult supervision.

Laila had stayed overnight at the Clinique Paris-Montmartre for observation and had stayed an extra day at the Crillon, just to be safe, while the others had taken the private 757, with its flight crew of six, onward to the next destination. Peter had toyed with the idea of postponing the flight so they could all travel together. But the pilot had already filed his flight plan, and Laila kept insisting that she didn't want to upset everyone's schedule. They would fly commercial and catch up.

Amy could have gone with the group. She'd been tempted, having grown quite fond of private travel, with seats that converted into beds more comfortable than her bed at home. And nearly the same size. Plus rose petals and a chocolate on the pillow every night. Under any other circumstances, she would have been fine with leaving a couple of tour members on their own for a day.

But these circumstances were unnerving. Maury had urged his wife to go to a Parisian brasserie and to order a dish that—and this was mentioned in the *Times* review; Amy had looked it up online—contained an ingredient that his wife was deathly allergic to. Then, once she was in the throes of anaphylactic shock, while fumbling through her purse for one of her lifesaving EpiPens, Laila would find that, inexplicably, there was only one pen and it was empty. She could have died.

And the kicker—the pièce de résistance, to keep the food theme going—was that just the night before, over a few rounds of brandy, Maury had grilled Peter about personal papers in the dead maid's apartment that might get thrown out without a second glance.

In reality, Amy's decision to stay in Paris couldn't have made much of a difference. The Steinbergs had remained in their room for much of the extra twenty-four hours, where Laila could have slipped "accidentally" on a bar of soap or entangled her neck in the cords of the venetian blinds. None of this happened. And Amy had spent the evening alone in her room, eating a room service burger but skipping the fries. She thought about watching something on the hotel's pay-per-view but decided to call Marcus instead. They had Skyped for over an hour, sharing small jokes and whispered intimacies, which turned out to be much more satisfying than any romantic comedy.

Peter and the rest of the tour were doing fine, as far as Amy knew. Her weather app was announcing fair skies. The new hotel was supposed to be great. And the wake's venue was booked and confirmed. True, during her check-in with Peter last night, he had sounded a little stressed. But Peter was like that. It could be the end of the world or a hangnail. She hadn't asked. And since he probably would have mentioned the end of the world, she was betting on the hangnail.

Amy was in a window seat toward the rear of the plane, trying not to think about the trays of warm macadamia nuts being served up front. She looked out the thick glass at the rugged terrain, then reached for her in-flight magazine and checked the map in back. They must be somewhere over Bulgaria. Did Bulgaria have mountains? She was vaguely aware now of someone settling into the empty aisle seat. When she glanced up, she saw Laila smiling at her sweetly across the empty middle seat.

"Why did you stay behind?" Laila asked.

It was unexpected, but Amy treated it as an innocent inquiry. "To make sure you were all right and that no travel complications popped up. All part of the service."

"It was my fault, you know." She was still a little weak from her ordeal. "Maury always warns me about having more than one EpiPen on me. Not that an incident happens often, but when you travel sometimes . . ."

A detective friend had once informed Amy that the best way to get away with murder was to give your intended victim an "accident" in a foreign country.

The change in routine made it easy. And the police were never as diligent about following through with accident-prone tourists.

"Why was your pen empty?"

Laila looked embarrassed. "It wasn't empty. It malfunctioned. Maury picked it up at the restaurant yesterday and had it tested. Anyway, I should have asked the waiter about nuts. Maury is always good about asking."

"Not this time." Amy tried to say it with a smile. "This time he recommended a dish with a chestnut stuffing."

"Please don't tease him about that," Laila said, her hand resting on Amy's forearm. "He feels so bad. You saw how he was."

That much was true. When he'd heard the news about his wife, Maury Steinberg had rushed to the clinic and had done everything a concerned husband should. And when he'd heard that his dining suggestion had been the culprit, he'd been nearly inconsolable. Laila literally had had to pull herself out of her sickbed to comfort him. Amy had seen it personally, both of them sitting on the edge of the bed, each Steinberg apologizing to the other for enabling Laila's near-death experience. Only a cynic would have doubted his sincerity.

"Are those the Dovetails?" Laila was staring directly into Amy's eyes, and it took Amy a few seconds to realize she was talking about her glasses.

"Oh, these. Yes. Not that I can afford Ellis frames. But I found them in a thrift shop in SoHo and had my prescription put in."

"I hope it was a high-end thrift shop. May I?" Laila reached out both hands and removed Amy's round, intricately checkered frames in one swift, professional move. She studied the temples and the frame and how the lenses were attached. "These are laser etched on acetate, as I'm sure you know. Your optician did a good job. I wouldn't have known."

Amy was stumped. And then she focused on Laila's own frames, also undeniably an Ellis pair. In fact, all of Laila's and Maury's frames, she seemed to recall . . . "Ellis is . . ."

"A cute version of my initials. Laila Santorini, my maiden name. But it still works for Steinberg, luckily."

"You're Ellis Eyewear? No." Amy was gasping. "No!" It was almost like meeting a rock star. Better. She had no interest in meeting a rock star. "Are you the designer? Oh, my God." She had to force her mouth shut in order to stop the gushing.

Laila blushed appreciatively. "We sold the company. But I still design a few, for fun." Laila removed her own frames and handed them over for inspection. They were oval, with an uneven, almost leopardlike pattern of spots. "These are limited edition. Twelve layers of buffalo horn." The frames were even more perfect close up. Amy felt as if she were holding the Hope Diamond.

For the next half hour, Amy forgot about "accidents" and mysterious "if I die" notes. For the next half hour, it was all about vintage Chanels and keyhole bridges and which celebrity wore what.

"Gwyneth Paltrow isn't even nearsighted," Laila whispered, evidently afraid that the Armenian family in the row in front of them might be listening. "Except when we have some fabulous design she can get for free. And don't even get me started on Rachel Maddow."

When the conversation finally wended its way

back in the direction of MacGregor and the Stein-bergs, Amy was actually disappointed.

"I was never sure what Paisley thought of us," Laila said, gazing unfocused at a seat-back screen where a soundless Adam Sandler movie had just been play-ing. "We were going through the sale of the com-pany and money issues. A lot of marital discord," she said softly, with an eye to the eavesdropping Ar-menians. "And, of course, she listened. I'm sure Maury confided in her, too. Like a marriage coun-selor who dusts and changes the sheets." She chuck-led at her own joke.

"But that's what she enjoyed. Being part of your drama. Did you ever give MacGregor a note?" Amy tried to make the question seem natural. It didn't.

"You mean like a reference?"

"No, I mean give her something for safekeeping. Something for her to read later on."

"You mean like a book?"

"No, like a letter. Never mind," Amy said and changed the subject.

As soon as the words hit the air, Amy realized how ridiculous it all sounded. It was ridiculous. All she had was an empty envelope. If it had indeed been given to Paisley MacGregor by one of her clients—a big if—well, that was years ago. And every one of these people was still alive. As for Laila Stein-berg, she didn't seem particularly frightened of her husband. And even if she was frightened, she knew that Paisley was dead and the note probably lost. She could write another. Or not write one. She could actually tell someone that her husband was trying to kill her. Or just leave him. She certainly had the resources to walk away. Not to mention the glasses.

"I should head back to my seat," Laila said as she unbuckled herself and got to her feet. Then she turned back. "Why aren't you in first class? You should have gotten Peter to spring for that. You can't let men walk all over you. Am I right?"

"You're right," said Amy. Suddenly, she felt better than she had in days. Laila was not going to be a victim. This murder obsession was just a reaction to Amy's last, very deadly escapade. As a result, she'd been seeing the shadow of murder everywhere. If she had done the second mystery road rally instead of this trip, it would have been the same, except there would be a different batch of prospective killers around each far-flung corner of the world.

Her whole body relaxed. It was like a revelation, a switch being flipped, and she giggled like a kid, a sound that finally did get the attention of the Armenian family in front. The husband and wife and son all turned and stared. But so what? This was Amy's moment. Either she had to forget about murder plots once and for all and learn to enjoy her job again or she had to find another. And she wasn't ready to find another.

"Ladies and gentlemen," came the announcement, a woman's voice lilting over the intercom. "Please return to your seats. The captain is now making our initial approach into Istanbul."

CHAPTER 10

"**H**e said to go past the sandal street, past the old jewelry kiosk on the left, and then a right at the jewelry shop on the corner."

"They're all sandal streets and jewelry shops." Barbara Corns looked down one long, confusing arm of the bazaar, then turned ninety degrees and looked down another. She did this once more and gave up.

The couple was an island of red, ample flesh bobbing in a moving sea of modest suits and head scarves and dark dresses. The Corns couldn't be called fat—they were, in fact, fairly athletic—but they were instantly recognizable as people of large appetites and passions. Typical Americans.

Evan Corns took his wife by the elbow and led the way, showing more confidence than he felt. "You're the one who forgot the alarm clock," he reminded her. "I distinctly remember——"

"I brought an alarm. I just didn't realize you meant that one." It had been less than a minute since that nice English-speaking man had come to their rescue and given them directions, and already she was disoriented. The sickening scent of two competing spice shops, one directly to her left and one to her right, didn't help.

"A digital? How are we supposed to do this with a digital clock?"

"I thought you brought it. You were the one in charge of the bomb."

"Shh." Evan pulled her into an alcove, away from the jostling stream of humanity, where their words might not echo quite so loudly off the vaulted ceiling. "I don't think it's smart to say 'Bomb' in the middle of an Arab street. Do you think it's smart to say 'Bomb'? I don't."

"You just said it twice."

Istanbul's grand bazaar was one of the largest and oldest in the world, a labyrinth of thousands of shops filling dozens of streets, all huddled under one roof, which could be seen from space, if anyone bothered to look. Back in Paris, after they'd discovered the missing clock, it had been Evan's idea to come here to buy a replacement, something small, with hands.

The bomb they were speaking of would be primitive. That was the point, to make it seem homemade and low tech. And the object wasn't to kill, per se, just to obliterate two specific people from the face of the earth. Afterward, if the police could somehow trace the remains back to the point of sale, then, Evan figured, a crowded Arab market would be just the place.

Evan and Barbara had tried to think up something other than a bomb. Nothing else seemed as easy or as final. They felt a little guilty about the prospect of setting off some kind of international incident. But who knew? If they got lucky and the bomb left no remains, the whole thing might get blamed on a faulty fuel line.

Paisley MacGregor's movable wake had been a godsend. It had materialized at just the right moment for the Corns, just as the walls were all closing in. They couldn't have suddenly gone off on their own. That would have looked suspicious, at least from law enforcement's point of view. But going off with a group of friends on a loved one's wake and then getting blown up by terrorists or by a fuel leak . . . that would be tragic. Barbara almost cried every time she thought about it.

Of course, they weren't going to blow themselves up. Their survival instincts were too well honed. They were going to rent a little motorboat tomorrow at Eminönü Pier and bring along their own little inflatable dinghy tucked into Evan's oversize backpack. Barbara would be bringing the bomb in hers—if they ever managed to find a windup alarm clock for their timing device. And then somewhere along the deep, treacherous Sea of Marmara, not far from a deserted cove they had already picked out—thanks to the wonders of Google Earth—they would leave the bomb, slip into the dinghy and . . . *ka-boom!* Two American tourists, tragically killed.

Barbara—as long as she was feeling sorry, for herself and her family and the people of Turkey, but certainly not for Evan, who had created this desperate need to disappear in the first place—was feeling especially sorry for Amy. Barbara had read about Amy's previous tour. The last thing the poor girl needed was another death, two deaths, taking place on another one of her high-end adventures.

"We'll never find a windup clock in this maze."

Barbara stepped back into the flow of traffic and headed back in the vague direction of daylight and the Beyazit Gate. With any luck, they could be out of here in half an hour.

"What do you suggest we do?" asked Evan as he rushed to catch up.

Barbara had thought it through. "We may not need to die," she whispered and made an arbitrary left turn.

"What?" Evan felt a pang of disappointment. He had put so much work into this plan.

"I overheard something. Come on. I'm hungry. If we have lunch at the hotel, it goes on MacGregor's tab."

"I'm not sure I can wait that long. I have to pee."

Barbara rolled her eyes. "You always have to pee."

"You need to eat. I need to pee. What's the difference?"

"Because you always need to pee."

"Let's take this one need at a time, okay?"

The Four Seasons wasn't far away. The hotel was comprised of a few dozen luxury rooms and suites, situated in the old city, in the picturesque shadow of the Blue Mosque. On reading the hotel's description, Barbara had been concerned that the windows might be a little small for her taste, given that the building had been built two centuries ago as a Turkish prison, but someone must have solved this problem, because the windows were fine.

By the time they made their way to a public bathroom, then out of the bazaar and back to the hotel, it was two hours later, lunch service had ended, and the Steinbergs were just arriving from Paris. Amy was with them, checking them in. All three were in high spirits. Laila was looking much better, Barbara noted, and whatever case of nerves Amy had been suffering from seemed to have dissipated.

The only one looking stressed was Peter Borg. His lanky frame had just loped down the stairs to the lobby, and despite his broad smile and warm greetings to everyone, he seemed eager to take Amy aside and share a few urgent words. Barbara would have been more curious, except that she was so tired from the walk and ravenously hungry.

Sandwiches and snacks, they discovered, were still being served at the terrace bar, and yes, they could charge them to their room. Evan and Barbara settled in with their strong, sweet mint tea and waited at a mosaic table in the shade, listening to the gurgle of a marble fountain. A hundred years ago, Barbara mused, this pleasant oasis might have been a cozy little exercise yard for rapists and killers.

The sandwiches arrived in short order—some kind of meat and eggplant. It was always eggplant. Why was that? Like a constant national sale on eggplant. They had just finished inspecting the sandwich contents when the Pepper-Sands, Herb and David, limped by on the far side of the exercise yard.

"Hey there. How was the massage?" Evan called out with a friendly wave.

Herb had been talking about a Turkish bath ever since New York. According to him, there was this straight, unbroken line between the baths of ancient Greece and the present-day *hamams*—from the Greeks to the Romans, who copied the Greek baths, then migrated to the eastern part of their empire in Constantinople. The Romans' descendants, the Byzantines, handed off the tradition to the Turks, who conquered this city and changed its name and built these amazing bathhouses in the fourteen hundreds that were still operating in exactly the same way today. According to Herb's theory, each generation of workers trained the next in the noble art of massage, so that a modern tourist could have approximately the same experience that Plato or Alexander the Great might have had on one of their days off. Herb found the prospect fascinating.

"Don't ask," said David in a voice laden with pain. His golden-red hair looked unusually flat and thin, almost plastered against his head. "It was like wrestling."

Herb nodded and kept on limping. "They rub you—more like squeeze you—up and down your arms and legs, then stretch you and throw soap and almost drown you. And blind you with the soap. And all the while they're talking incessantly about how big a tip you should give them."

"Not a sensual experience at all," David said, loud enough for anyone to hear. "Not that we were looking for one. But we were expecting something pleasant. Or historical, at least." He glared at Herb. "So much for your theory."

"The Greeks would never have put up with this," said Herb. "And no one was even remotely cute," which was his final, damning critique.

Evan couldn't repress a smirk. "Well, at least you're clean."

"Right," Herb said. "I'm going up to the room and taking a shower."

When the Corns finally got up to their own room, Evan had to pee again. Then they continued from where they'd left off at the bazaar.

"You can't change the plan," Evan insisted. "Everything's in place."

"What if we don't disappear?"

"Then our lives are ruined, and we go to jail."

Barbara hated when he said "we" instead of "I," but she let it pass. "Peter said something the other night. He said MacGregor didn't unwrap most of the things people gave her, that they all just sat in some closet forever. Unopened."

"Unopened?" Evan immediately knew. He knew the exact package she meant. "You're kidding me. You're saying she never opened it? It's just sitting there in her damn closet? Right now?"

"We can get it back. It's worth a shot at least."

"So you're saying she never opened it."

"I'm thinking no one's going to open it. No one will ever know. It'll just get thrown out. But if we can somehow get it back . . ."

They stood there, side by side, looking out at their partial view of the Blue Mosque through their adequately sized window and doing some mental calculations.

"This could solve our problem," Evan whispered. "Are you sure it's in there?"

"Where else would it be? If you can somehow get it back—maybe volunteer to help clear out her apartment—it'll give you some breathing room at least."

Evan hated it when she said "you" instead of "we." "You're the one who gave it to her in the first place," he replied. "If you hadn't given it to her in the first place . . ."

"I know, dear. We've been through this a million times. I'm sorry."

"This means going back home and giving up our plan," he said, half relieved, half regretful. "Our one chance to escape."

"You can always bomb a boat in the Long Island Sound." She said it, not knowing if she was being serious or not.

Evan took her seriously. "It's easier done in Turkey, both the bombing and the disappearing." He turned away. The sandwich was not settling well, and he suppressed a fragrant little burp. "I'm not going to prison. It doesn't matter what. I can't get caught."

"Honey, if this works out, we'll have everything. Our old lives back. And no one will ever find out."

"What if it's not there? We'll be taking a risk."

"A risk? Bombing a boat and disappearing forever? That's not a risk? Evan . . ." She took his large head between her hands, looked him in the eyes, and ignored the smell of eggplant on his ruddy face. "I don't want to be on the run for the rest of my life. Let's give it a shot. Please."

CHAPTER 11

"**W**hat can we get that resembles human ashes? I never looked that close at them. If we buy some charcoal . . ."

"No." Amy had never examined Paisley MacGregor, either, not recently, but she felt sure the woman did not resemble lumps of charcoal. "Just ashes. Maybe a few bone chunks? I don't know. Not charcoal."

"And where do you suggest we get ashes?" Peter Borg was trying to keep the panic out of his voice. "Other than buying a charcoal shop and burning it to the ground."

"Let's make that Plan B."

Replacing Paisley's urn, they'd thought, would be the tough part. But the original urn, purchased off the shelf at Frank E. Campbell's, had been silver and fairly generic. Among the hundreds of silver shops in old Istanbul, it had been relatively easy—twenty minutes, no more—to find a passable substitute. Paisley herself was turning out to be more problematic.

The disaster had started yesterday at the Istanbul airport. Peter had been stopped randomly and been asked to open his luggage. The silver urn, wrapped in a few protective layers of dirty underwear, drew the customs agent's immediate attention. As Peter tried to explain and grew more nervous each second, the heavyset, scowling agent with the stained uniform grew more curious. Peter was then taken into a small back room. It was only by turning over his passport, Paisley MacGregor, and nine hundred dollars cash U.S., which he suspected he might never see again, that he managed to get away.

Amy wondered how she might have handled such an emergency. Someone like Marcus might have been able to charm his way through. Someone like Fanny might have avoided blurting out that this powder was the remains of a maid who had financed a trip around the world for a troupe of rich New Yorkers. Someone like Marcus or Fanny wouldn't have started sweating and mumbling like a drug addict in desperate need of a fix.

Even someone like Amy, after being forced to leave the ash-filled urn at the airport for testing, might have figured out some solution on her own. Not Peter. He had gone catatonic for nearly a day, not sending as much as a heads-up text, for fear that she might misunderstand or accidentally spill the beans. So now the situation was even worse, with only a few hours to try to make things right.

"We should just tell them," Peter moaned. Suddenly Amy missed Marcus and her mother so much.

"Really? Tell them the wake is on hold, that Mac-Gregor is in Turkish custody, may never be released, and there's nothing left of her to scatter, so they might as well go home?"

"When you use that tone, sure, anything sounds bad. It's your fault."

"My fault?"

"If you hadn't stayed behind to babysit the Steinbergs, I wouldn't have had to pack her myself. I told you I was no good with customs. Especially Turkey." Peter held the new, empty urn, wrapped in brown paper and tied with string, and pressed it to his chest.

They were in the old city, a dozen blocks from the Four Seasons, on the outer edge of the tourist district, where the jewelry shops were gently giving way to copper shops, the rare bookshops giving way to secondhand bookshops. Only about once a minute did Amy have to wave away a peddler offering her a rug or an armful of watches, which was a vast improvement over the tourist district.

"Can I be of some help?"

He was a middle-aged man, large featured, with thin limbs and the hint of a potbelly. He could have been a local—a well-fed, Western-dressed, well-groomed local, the kind who came up and offered their services as a guide, only to wind up leading you to their cousin's rug shop. She might, in fact, have already waved him off a dozen times without knowing it. Amy was halfway into the gesture: no eye contact, a polite but firm lift of the hand. But then the voice . . . He was American, tristate area, maybe Brooklyn. *Not a tourist*, she thought. The man exuded a confidence in his surroundings that said "ex-pat" or "businessman," someone who might actually be able to deliver on the help he was offering.

All of this went through her mind in those first seconds of hesitation, and the man took it as an invitation. "I noticed your confusion. Istanbul can be a rough town."

"You're not a guide," Amy said, with the hint of a smile that asked him not to take offense.

"My name is Bill. Bill Strunk. Call me Billy." He might have shaken hands, but his right hand was curled around a Turkish cigarette. His left was busy with a plastic shopping bag, full to the brim and probably heavy. "My wife's birthday is tomorrow, and I had to pick up a few things. She loves this market."

"So you're a local?" The smell of strong tobacco said yes; the accent said no.

"For a few years now. Half retired. Dabbling in things here and there. Are you guys looking for—"

"Where can we get some ashes?" The words shot out of Peter's mouth, like the arm of a drowning man reaching for a lifeboat. "They don't have to be human ashes, but the closer, the better. And if you can get some tiny bone fragments . . ."

Billy might not have physically taken a step back, but it certainly felt that way.

"No. Let me explain," Peter stammered. "Sorry." Then he started right in, trying to tell it all, the words cascading over each other, reaching even harder for that lifeboat.

To Billy's credit, he didn't run. Instead, he put down his bag and listened. Amy noticed that his hands were shaking. Then she realized this was a medical condition, some sort of palsy, perhaps Parkinson's.

An amused twinkle spread lightly across Billy's eyes, and she could see he believed them. It wasn't the kind of story that anyone, even a suspected drug smuggler like Peter, would make up.

"The customs officer was being a prick."

"Thank you," said Peter.

"If he suspected drugs, he wouldn't have let you go. He just wanted the urn and your money."

"You see?" Peter nudged Amy. "It wasn't my fault. Wait! What about my passport?"

"You'll get that back. But your maid is already down a toilet."

"A toilet?" Amy was shocked. "You think he just dumped her. No!" It seemed so sacrilegious.

"I think so, yes."

"And he's never going to return her?"

"Why should he?"

"Oh."

It sounded reasonable. But it had never occurred to her. Amy allowed herself a moment to grieve. Poor MacGregor. The woman had meticulously planned and taken comfort in this deathbed dream. She'd spent many thousands on making it happen, only to wind up floating in a Turkish sewer. Ah, well, at least she'd had Paris.

"Sorry," Billy said, taking another puff. "You know, I like meeting Americans. Reminds me of home. Sometimes I take them out for a mint tea, and we chat. Talk about the States. About life in Turkey. But you guys . . . I gotta say . . ."

"You weren't prepared for something this crazy. I understand." Amy shrugged and pointed to his plastic bag. "You should get home for your wife's birthday."

"No." Billy stubbed out his cigarette, then raked

a hand through his thinning black crew cut. "This is much more fun. Do you think chicken bone fragments will do?"

Amy and Peter exchanged a look. "Maybe," said Peter. "No one looks up close. It's so solemn."

"Besides, what are they going to say? 'Wrong ashes'? We just need something not too obviously fake. And it shouldn't smell of chicken," Amy added.

Billy's chuckle was throaty and warm. "My wife says Americans are dull and unimaginative."

"I wish," Amy said with feeling.

"My wife's cousin has a kebab shop." Billy pointed down the narrow and endless line of wooden storefronts, with their obstacle course of stalls pushed out into the street. "It's not far from the Four Seasons. I'll have you back in plenty of time."

"That's very nice," Amy said. "Thank you."

"No problem," said Billy. And without wasting another second, he led the way, the two travel agents falling in line behind him. "You'll like Theo. He grills the chicken and beef over a charcoal pit."

"Charcoal?" Peter asked.

"It turns to ash. You'll have all the ash you want. What shade of gray was your friend?"

Peter thought as he dodged through the stalls and the tide of customers. "Actually, I think she's kind of charcoal colored."

"Good," Billy called back over his shoulder. "You're in luck."

The Basketmakers' Kiosk was technically part of the sprawling Topkapi Palace, home to sultans and their wives and concubines and eunuchs for over four hundred years. The building, Amy discovered that evening, was in no way a kiosk and had never had anything to do with basket makers. In fact, the only thing romantic about the four-story, monolithic structure was its quaint name—and the fact that it had been used historically as a pleasure palace, as if the sultan had needed another excuse for pleasure seeking, given all his wives and concubines and eunuchs waiting just up the hill.

For this second leg of MacGregor's wake, they had rented a restaurant/disco that had been carved out of one section of the kiosk's ground floor, although they wound up not using the indoor space at all, except for the bar. Amy and Peter had arranged the linen-covered table and the silver spoons and MacGregor's photo by the seawall, in a conveniently shadowy nook. The new urn and new ashes became little more than outlines in the growing sunset, which was exactly their plan.

One by one, the mourners did their duty, stepping up to the far edge of Europe, saying a few somber words this time, and tossing spoonfuls of chicken charcoal out toward the Bosphorus and the soft, twinkling lights of Asia.

Amy had been concerned that the ashes might still be warm, a difficult thing to explain, or that the smell of chicken might be in the air, an easier thing to explain here on the grounds of a restaurant. But the only hiccup occurred when Laila Steinberg mentioned offhandedly how, after two wakes, so much of Paisley MacGregor seemed to be left in the urn.

"We'll have to start doing two scoops from now on," she said. Peter pretended to find this amusing.

In the end, they seemed to have gotten away with it. Amy felt euphoric at having so deftly dodged a bullet, and more than a little sad. "Don't you feel sad?" she asked Peter, seeking some confirmation of her muddled emotions. The two of them were sipping the mandatory champagne by the boat slip, far enough away from the best view and from the others to speak freely.

"Not really," said Peter. "When you break it all down, it's just symbolic. Even with real ashes, the funeral home gives you only a fraction of them. And a lot of that is the casket she was burned in. Memorials are for the living."

"You're right," Amy had to agree. "It's the thought and the memories."

"And you were right not to tell them the truth." Peter looked back at the figures silhouetted in the sunset's last red glow. Their voices echoed off the waves, telling stories they'd already told a dozen times. He sipped again and smiled. "But a couple of chickens are getting one hell of a send-off."

When Amy laughed, the chilled champagne almost flew out of her nose.

"And on that high note . . ." Peter checked his watch. "I gotta go. You'll take care of getting the mourners back home?"

"Sure. Where are you going?"

"Billy wanted to get together for a drink. I think he's homesick."

"And probably curious about our little group."

"It's a curious group. Anyway, I certainly owe him a drink. Is that okay?"

"Buy him one for me."

Amy walked Peter to the bottom of the stairs leading up to the street, then circled around the cobbled plaza, taking the long way back to the waterfront site. Evan and Barbara Corns were leaning on the railing, gazing out at a lone motorboat, little more than a pair of red and green lights making their way across to a new continent. And that, of course, reminded her. Amy caught their eye and joined them.

"I hear you're renting a boat tomorrow morning, which is totally doable," she said. "Our flight isn't until six fifteen in the evening, so—"

"We canceled," Barbara said quickly. "The water's supposed to be choppy."

"Are you sure?" Amy had checked the forecast a few hours ago. Tomorrow was predicted to be another perfect, calm day.

"We thought it over." There was a note of true reluctance in Evan's voice. "It seems a little risky." He turned to his wife. "Don't you think?"

"Yes," Barbara said emphatically. "Too risky."

"We can still do it, honey. What do you think?"

"Come on, Barbara," Amy blurted out and was surprised by her passion. She had seen instantly what this was. It was like her own life with Eddie. "Do it. How many times will you ever get to sail on the Bosphorus?" It almost sounded like pleading.

"I think it's safer if we don't," said Barbara.

"What about adventure?" Amy looked up over the rims of her glasses, her eyes meeting Barbara's. "It's the adventures we remember, not the perfect days. You remember getting caught in a thunderstorm. Running out of gas in the French countryside. What's the worst that can happen? You get a little lost and you miss the flight? There'll be another." She saw Barbara's look of alarm and instantly backtracked. "Okay, that's not good. That's a worst-case scenario. It'll be a gorgeous day, and you'll be so glad you did it. How many chances like this will you get?"

"How many chances will we get?" Evan echoed. "Honey?"

Barbara turned back to the railing and focused on the disappearing red and green lights. "We'll get another."

CHAPTER 12

"I don't think I've ever seen you in a suit," Fanny said. Her tone was admiring and supportive, even as she reached up and picked an imaginary speck of lint from his breast pocket.

"It's a uniform." Marcus spotted himself in a mirror halfway across the store and felt he was looking at his own evil twin. The same crooked smile; the same hair, wavy and jet-black, but now combed straight back to reveal the beginnings of a widow's peak. The black suit was evil twinish as well, sleek and slick. Not suit. Uniform. He still wasn't used to the concept.

Fanny Abel went from picking imaginary lint to straightening the very real pins on his jacket lapels. Each was shaped like a pair of golden keys crossed in the middle. "Very snazzy," she cooed. "I didn't realize every concierge got the golden keys. Some hotels I've been to . . ."

"The keys are special," Marcus said modestly, lowering his voice in the elegant, mostly deserted boutique. "You need five years of experience to earn them. I think there are other requirements, too. I didn't check. The keys are a big deal."

Fanny was impressed. "Five years' experience. So that means you've been on the job at the Ritz-Carlton . . . ?"

"Two days. And yes, I came by them honestly. Bought them at a flea market in Tribeca maybe three years ago."

Fanny wasn't disappointed by his admission. Quite the contrary. "And you just knew they might come in handy one day? Bravo to you."

"The Ritz-Carlton loves my keys. Unfortunately, the hotel where I earned them happened to burn to the ground, so they weren't able to send over my employment records."

"Pity. Burned to the ground, you say?"

"Electrical fire in Chattanooga. I found it online. Half an hour on Google and I pieced together a whole backstory for myself. By the way, if someone calls you for a reference, your name is Anita and you used to be my boss."

"Wasn't I killed in the fire?"

"It was your day off."

Marcus would make a terrific concierge, Fanny was sure. His job would consist of getting his guests whatever their hearts desired, provided it was legal and they had the money. And there was no doubt that he had already proven his qualifications—by, in fact, getting the job without any qualifications.

"Is this going to happen soon?" Marcus shot back his left cuff and checked his shiny Faux-lex. It was still ticking. "I can't be late for work, at least not for the first month."

For the past ten minutes they had been browsing, wandering the display aisles in the Ellis Eyewear shop

on Lexington Avenue. The boutique was filled with
nothing but frames, although, in Fanny's opinion,
the price tags might have been borrowed from
Tiffany, a few blocks away. She had never understood
her daughter's obsession with fancy eyeglasses, although she supposed they made her feel more interesting. Of course, if Amy really wanted to stand out
in a crowd, she would follow her mother's example
and adopt a pageboy cut. Seventy bucks max, including a henna rinse.

"I'm sure we'll get served in a minute," Fanny assured him. It wasn't that the service at Ellis Eyewear
was bad. It was, as in many overpriced shops, quite
good, with several well-dressed, well-spoken sales-
people circling the premises like vultures.

"Are you sure I can't help you?" a tall, toothy girl
of twenty asked for the third time. Fanny inspected
her green- and red-striped frames—really quite
stunning, she had to admit—and wondered if the
girl actually needed glasses or was just using herself
as a walking advertisement.

"Thanks," she said sweetly. "We're still waiting for
Gary." She tilted her head toward the far side of the
shop, where Gary, the oldest member of the staff,
perhaps thirty-five, was sitting with a pair of teenagers
in front of a mirror, trying on endless versions of
black-rimmed, Justin Bieber–like spectacles. "Gary's
been dealing with me for aeons."

"I'm sure I'd be able to assist you," the girl said.
"I'm quite experienced." Moments later and she
was slinking away under the glare of Fanny's sweet,
withering smile.

"Have you told Amy about your job?"

Marcus winced. "Not yet. Do you think she'll approve? I mean, it's a similar business . . . hospitality.

She should like that. Of course, I'm still in my probationary period. But it's the Ritz-Carlton."

"Just don't let her see your golden keys."

"Oh, I can make up a story about those."

Fanny patted his hand. How could her daughter possibly prefer that stick-in-the-mud Peter to a man like this? "Did you get this job because of her, dear?"

"Depends. Would she prefer it if I got it because of her or because I'm suddenly a reliable, responsible individual?"

"Responsible individual."

"Then I did it for that reason."

"Sounds like you're serious." Fanny looked up into his hazel eyes, a little more green than brown. "Or are you just jealous about Amy being away with Peter?"

"Which would she prefer?"

"You are serious."

"No," Marcus said, not even pretending to mean it. "I just miss talking to her. And seeing her. And fighting with her incessantly."

"Excuse me." Gary had managed to extricate himself from the Bieber teens and had silently sneaked up on them. "You wanted to see me?"

It took Fanny a mere second to turn her focus to the man with the shaved, perfectly shaped head and switch from heartfelt to devious. "Gary, darling," she said in her best Long Island accent. "Haven't seen you in ages." She tilted up her lips and air-kissed in the direction of both his cheeks.

"Good to see you again," Gary said, without a hint of hesitation. "You're looking wonderful, dear. New diet?"

"Oh, you flatterer." Fanny slapped at his hand. "I

must have put on five pounds. By the way, those Chanels you sold me are fabulous. Fabulous. I wear them all the time." She saw the salesman's eyes focus on her eyes. Seamlessly, she amended her statement. "Except sometimes they pinch the bridge of my nose, so I'm taking a break today and wearing my contacts."

"Chanel?" Gary winced and looked wounded. "We don't sell Chanel frames. You must have bought them somewhere else."

"You're right," Fanny corrected herself. Two mistakes in five seconds. She had to pay more attention. "Well, no wonder they pinch. If they were Ellis, they wouldn't. Serves me right. Gary, dear, I'd like you to meet a friend." She slipped her hand onto the small of Marcus's back and gently pushed him forward. "This is Marcus . . . Aveeno."

"Aveeno," Marcus repeated, trying to make sure he'd heard the name right. Was that a body lotion? The two men shook hands. "Marcus." He had no idea why Fanny hadn't invented a first name for him, too. Apparently, even she could get flustered.

"Marcus is visiting town from Potsdam. Not the one in Germany. Somewhere else."

"Potsdam, New York?" Gary offered.

"It could be. Is there a Potsdam, New York?"

"That's the one," Marcus said with an indulgent grin.

"Of course. I always get it mixed up with Potsdam, Connecticut."

"Is there a Potsdam, Connecticut?" asked Gary.

"I don't know. Is there?"

"She's a kidder." As much as Marcus was fascinated by Fanny's brain melt, he felt it best to step in now and take control. "Every time I visit Fanny, I always tell her how much I love her glasses—except today, of course."

"Yes," said Fanny, "because I'm not wearing them."

Were the two of them just bored? Marcus wondered. Or morbidly curious? Or perhaps really concerned about Amy and Laila Steinberg and the "if I die" note? That was also a possibility. Amy had called them from Istanbul and had told them about the near-death experience, and even though Amy no longer seemed as interested, they themselves had gone through more than a few bottles of wine in Fanny's back garden, mulling over what it could all mean.

Their conclusion was, "We don't have enough information," which was the whole reason behind their little outing today on Lexington Avenue. In retrospect, Marcus thought, they should have rehearsed a bit more.

Early in their conversation with Gary, Fanny brought up the brilliant designer Laila Santorini. The things that woman could do with plastic and bone and whatnot. "Didn't she get married some years back? To a Steinbeck? Steinberg? Maury Steinberg." That was it.

"It so happens I knew a Maury Steinberg years ago," Marcus said, picking up his cue.

"In Potsdam?" asked the salesman, looking dubious. "I don't think either one of them is from Potsdam."

"No, not Potsdam. From here in the city." Yes. A rehearsal would have been a definite plus. "Short guy, gray hair, full of energy, maybe in his fifties by now."

"That could be Maury," Gary said.

"I'd love to say hello. Is he here, by any chance?" Marcus asked, knowing better, of course.

"No, no. They sold the business a few years back."

"I assume it's the same Maury Steinberg. Do you know him well?"

"I met him before Laila did," Gary said, then chuckled. "By a few minutes. He came in the store one day, looking for frames. I called her out from her office and introduced them. I was the best man at their wedding."

"So you knew him," Fanny deduced.

"Is he still the same crazy guy?" Marcus asked. This was always a safe bet. Everyone in the world called everyone else a crazy guy. The phrase had a million definitions.

"Totally crazy," Gary confirmed.

"I'll bet you have a hundred stories," Fanny prodded.

"A million stories," said Gary with a thin, mischievous grin.

Good. They were back on track, Marcus thought. Who needed rehearsals?

CHAPTER 13

The morning mist flew by in layers, now thicker, now thinner. Occasionally, she could see the silhouette of a hill chattering by. But mostly it was the scrub and a few rows of trees, each row away from the train a little fainter in the distance. And, of course, the mist. Amy had assured her guests that it would burn off, and that once they pulled into the Agra station, the day would be fine. But several of them had been on this journey before and knew how unpredictable it could be. *Mist* was a better word than *fog*, and she would continue to call it mist, even if it lasted all day.

The train from Delhi to Agra was easily the best way to get to the Taj Mahal. Peter had done the trip once with a car and driver, but the anarchy of the roads, even at 7:00 a.m., had made it a long and harrowing ride. Here in the first-class compartment, officially called the AC chair class, the trip took a comfortable two hours, not counting delays for the occasional bull found lounging on the cool tracks.

Amy yawned and nodded and fought the urge to

nap. The early call this morning at the Imperial New Delhi, the three-and-a-half-hour time change from Istanbul, and the smooth rocking of the train all conspired to close her eyes. But the sight of MacGregor's urn under the seat in front of her kept her awake. All right, perhaps this wasn't precisely the maid or precisely her urn, but it did occupy the same emotional space that MacGregor would have if she hadn't been dumped down a Turkish toilet. The last thing they needed now was to lose her to a theft of opportunity.

One row in front of her and across the aisle, Peter was seated at a small club table with Herb Sands and David Pepper. Back in Paris—it seemed so long ago—he had suggested that the Pepper-Sands organize an anniversary trip with friends. Herb had leapt at the idea, but the exact anniversary to be celebrated remained hazy. It would be sixteen years since they'd moved in together, thirteen since their commitment ceremony, nine since a civil union in Vermont, and two since their official marriage in New York City.

"We want to celebrate something," Herb said. "But a second wedding anniversary . . . ?" He scrunched his mouth.

"Sounds small," Peter agreed. "Maybe if we add the numbers together . . . combine your sixteenth, your thirteenth, ninth, second . . ." It took him a few seconds. "Perfect. We can call it your fortieth."

"Cute," said Herb, clapping his hands together. "I like it."

"No," said David and shook his head. "Makes us sound too old."

"No it doesn't," said Peter. "It's funny. People will get it."

"They would," said Herb. "But I'm afraid the invitation would freak David out. He doesn't want to be associated in any way with the number forty."

"Why not?" Peter's surprise was genuine. "You mean the age? David, you're not anywhere near forty."

"Thank you."

"Not anywhere near?" The look on Herb's face was priceless, and it was only the chattering of the wheels that kept Amy's little yelp of laughter from being noticed. "Sixteen years together. Do you think I stole him from a nursery?"

"No, no. I guess I didn't think."

"Leave the poor boy alone," said David and reached out a hand to Peter's knee. "He was being nice."

"And how old do you think I am?" Herb demanded.

Peter turned white and stammered.

"He's sixty-two," David said.

"You sure don't look it." Peter almost shouted the words.

Amy straightened her smile and returned her eyes to the urn. The older man had been shamelessly pursuing Peter the whole trip—eye contact, compliments, fixing collars and brushing shoulders. Amy had finally decided to warn him. She had mentioned just last night, over drinks on a foggy, viewless balcony in New Delhi, that Herb's interest in an anniversary trip might come with a few strings. But Peter continued to see it as nothing more than harmless flirting.

"You should see him in the morning," Herb sniffed, refusing to let it go. "Then he looks his age."

"I'd love for Peter to see me in the morning."

"I've seen you both in the morning." Peter wasn't sure where this was going. Both men had taken his involvement as part of their game, something that could subtly change the balance in their ongoing power struggle. Peter Borg had gone from being a flirt to being the rarest kind of pawn, one that could be used by both sides, depending upon his position on the board.

"Don't play innocent," Herb growled.

Peter didn't know who this comment was meant for. Had he been playing innocent? Had David? Luckily, it didn't matter. A series of electronic chimes and a recorded voice—in three languages: Hindi, English, and French—filled the air and announced their impending arrival in Agra.

Amy got to her feet, along with most of the other first-class tourists, inserting herself into the aisle and gathering her things as quickly as she could. The plan was to assemble on the platform and make their way en masse past the army of hawkers and food sellers and beggars and rug-shop guides to the row of chauffeured Audis waiting for them out at the curb.

Amy checked in front of her and behind. All her people were up and moving, a good sign. And then, out of the corner of her eye, by the door to the second-class car . . . It was one of those moments where a familiar size and shape and physical bearing somehow coalesced. Billy. Billy Strunk. Their savior from Istanbul. And then the mirage, whatever it was composed of, disappeared, leaving nothing but a fleeting sense of gratitude—and a reminder not to leave MacGregor under the seat.

Outside the train, the stubborn mist solidified into fog, and a directive as simple as "gathering on the platform" was proving to be tricky. First off, Amy saw, there was no space, just chaos. Meanwhile, the things filling up that chaotic lack of space were constantly moving and oddly disorienting—fruit vendors and water vendors going from window to window, whole families disgorging from a door and meeting other whole families waiting for them. Brazier fires somehow seemed to be moving, too. And the saris and suitcases. And everywhere the fog.

Peter was tall enough and brightly dressed enough to act as an assembly point. One by one and two by two, the others drifted toward his red Windbreaker, forging a brave little island amid the buffeting tides. Amy was counting them as they came—the Steinbergs, gray and thin and arm in arm; substantial Herb and golden David; the petite Nicole, falling into the wake of Evan and Barbara, large and ruddier than a pair of cherries. And, in the near distance, disembarking from the second-class car, Billy Strunk. Again.

Amy stood on her toes, stretching an inch or two higher than her full five-ten. This time it looked more substantial than a mirage of shape and size and bearing. It looked exactly like Billy, from the thinning hair to the slightly pear-shaped body. The man was facing her way, and their eyes met for a second over the bobbing sea. His eyes seemed to react in recognition. Then he turned away and began to barrel his way down along the platform.

A second later and the man disappeared into the fog.

CHAPTER 14

"Is that the Taj Mahal?"

On the surface it seemed a silly question. Here they were in Agra, just half a mile away, at a hotel known for its magnificent view of the Taj Mahal, standing by the balcony at the rear of the lobby, overlooking a pale dome reflected in a pool of water. "Is that the Taj Mahal?" Really? One of the most famous buildings in the world?

"I don't think so," said Amy. She waved her arms, as if trying to brush the fog away, but a bright blanket of gray enveloped everything except the faint, hopeful outline in the distance. "I think it's part of the hotel," she answered. "Maybe a pavilion on the far side of the swimming pool?"

"Are you sure?" Nicole Marconi asked, giving her a second chance.

"I'm kind of pretty sure."

"That it is?"

"That it's not." Amy would have loved to confirm the sighting—for herself as much as for them. It was one of the dream destinations still on her list. But when the fog lifted, if it lifted, there it would finally be, the iconic white dome with its minarets, a bit higher up and farther away to the right, leaving the pool pavilion to look like the fanciful pool pavilion that it was.

"Are we ever going to see it?" Nicole asked almost accusingly.

"Of course." Now, that was a silly question. You could see anything if you were close enough.

Nicole turned away, disappointed, and approached the hotel doorman for a second opinion. Amy watched as the doorman, undoubtedly experienced in this situation, nodded agreeably. Then they stepped outside, and he patiently pointed Nicole through the gray, toward what might be a footpath. She began walking in that direction and quickly faded from view.

The fog can play tricks, Amy told herself. It was one of the oldest weather-related clichés, right up there with "It's not the heat. It's the humidity." But she wasn't thinking about the Taj Mahal.

Billy's appearance couldn't have been a trick of the fog. She might have mistaken the face. Although a little taller than average, Billy had that generic middle-aged, swarthy look common the world over. But the way he'd reacted upon seeing her . . . the way he had met her eyes, then had turned and disappeared . . . All right, the disappearing part had been easy, given the weather.

"Miss Amy Travel. Hello." The doorman approached her now across the lobby's marble expanse. He had obviously learned her name from someone who had learned it from the tour documents. "Did you talk to that nice man?" He smiled and twisted the pointy ends of his long, well-groomed mustache. From the look of them, the mustache received a lot of proud twisting.

"What man?"

"After you and your friends come. He said he did not want to disturb."

"He came to see me?" She was puzzled. Could it have been a representative from the India tour booker? She knew from Peter that Indian businessmen took the personal connection very seriously. "Did he ask for me? Or for Peter?"

"He said your names, yes. And how many days you be here? And if all your days be very busy? I said, 'Yes, yes. Very busy. Very important.'"

"Did he leave a card or a name?"

"With me?" He said it with a typically Indian blend of modesty and pride. "No, no. That's not for me."

Of course, Amy thought. Which brought up a good point. Why would a travel rep ask a lowly doorman such questions? Besides the fact that a reception clerk or a concierge would have much better information, no Indian of any stature would engage in a conversation like this with a doorman.

"Was this man a foreigner? Like me?" Even as she said the words, Amy had a sinking feeling.

"Yes, yes. American."

"Did he say his name? Did he say who he was? Did he leave? How long ago did he leave?"

The doorman frowned, confused by her sudden intensity. His right hand rose to the comfort of his mustache, while his left pointed to a corner. "He sat there. I'm so sorry I did not get his name."

"Thank you." Under normal circumstances, she would have taken the time to talk and be polite. Instead, she turned on her heels and clicked across the patterned marble and around the coffered wall. No one was sitting in the little alcove, not now. But a cigarette smoldered in a silver ashtray, defacing the Oberoi hotel crest that had been impressed into the white sand.

The strong, bitter smell of tobacco lingered. And if there was any doubt in her mind, it was dispelled by the cigarette pack that lay crumpled on a side table. The red and white diagonal pattern. TEKEL 2000 printed on the upper white half. Probably the most popular brand in Turkey. And Billy Strunk's brand.

"Is that the Taj Mahal?"

Amy was so focused that she hadn't heard them until now. Evan and Barbara Corns had changed their clothes and were ready to attack the sights.

"Sorry if I startled you." Evan pointed behind them at the lobby balcony and the gray shadow of the pool house. "Is that the Taj Mahal? You can barely see. . . ."

"Yes," Amy said. "Yes, it is."

"Really?" Barbara seemed skeptical. "It looks small."

"Everyone says that," Amy agreed and, without another word, headed out toward the doorman and the door.

She had no idea where Billy had gone or how she would find him. As odd as it seemed, she knew that he had come to India to follow them. To follow someone. Perhaps she would ask the parking valet. Or better yet, Peter. Peter was right there on the white gravel by the Oberoi gates.

"Billy," she called out as soon as she managed to catch his eye. "Remember Billy from Istanbul?"

"You saw him, too?" Peter laughed. "I thought I was hallucinating."

"Where did you see him?"

"Just now. He got into a taxi."

"Did he see you?"

"I don't know. Quite a coincidence."

Amy didn't argue. She turned to face the parking valet a few feet away. "Excuse me." *Calm and polite,* she had to remind herself. Otherwise, she would seem unforgivably rude. Again.

"Good afternoon, madam." The valet greeted her with a broad, engaging smile. "Are you enjoying your time here? I think the mist will be lifting anytime soon now."

"Very good to hear." Amy tried to smile back. "There was an American gentleman here a few moments ago. He got into a taxi."

"Ah, yes," the valet agreed. "He is a friend of yours?"

"What makes you say that? Never mind. Do you know where he went? Where did he tell the taxi to go? Was he following someone?" She was trying to keep her voice slow and friendly but wasn't succeeding.

CHAPTER 15

"The Protected Forest." That was what he said. Amy got her bearings quickly, almost on the run. The Protected Forest, she knew, was a patch of parkland on a rolling hill overlooking the Taj. Although it was created as a pollution buffer, the views of the monument were magnificent and on non-fog days the forest was a popular destination. It was, in fact, the only thing standing between the Oberoi and the Taj and was an easy walk from the hotel. But Billy had taken a taxi, so they took a taxi.

"You think he's following us?" Peter buckled up beside her in the back of the pink Ambassador.

"He's following someone," Amy said, leaving herself unbuckled. "Think about it. He strikes up a conversation with us in a market in Istanbul? That wasn't accidental."

"He wanted to help."

"He would have found some way to talk to us." She went back over their first conversation in her mind. Something clicked. "We never told him we were staying at the Four Seasons, but somehow he knew."

"Are you sure?"

"We were worried about the time, remember? He said that he'd get us back to the Four Seasons in plenty of time. He knew because he'd followed us from the hotel."

"But he's not following us now. We're following him."

"That's probably because he's following someone else."

"He likes following people?"

She wanted to slap him. "He's not interested in us. It's someone from our group. When you met him for drinks in Istanbul, what did you talk about?"

"Talk about?" The taxi was stalled, waiting for a parade of oxen to decide which way they were going before it could pull out on the road. Peter undid the second button on his polo. "I don't know. We were drinking."

"Did he ask about the tour? The people on the tour?"

"Sure he did. Or I volunteered. Amy, the guy helped us out. He had a right to be curious."

"Did he ask about anyone in particular?"

"You're saying he followed one of our people from New York? That's crazy. He lives in Istanbul. He speaks Turkish. People knew him at the bar."

"Then how do you explain him being here? On the same train? Hanging out at our hotel?"

A minute later the taxi turned into the parking lot by the entrance to the forest trail. Amy got out and paid the driver and waited as Peter struggled to unbuckle himself.

"Sorry. Hold on. Damn these seat belts. Where the hell are you going?"

It was a great question. And Amy didn't have a great answer, except to say, "I need to find him."

"And then what?" Peter was a few yards behind her now, running to catch up. "If he wants to lie, he'll make up a story." She was already fading in the fog. No one else was in sight, undoubtedly a result of the weather, but still an odd sensation in India, where there were always people. When the path divided, he followed her on the left one . . . he thought.

"I can't just do nothing," she shouted.

"Why not?" he shouted back.

Another great question. Because I did nothing last year, and someone got killed, she thought. Because I did nothing three years ago, and Eddie got shot. Because right now I'd rather do something, anything, no matter how useless, than do nothing again. A small sign with a silhouette of the Taj pointed up a second path, and for some reason, she obeyed.

"You're never going to find him."

She could barely hear his voice. Why couldn't he keep up? He was young. His legs were certainly long enough. "Fine. Then I'm getting exercise."

"We're going to get lost."

Amy could hear his last complaint, but barely. And that fact, combined with the complaint itself, brought her to a stop in the middle of the dirt path. She spun around and saw nothing behind her. Then she listened for the sound of his footsteps and heard nothing. "Peter?" The adrenaline of the past ten minutes was just beginning to ease.

"Hello?" At least he was within shouting distance. "Amy? Where are you?"

"I'm on the path." She looked around for land-marks. "I don't know how else to describe it." As the fog finally started to blow off, there still wasn't much to see. "Follow the signs."

"There are lots of signs," he yelled back.

"The one pointing to the view."

"They're all pointing to the view. There are lots of views."

"Oh." She hadn't thought about that. "Just stay there." It was common knowledge that the best thing to do when lost was to stay where you were. But Amy didn't understand how that would possibly help if they both stayed where they were. "Keep talking," she said. "I'll follow the sound of your voice." Then she turned around and headed back on the path.

"What? So you're no longer trying to catch him?"

"Not if there are lots of paths and lots of signs." Even she realized that. "Peter, keep talking."

"Okay."

Amy waited for more. "Peter? Talking?"

"I'm thinking. Okay." He cleared his throat. "Four score and seven years ago our fathers brought forth on this continent . . . Okay, that's all I know. Amy, you know you're being crazy, right?"

"Keep talking."

"Just because you had a bad experience . . ." He sounded more than a little exasperated. "I mean, we find an envelope in a piano. So what? And a guest has a nut allergy. And we meet someone, and we see him in a different country—if it even was him to begin with. That doesn't mean murder. It doesn't even mean bad. I don't know what it means."

"Keep talking." Amy wasn't listening to his words, just the sound and the direction. "I'm getting closer."

"I wanted to get to know you," he shouted into the gray. Even as the visibility grew, their conversation still felt private, cut off from the world. "This was a simple boondoggle. Idiot proof. No offense. And nothing's gone wrong, outside of the ashes thing, and we fixed that. We should be happy. Can't you enjoy yourself anymore? I don't know. Maybe you need to talk to a doctor or get medication. Or change your line of work. Because no one's going to die. I've been on hundreds of trips, and no one ever dies."

"Shut up." Her voice now sounded slightly farther away.

"That's no way to communicate."

"No, shut up. I hear someone."

"What do you hear?"

"Shut up."

It had come from the other side, away from Peter. At least she thought so. Was it a shout or a scream? No, she didn't even want to think that. But it had been human. They couldn't be the only people wandering through the haze, hoping for a photo op.

There it was again. A human sound, definitely, but different this time, higher in tone, like a cry of pain. Okay, maybe someone had twisted an ankle. Or dropped a camera. There was no reason for the adrenaline to start pumping through her again, but it did. Maybe Peter was right. Maybe she did need to see a doctor. She would consider this option, seriously consider it, just as soon as she discovered the source of the human cry of pain and knew it wasn't murder, although it probably was murder. She could sense it.

The extra little surge focused her senses and sent

her scurrying around two or three of the meandering bends. The scrub caught at her ankles. And when the path split again—one downhill, one up—she instinctively took the up. The cry had come from up.

"Amy! Where are you?"

Damn. Couldn't the guy take direction? She tried to shut out his voice and made another choice at another split in the path. Up again. Not far ahead of her she could suddenly see a clearing and an outcropping of rocks and ran toward them. A second later she saw it and stopped in her tracks. "Oh, my God!"

The sight was unbelievable.

"Oh, my God," she said again, almost in a whisper. *As much as you think you're prepared for this moment*, she thought, *it probably takes everyone by surprise.*

The mausoleum of Shāh Jāhan was directly in front of her, its dome dominating everything, perfectly framed among the green, scrubby hills, parting the river haze, a smoky white butterfly edged in pink emerging from a soft gray chrysalis. A sight at once so familiar and so startling. *Like seeing a unicorn*, she imagined. The Taj Mahal.

It took her several moments—long, blissful, utterly satisfying moments—to tear her eyes away from this amazing view and notice the dying man.

He was sprawled by a stone bench on the grass, facing the view, perhaps ten feet back from the outcropping's edge. He might have been sitting there when attacked. Had he come here to meet his attacker? Or had he been caught unawares, knifed in the side with this long, colorful, almost laughably ornamental dagger? He wasn't dead, not quite.

Amy just stood there, watching the man gasp and

bleed out. What could she do? Give first aid? She had no supplies, and it would do no good. Use her phone? She hadn't bothered to bring her phone. Put her ear to his lips and ask him who had done this to him? Too late. He had just eked out his last senseless, wet gurgles, and his eyes glazed over.

Once again, Amy had done nothing. And Billy Strunk was officially dead.

She could hear footsteps now—hurried, frantic footsteps—and turned with a start. It was Peter. His feet stumbled over the pebbly grass, and his gaze took in everything that Amy's gaze had taken in a few moments before. After it finally registered in his mind, he turned to her and frowned and shook his head in disbelief.

"Are you happy now?"

"He was just killed. That's the sound I heard."

"Do not say, 'I told you so.' "

"I'm not saying, 'I told you so.' A man's been murdered."

Peter looked at the dead man a little more closely this time. "Is that Billy?"

"Yes, it's Billy."

"Then you can't even say, 'I told you so.' He's supposed to be the killer."

"He's not supposed to be anything," she protested. But Peter was more or less right. And he was taking this very calmly. "I think you should call the police."

Peter pulled out his phone, then hesitated. "I don't know how."

"Dial nine-one-one," Amy said, then stopped herself. "Wait a minute. Isn't that the country code? What's the country code for India?"

"It's nine-one."

"Then what do they use for nine-one-one?" Amy demanded.

"They don't have nine-one-one. I don't even think they have emergency services. Have you seen the inside of an Indian hospital? The whole country is one big emergency. Why would they have a special number?"

"Call the hotel. They'll know."

"Good idea."

CHAPTER 16

Amy called Fanny that night, which was mid-afternoon in New York, nine and a half hours earlier due to some strange Indian finagling with the international time zones. For once, Marcus wasn't at the house. Fanny mentioned that he was at work, starting a new job, but Amy was more in the mood for talking than listening. She reviewed the facts in great detail—from Billy's appearance in Istanbul to his death in Agra—then finally listened as her mother claimed that Billy Strunk's death must have been a coincidence. It was something that neither of them believed.

For the rest of the night, Amy lay awake, eyes staring unfocused on the ceiling. This was her usual reaction after a murder. And the fact that she realized she had a usual reaction only made it worse.

True, no one on the tour had died. In fact, no one in her group seemed to know the man. And while Amy doubted the police version of events, at least she wouldn't have to deal with the aftermath of another murder on her watch—the worry and suspicions among her guests, the headlines back home. Not for now.

When she noticed the room growing brighter, Amy dragged herself out of the comfortable but useless bed, slipped on a hotel robe, and groggily drew back the curtains. It took her eyes a few seconds to adjust, but the view was unobstructed and astonishing: She gasped. Many of the rooms at the Oberoi Amarvilas had this view. It was the whole reason behind the hotel. But still . . . to open your curtains and suddenly bask in the pinks and purples of a new day over the creamy white dome and minarets? The Taj Mahal looked almost translucent.

She stepped out on her balcony and stood there for maybe half a minute, bathing in the reflected glow. Then she went back inside, shut the French doors, and closed the curtains tight. The last thing she needed now was a glowing reminder of yesterday.

They had stayed at the overlook with the body for what had seemed like forever. Three groups of tourists had come to the spot and gone before the police arrived. An English family of four, full of smiles and wonder, had turned and seen the body and heard Peter's makeshift explanation about a mugging. The two boys were fascinated. But the English couple dragged them away with the promise of even more fun somewhere else. A small Chinese tour group were less upset with the bloody corpse. They stayed for several minutes and arranged their photos of each other so that the body was safely out of frame. Two Indian couples then arrived together with a blanket and the makings of a picnic. They were the hardest to get rid of. But through it all, Amy and Peter managed to keep an untrammeled perimeter around the crime scene. It turned out not to be that important.

Minutes later several khaki-clad officers strode up the path, then proceeded to touch the body, move the body, try to wake the body. The officer in charge removed the knife from the wound with an ungloved hand, then reconsidered his action and placed it back in the hole.

If the crime scene was chaotic, the local police station, the tourist *thana* on Fatehabad Road, was chaotic to the power of ten. When Amy and Peter arrived, the big event, apparently, was the aftermath of a collision between a goat and a motorbike, with about a dozen witnesses there to give their stories. A Norwegian tourist had come to report a stolen watch. And a trio of shopkeepers was trying to establish who had cheated whom, the prize obviously going to the one who could shout the loudest and wave his hands the most.

Assistant Superintendent Badlani seemed unfazed. He exchanged a few words with his subordinates, then ushered Peter and Amy outside to a scruffy dirt courtyard. The short, neat man with a pencil-thin mustache offered them a cigarette and, when they refused, lit one for himself and leaned against a concrete post.

"Very unfortunate," he said, taking his first puff. "We are trying very hard to make life good for our visitors. That's why we made this special *thana*, to deal with tourists." He must have deduced their skepticism. "Believe me," he laughed, "you do not want to be in a typical *thana*."

Amy smiled obligingly. Out of the corner of her eye, she couldn't help seeing a police car with a roof rack. It had just pulled in through the gates.

What drew her attention most was the large object, almost the length of the car, wrapped in a blue tarp and tied securely on the rack. It wasn't until the police car disappeared around to the back that she realized what was inside the tarp.

Badlani saw that she saw. "Did you know this man? The deceased?" For the first time in the investigation, he took out a notepad and pen.

She and Peter had argued about how to answer this question. "His name is Billy Strunk," she said. "William, I suppose." It was better to stick to the truth, or some close version of it. "We met him in Istanbul a few days ago."

"An American tourist?"

"He was an American living in Istanbul. I'm not sure what his citizenship was."

"Was he staying also at the Oberoi?"

"We don't know," Peter said. "We only met him for a few minutes at a bar in Istanbul. We were very surprised to find him here. Especially dead."

The inspector found nothing strange with this coincidence. "Everyone comes to Agra," he noted proudly. "The man had no wallet or identification, which is normal for a robbery killing."

"You think it was a robbery?" asked Amy. She could almost feel Peter's eyes boring into the side of her head.

"We have had nasty robberies in the forest, yes. But very few robberies go nasty like this."

"I'm sure you're right," Peter agreed. "Robbery."

"How do you know?" Amy demanded.

"Because it was in the forest, where robberies happen. And everything was gone," Badlani added patiently. "No wallet or ring or jewelry."

"Or the murderer took his possessions in order to make it look like a robbery."

The assistant superintendent nodded. "Perhaps. Do you have many such experiences with robberies and murders, miss?"

"No," blurted Peter. "She watches too much American TV."

Amy had never considered the possibility that they themselves might be suspects. But they had known the victim. They had discovered the body. And it didn't help that they—she, actually—were trying to eliminate the option of a mugger.

"You are not leaving today?" the inspector said; a statement in the form of a question. "And you will be staying at the Oberoi? They have your passports at the desk?" Yes and yes and yes.

"We are not leaving today," Amy assured him.

"Good. We will inquire at the hotels and find out more about your"—he checked his notes—"Billy Strunk. Is that a sentence?"

"A sentence?"

"A statement about a man who drinks."

"What . . . Oh! Billy's drunk?" Amy hadn't thought of that. "No, it's Billy Strunk. Or Bill. Or William Strunk."

"Was the man drinking when you first met him?"

"No," Amy said, then remembered Peter's white lie about having met him in a bar. "Yes, I suppose he was drinking. But that was his name."

"Are you sure he didn't just shake your hand and say, 'Hey, Billy's drunk,' a kind of apology, and you misunderstood his words?"

"No, that's his name."

The conversation with Badlani played once again in Amy's mind as she took her long morning shower.

It had played all night, along with all the other scenes from yesterday. She took her time pulling herself together. Today would be her brown, slim ankle pants, topped by a caramel cowl-necked tank. It was easy and stylish, one of her best travel outfits, especially in the evenings, when she added a matching cardigan. She topped it off with her red Lafonts, the same glasses as yesterday; that was how distracted she was. When she left her room, ready to face the day, she was still too early for breakfast and not hungry at all.

Instead, she roamed the corridors of the Oberoi, wandering aimlessly out to the gardens and the ornamental pools and back again, keeping her eye off the glistening Taj and focusing on little things. It was like a form of meditation, and it helped to calm her as she tried not to think. The modern oil paintings of somber, ancient shahs; the gold ornamental Sanskrit done in relief on the ceilings; the colorful daggers, identical in their curved sheaths, mounted in the long hallways; the silver shields, the size of hubcaps, festooned with tassels . . . the colorful daggers. *Wait a minute!* And she took a closer look.

She must have glanced at them a dozen times before making the connection. These daggers were exactly the same size and design. A pair of them hung high by the entrance to a lounge. *Yes. Exactly like the murder weapon.* Just saying those words mentally—*murder weapon*—gave her the shivers. And they had once been such fun words, as in Sherlock Holmes or a game of *Clue.* There were dozens of identical daggers, maybe hundreds, fastened to the walls throughout the hotel, the blades clipped tightly into their sheaths, the sheaths clipped tightly into the stone.

Before she knew what she was doing, Amy was pacing the hallways, examining the walls for a missing knife. Every blank space of wall drew her eye. Had it once been hanging here? Was that a chip in the stone? Only gradually did it dawn on her that she was trying to prove a negative, trying to find a knife that wasn't there.

Anyone could have done it on the spur of the moment, needed a weapon and pried it off the wall. She was looking high on the walls, knowing the search was pretty much futile, but she eventually found it under the sole of her right flip-flop. Not the murder weapon, of course, but something just as good.

Amy had just rounded a corner, facing the third-floor corridor right above her own corridor, when something under her arch made her yelp in surprise. She picked up the pointed silver clasp, like a large, thick staple. It took her a few seconds to recognize it, as it lay among a few scattered bits of stone chips. Her eyes went from the clasp to the wall above her head. And there it was. Or rather, wasn't.

A lonely dagger pointed inward, trying to form a pattern with a mate that was no longer there. Two thoughts came quickly to mind as Amy stared at the empty space and the almost invisible chip in the stonework. One: this was all very recent, probably since this corridor was last vacuumed by the attentive staff. Two: this was the same corridor, one floor above hers, where all her guests were spread out in their suites, enjoying the best views.

Make that three thoughts. Three: Amy knew she was suspecting one of her own.

CHAPTER 17

This leg of the wake was supposed to have been held yesterday, at sunset, at the most dramatic of the many overlooks in the Protected Forest. But an hour before sunset, Assistant Superintendent Badlani had ordered the entire forest cordoned off. *Just out of spite*, Amy thought.

All evening long they had scrambled to find an alternative and had settled on the Mehtab Bagh gardens, on the banks of the Yamuna, directly across the river from the Taj. Dawn would have been a perfect time, with the sun hitting the eastern side and throwing its long, misty shadows across the winding water. But dawn wasn't a viable option for this bunch. Mid-morning would be much more acceptable.

The Mehtab Bagh was technically part of the Taj Mahal complex, literally a stone's throw across the river. But it was miles from the nearest bridge, and these formal gardens were spared the hordes of mid-morning visitors who daily jockeyed for position in front of the white marble and who employed a platoon of local entrepreneurs who made their living by taking your picture.

An unfortunate bend in the Yamuna had formed a permanent, marsh-like effect, at just the most picture-worthy spot on the bank. But Peter had been here before, and he knew enough to hire someone who knew where nine people might stand, prop up a photo of their maid, and throw even more dust into the silty marsh.

Everyone had heard about the murder, of course. It was the talk of the hotel, and the legend grew in the retelling. Strunk had been a wealthy businessman, they said. He had been assaulted by a gang of underage thieves and had fought for his life. "If only he hadn't fought," a concierge had bemoaned to a desk clerk, wagging his head, "he would easily be alive."

None of Amy's guests seemed overly troubled by the news, although Evan Corns did take her aside and point out the coincidence. "Weren't you just involved in a murder? A few months ago? You and your mother?"

"Seven months ago," answered Amy. "And this one doesn't count, does it? It just happened nearby."

"All the same. Being around for two murders?" He raised an eyebrow. "What are the odds?"

Amy studied the group of eight in their solemn semicircle facing the marshy expanse and tried to conjure up an alternate explanation. None was coming to mind. Strunk had followed one or more of them for thousands of miles, had asked questions about one or more, had followed one or more into the Protected Forest and, lacking an alternate explanation, had been murdered by one or more.

"The little beggar girl had to be ten years old at

the most. Popping up out of nowhere in the middle
of that big, crazy square in Marrakech. You know
the one, the famous one. Anyway, before Herb
knew what was happening, she tied this little string
bracelet on his wrist. Tight, with a double knot. He
tried to take it off, of course, but he couldn't. 'It's a
present. It's a present,' she kept saying, with this big
smile on her face, holding on to his arm. 'No
money. Free for you. No money.'"

David Pepper was center stage beside the now
slightly tattered photo of MacGregor on the easel. A
few feet away stood his husband, the subject of this
travelogue, which, given the uncomfortable look on
his face, had been told before and was going to be
embarrassing. David paused for just the right amount
of time. Then, still in the little girl's voice, he added,
"Now you give me a present, too. Money."

The laughter was polite. It was a common enough
anecdote, but perhaps a bit mean-spirited in the
telling, Amy thought. Could they really begrudge a
ten-year-old Moroccan girl working the Jemaa el Fna
square, trying to make a little money off the rich
tourists? But David wasn't through.

"I told Herb just to walk away. But now the girl
had ahold of his wrist, and she was starting to shout,
'I am your friend. I give you something. You give me
something.' That's when my Herb made the mistake, dumb mistake, of taking out his wallet. And
worse than that, taking out a wad of bills and waving
them around. There must have been at least a dozen
kids right close by, working the same scam, and as
soon as they saw the green bills out in the open . . ."
David paused, relishing the memory. "Like a flock of
pigeons diving on a crust of bread."

"My big mistake was running," Herb said, reluctantly joining in.

David's laugh didn't even try to be affectionate. "He must have done three laps, lumbering around. And you know how big that square is. It's like a racetrack."

Amy smiled dimly and tuned out the rest. By stop number three, the wake stories had grown less relevant, devolving into the normal anecdotes that people on trips told strangers about their previous trips, just to show off how worldly they were. This one didn't even mention Paisley MacGregor, except David's claim that the framed photo of a sweaty Herb showing his now empty wallet to a horde of disappointed Moroccan children had always been one of her favorites.

They were scheduled for the first-class train back to Delhi late that afternoon, but it was all dependent on getting their passports back. When the hotel manager said the police had come by and confiscated them, Amy screwed up her courage and paid another visit to the tourist *thana* on Fatehabad Road.

She located Assistant Superintendent Badlani at his desk in a small, windowless back office. The bedlam was not nearly what it had been the day before—a simple dispute over a taxi fare, plus what looked like a drunk and disorderly backpacker. Amy looked forward to being able to think and talk at the same time.

"Ah, Miss Abel. Come in, come in. Take a seat. Make yourself uncomfortable." He laughed at his joke and motioned to a metal chair positioned across from his desk. He had remembered her name, she noticed, without checking his notes, which she did not really consider a good thing. "You are here, no doubt, about the passports."

"Yes," Amy said. "I'm sure it was just a mix-up."

"No, no," he said, still smiling. "No mix-up. I wanted you to visit me." She didn't reply but simply lowered herself into the metal. He'd been right about the uncomfortable part. "We have been continuing our investigation."

"Good. Were you able to trace the murder weapon?" She wasn't yet prepared to tell him about her dagger discovery.

"Murder weapon?" He seemed almost puzzled. "Oh, you mean the dagger. It is very, very common. Your hotel has many such daggers decorating the walls."

"I didn't notice," Amy lied.

"Yes, yes, dirt common." Then, still smiling, he added, "Are you sure you knew this unfortunate man from Istanbul? No confusion with someone else?"

"Yes," Amy said. "I mean no. Yes, I knew him, and no, no confusion. We spent maybe an hour together. And then I saw his face clearly when we found the body. It was him."

"Yes. Good for you." At this point, he finally consulted a page of notes. "Unfortunately, there is no hotel renting to a Mr. William Strunk."

"That's the name he said. And he wasn't just saying he was drunk."

"I am not doubting." Badlani's smile vanished, like a switch had been thrown. "The lack of a hotel made us curious. No Mr. Strunk from anywhere has entered India. Not in six months. We are speaking to your country's Department of State to see if we can get a name match. Also Turkey."

"You mean, you don't know who he is?"

"We are hoping you can help us."

"Me?" Amy's mouth went dry.

"You are the person who found him, dear woman. You and your friend were alone with the body. You knew him from before he came here. So you say."

"No. I told you everything. You don't . . . You can't suspect me."

"I can suspect anyone I want."

He let the harsh, impatient words hang. It was only ten seconds, but it felt like ten minutes. The room, Amy noticed for the first time, was made of cracked sandy concrete, like a cell, and a small air conditioner inserted crookedly in the concrete wall chugged away.

"No, that is a joke," Badlani finally said with a comical shrug. "Yes, I can suspect anyone. I am assistant superintendent. But I do not suspect you. Or your friend."

"Why not?"

"Why not?" His laugh was almost a giggle. "Are you wanting to be a suspect? Missy, you had no blood. The killer would have blood. It spurted from him like a pig. You see, investigation is not all fingerprints. It's common sense. My officers were bloody just from touching him."

"I was going to mention that, about them touching the body."

Badlani nodded. "I believe you knew him, yes. But he had another name. Or he lied to you. Is there maybe a reason why he would lie?"

She gave the matter some thought. Yes, there was a reason Strunk would lie—if he didn't want them casually mentioning his name in front of a tour member. Amy wondered if there was any way she could offer this information, more of a theory than information, without subtly implicating one of her own guests. No, there wasn't, and she couldn't.

Besides, she had no proof that one of them was involved. And if she were to reveal her unfounded suspicions, Badlani would undoubtedly keep hold of their passports and interview everyone tomorrow and let it slip that she had named them all as suspects. That would make for a very awkward last few days. No, Amy would try to avoid any real police investigation, at least for now.

"You are thinking long and hard."

The words startled her, and her shoulders twitched. "Sorry. No, I don't know why Mr. Strunk would lie. We were just acquaintances, fellow Americans at a bar."

"You met by accident? With no friends in common? Did he tell you about his life?"

"Peter talked to him more than me." She was only three words into the sentence when she regretted it. "But they didn't talk much. Can you arrange for our passports to be returned? That would be great."

Badlani responded by steepling his fingers on top of his belt buckle. He breathed in slowly through his nostrils and out through his mouth, reminding her of Danny, her middle-aged yoga instructor back home on Barrow Street. "Not yet, I am afraid. I will be needing to talk to Mr. Peter Borg again."

CHAPTER 18

Peter was not going to make the afternoon train back to Delhi, and neither were the passports.

Assistant Superintendent Badlani hadn't told them not to leave Agra. That would have weakened his official line that the murder was a mugging. He just wanted to make things inconvenient.

When her people gathered in the lobby late that afternoon, Amy smiled, embarrassed, and invented a teeny-tiny medical emergency for Peter. He would be joining them in Delhi, she said, in plenty of time for their morning flight. "Tourists are like wild animals," Peter had once explained. "They can smell fear." As for the passports, only Herb asked. Amy replied that it was simpler for her to hold on to them until tomorrow at the airport. She didn't even want to think about tomorrow at the airport.

On the train back to Delhi, Amy roamed the aisle, chatting amiably, laughing at everything, then ducked into the bathroom to spray herself lightly (Happy by Clinique) just as a precaution.

At the Imperial New Delhi, the same suites were waiting for them, except for Amy, whose room had been upgraded to an Art Deco suite. "We would be privileged also to upgrade Mr. Borg to the other Art Deco suite," the smiling desk clerk said with what was almost a bow. It always paid to be nice to travel agents.

Amy thanked him. "But I'm not sure when Mr. Borg is arriving," she said in a whisper. Her guests were out of earshot, following their luggage and bellmen toward the elevators. "It may be tonight. It may be in the morning."

The Art Deco suite, she discovered, wasn't particularly Deco—less Astaire and more *The Godfather Part II*, it seemed, with burled-wood lamps and comfortable 1950s sofas and chairs. But the bar was free, and the selection surprisingly complete.

Amy went with her favorite, Campari and soda, and made room for a chair on the little balcony overlooking the hotel's Spice Route garden. Ever since her teenage years, she'd loved Campari, the deep red color and the combination of sweet and bitter. It had seemed so sophisticated and European for a girl who longed to be both. Campari was the only thing she'd ever filched from her parents' liquor cabinet, gradually replacing it with water until it faded into a light pink. Every now and then, two or three times a year, the bottle would disappear and be replaced by a fresh one. She hadn't thought it through at the time, but her mother had obviously known. Keeping track of the shade of the bottle and replacing it a few times a year had just been Fanny's way of monitoring her daughter's alcohol intake.

She was on her second drink, enjoying the di-minishing echoes, the jasmine, and the growing calm that filtered up from the garden. This was her first relaxing moment in two days, artificially en-hanced though it was, and she wanted to enjoy it. She barely noticed when, across the suite, a mecha-nism whirred softly and a handle turned and the door opened.

"Amy?" It was Peter, tiptoeing gently in and pulling his luggage behind him. "They gave away my room. They said they had upgraded me to a suite, and then they gave away my suite because I wasn't coming till morning."

"That was probably my fault." Amy felt a wave of relief. Under other circumstances she might have jumped up and run into his arms and hugged him and jabbered on with a hundred questions. But to sit on the balcony and smile and just feel the relief . . . This was better.

"Can I sleep here?" Peter looked dead tired. "I'm not making this up, not like Paris. You can check with the front desk. I'll sleep on the sofa."

"I believe you. Did you get the passports?"

"Of course I got the passports. That was the whole point."

It took Peter only a few minutes to settle in, grab a giant Kingfisher from the refrigerator, pour half of it into a pilsner glass, and pull a second chair to the edge of the French door balcony. Amy didn't move, except to nurse the ice cubes of her second Campari and soda. She waited until after the foam had settled on the rim of his glass and he'd taken his first sip.

"How did you get here?"

"Car and driver. The roads are even worse than I remember."

Peter told his story. He had been in Badlani's office for two hours, sitting in the metal chair and swatting bloody mosquitoes against the concrete wall, while the assistant superintendent was off dealing with some more pressing piece of business. "Two hours! I think he just wanted to unnerve me."

"Why would he want to unnerve you?"

"I don't know, but it worked. I wound up telling him everything."

Amy was ready for another Campari. "How much of everything? You didn't tell him we suspected one of our own?"

Peter almost coughed up his second sip. "I don't believe that myself. No, I told him about the ashes and how Billy saved our butts and how we had drinks later that night. At this point he's just trying to find out who Billy is."

"An American living in Istanbul with his Turkish wife and in-laws."

"That's what Billy told us."

"And the whole deal about him showing up in Agra and following someone and being killed by a dagger from the wall of our hotel?"

"The dagger came from our hotel?"

Amy had forgotten to mention this. "Yeah. I found an empty spot on the wall. You know all those wall decorations?"

Peter shook his head and chuckled. "I knew it looked familiar. So, wait. The killer . . ."

"Pried it off the wall. And here's the kicker. It was from the same hallway where all our people were staying."

"Wow." Peter mulled over the information, then sipped again, taking more of a gulp than a sip. "I'd never seen a murdered person before," he admitted softly. "I'm sorry if I was ever cavalier about it. I can see why you'd be skittish about going through it again."

"And I'm sorry for always thinking murder."

"Except this time you were right. Are they always that bloody?"

"Except for poisonings and strangulations." Amy had never seen a strangulation, but that didn't stop her from being an expert. And it was kind of sweet to see Peter so thrown and vulnerable and out of his element. "Peace?" She toasted the air between them.

"Peace. What did you tell everyone about me? Why I missed the train?"

"You had diarrhea. Delhi belly. It was the first thing that popped into my head."

"Diarrhea? Now I have to talk about diarrhea all day tomorrow. Listen to their homemade cures. Thanks."

Amy got up and crossed to the bar, tired of sucking her ice cubes. *Just half of one this time.* "So it's just going to go unsolved?"

"I suppose. Like most murders in the world."

"And that doesn't bother you?" How could it not bother him? She didn't understand.

"It doesn't matter if it bothers me. It's not my business. There's nothing we can do, and I don't see how it's going to affect us, to be honest."

"But if one of our people is a killer?"

"Unless he's a serial killer with a bloodlust that's going to need quenching in the next few days . . . Badlani wouldn't be making this big a fuss, except that the victim was an unidentified American. He's probably mad at us for saying he was American."

As she poured her Campari, she could feel Peter's eyes on her. Did men suspect that women had this power to know when they were being watched? She didn't even turn her head for confirmation. "The sofa looks pretty comfortable," she said.

"I was thinking just the opposite." He followed this with a yawn, as loud and as exaggerated as a yawn in a cartoon. "Ah, Amy! I need my sleep. I can't sleep on that thing."

"Poor boy." Amy smiled as she added an ice cube. She was almost tempted to let him have the bed and take the living room sofa herself. Peter deserved a bed after what he'd been through. So what if they disagreed? Peter could be a selfish wuss, but this time he was right. Outside of rooting for justice, there was little they could do. An unknown man had died in a country they were leaving—with any luck, tomorrow morning.

"Shoot. I had one, after all."

"What?" Amy turned and saw Peter checking his phone.

"Nothing."

There was something furtive about his "Nothing" and the way his eyes darted as he set his phone on the arm of the chair. "It's not nothing."

"Um . . ." He looked too tired to lie. "Badlani asked if I had any pictures of Billy, and I didn't think I did."

"Wait. You took Billy's picture?" Amy forgot about her Campari and crossed back to the balcony. "That night at the bar?"

"I honestly didn't remember. God, I must've been

drunk." Peter focused on the phone again, and something told Amy what he was planning to do.

"You're not going to erase it," she said and grabbed it out of his hand.

"Why not? Then I won't be a liar."

"But it's evidence."

"No it's not. The cops know what he looks like. They have his corpse. Badlani just wanted a picture with his eyes open."

Amy nodded and shrugged reluctantly. "I guess you're not wrong."

"You mean, I'm right?"

"You're not wrong." She examined the image on the screen. Billy Strunk, sure enough, was on a bar stool, his bleary, drunken face illuminated by the flash. His right hand was reaching forward. "Did Billy try to stop you from taking it?"

"Kind of."

"Either he did or he didn't."

"He did, okay? He said he was self-conscious about his weight. Boy, we're full of semantics tonight. What are you doing?"

It was an iPhone like her own, which made things easy. Amy pressed a few buttons. "I'm sending it to my phone."

"You're not sending it to Badlani, are you? That would be stupid."

Amy hadn't considered this, but now she did, just for a second. "No, not until we're out of Indian airspace."

"Good. Because the last thing you need is to get mixed up in another murder."

"You're not wrong," Amy said. Murders, she knew, happened every day and got solved or not, without her being involved. This was probably the best thing for her, for Peter and their business, and for Mac-Gregor and all her guests. "But you're not right."

"Amy, sweetie. Don't be naive."

"Naïve? I am not naïve. And you are not getting the bed."

CHAPTER 19

Under normal circumstances, Marcus found it easy to text and talk at the same time. "Very good, sir," he told his hotel guest, glancing up and smiling warmly. Then he went back to texting Amy, his phone and hands hidden under the antique concierge desk.

Amy had just gotten off the plane in Beijing, the fourth of their five memorial stops—Paris, Istanbul, Agra, and now Beijing. Last night she had called, filling him in about Billy Strunk's death and adding, almost as an afterthought, how much she missed him. Marcus had reacted with more than a twinge of jealousy—not about her platonic night with Peter Borg, but about the murder. It should have been him with her in India, not that clueless jerk, who wouldn't know an alibi from a hole in the ground. Murder was their thing, his and Amy's, the thing that had brought them together in the first place. And now she was involved in another one. With another man.

Amy texted that she loved him. Marcus texted

the same thing back, along with a heart-shaped emoji. But then something that his guest said caught his ear. He repeated the man's last phrase, just to make sure. "You want to propose to her on top of the Empire State Building?" Marcus was beaming on the outside, frowning inside. "Very romantic. That should be quite a moment." *What will the request be?* he wondered. *Closing the observation deck to the public? Special lighting on the building's spire, spelling out the woman's name?*

So far, his job as concierge at the Ritz-Carlton had been a piece of cake: the usual tickets to sold-out musicals, a new puppy waiting in the suite for a ten-year-old's birthday party, a rather intimate item of clothing purchased for an anniversary. He had been forced to guess the recipient's size from across the lobby and had been right on the money. Reportedly. But this guy standing in front of his desk—midforties, rich as hell, sky-high sense of entitlement —was going to be trouble; he could tell.

"I want you to get Michael Bublé to sing for us. Can you do that?"

"You mean at your proposal? On top of the Empire State?" Marcus didn't flinch.

"Yeah. Calista loves this Bublé guy. Oh, and he's probably going to need a band. Piano and a small band. Whatever it costs."

"It might be hard getting a piano up on the observation deck."

"It can be a keyboard," the man said magnanimously. "Maybe a couple violins and a drum set. Make it sound good."

"Do you have a date for this proposal?" Marcus glanced across the beige wainscoting of the Ritz-Carlton lobby and saw his boss, Gavin, head concierge, eyeing them with what, even from a distance, looked like a smirk. "I'll need a few days."

"You got a week. Then we're back to Columbus and my second choice—Ohio Stadium, midfield. It's all the same to me, but Calista has this notion about the Empire State Building. . . . Sunset, by the way. It's gotta be sunset. And private. No tourists gumming things up."

"I'm sure we can make it happen." Marcus had no idea which continent Michael Bublé was on at the moment, or if he was previously engaged or averse to performing at proposals, or even if the singer had a fear of heights. "Any particular song?"

"Bublé can choose. You sure you call pull this off?" The man looked doubtful. "'Cause I don't want you calling me up at the last minute, saying, 'Sorry. It's the Rainbow Room, and all I could get was Tony Bennett.'"

"Bublé with a band on top of the Empire State. I don't foresee a problem."

"Good." The man finally looked impressed. "Gavin said you'd be the guy to handle this."

"I'll get right on it." Marcus was almost tempted to laugh. He knew Gavin regarded him as a threat, so it might just be his version of a practical joke. But Marcus was a fine connoisseur of smirks and could tell, even across the lobby, that Gavin's smirk was deadly serious.

As the Buckeye billionaire lumbered away toward the elevators, Marcus caught Gavin's eye, returned his smirk, then reached up and fingered the crossed golden keys on his lapels.

By morning's end, he'd done a few Internet searches, made a few phone calls, and had a few ideas fomenting in his mind. He looked forward to reviewing them with Fanny. She was the one person he knew who thought the way he did. Amy was pretty good, but he always found himself wasting time discussing morality or what could go wrong, whereas Fanny was always right there.

He had just walked into the Astro on Sixth Avenue. Fanny was waiting for him, looking tiny and oddly vulnerable on a blue leatherette banquette in a booth toward the back of the diner. She was always early for these lunches. By the time Marcus recognized the man in the gray suit sitting across from her, it was too late. Not that he would have turned and run. He just would have liked to be a little more prepared.

Rawlings saw him approaching in the mirror and got to his feet. He was a deceptively friendly man, Midwestern and boyish, with wide features and sandy hair, now growing out just a bit. Despite the conservative suit and tie, he looked even younger than he had last year, when he'd thrown Marcus in jail for murder.

"Sergeant." If only he'd had an extra second to put on his game face.

"It's Lieutenant now." The officer had a self-deprecating smile, which helped to disguise the fact that he was pretty much a jerk. He extended a hand. "Marcus, buddy, how's it going?"

"The lieutenant pulled up just as I left the house," Fanny apologized.

"She said she was meeting you, so I gave her a lift." Marcus had only half extended his hand. But Rawlings grabbed it and used the handshake to draw him into the banquette, next to Fanny. "Turns out I want to speak to you both. Together. The timing was perfect."

Together? Marcus tried to settle in, squeezing in next to Fanny. "Congratulations on the promotion."

"Well, I had a big case six months ago. Guess I'm the flavor of the month."

You mean the big case that Amy and I solved for you? Marcus wanted to say it but didn't.

"By the way, how's Amy?"

"She's away," Marcus said, keeping a casual tone. "I think in China."

"No longer in India. That's what I hear." Rawlings's smile maintained its shape but lost its warmth. "There's an inspector over there who's pretty mad." He spoke as if he already knew everything. "Amy called you both, so don't act innocent. The Indian police have her phone records."

"Is my daughter in trouble?" Fanny asked in wide-eyed wonder. "No! My God! What happened?" Her performance was interrupted by the waitress, who wiped their table, set out three place mats and menus and sets of silverware. "What happened?" Fanny asked again, but this time without any real conviction.

Rawlings pulled a photo off the banquette beside him. "Do either of you know this man?" He put it on the table, facing them, between their place mats. It was the shot of Billy Strunk, bleary-eyed on his Istanbul bar stool.

"That's the guy who got killed?" Marcus asked.

"Good. Things go faster when you don't lie."

Fanny raised a single eyebrow. "Of course she told us. What kind of daughter do you think I raised?"

"So the question remains. . . . Do you have any information that can help us identify him?"

"No," Fanny said. "We know nothing more than you."

"That's hard to believe."

"What? That we don't know more than the police?"

Lieutenant Rawlings grunted, lowering his eyes to his closed menu. When he raised them, he was back on track. "Amy and her friend happened upon a murder. They told the police some unsubstantiated story about the victim and misled them with a false name. Then, as their plane was taking off, they e-mailed in a photo, which they'd previously denied having taken."

Marcus pretended to be confused. "I thought it was a mugging."

Rawlings stretched his smile thin. "That's a placeholder. Every unsolved murder is a mugging. I'm not sure even Badlani believes that. Did one of Amy's people kill this guy?" The question had come out of nowhere.

"No," Marcus sputtered. "I mean, I don't know."

The homicide detective turned to Fanny. "Your daughter has withheld evidence in the past. She was never charged, because . . . well, it all worked out, if you don't count Marcus here getting shot." He reached across and punched Marcus on the left arm, the arm where they'd dug out the bullet.

"Is the Taj Mahal within your jurisdiction, dear?" Fanny asked, as sweet as syrup. "Just curious."

Rawlings cleared his throat. "Amy mentioned a New York accent, so the Indian foreign ministry asked for our cooperation. If evidence develops to connect a New York resident to this John Doe's death, then, yes, it will become a joint investigation."

"You have to identify the victim first," said Marcus. "And we can't help you."

Fanny had retrieved her reading glasses and was bent over, staring at the photo. "He doesn't really look American. Can we have a copy of this?"

"Don't insult my intelligence. Amy already sent you one." The waitress was about to return to take their order, but Rawlings waved her away. "I'm not staying. I just wanted to warn you so that you'll warn Amy. If she's withholding evidence or protecting a killer, for any reason . . ." The detective let the words hang. Then he pushed himself up from the plastic tabletop and pulled out his phone. Before they knew it, he had taken their picture, Marcus and Fanny, sitting side by side in the booth.

"What's that about?" Fanny demanded.

"I just wanted to record the moment." Then the lieutenant turned and headed for the door.

"What was that about?" Marcus said, his eyes following Rawlings until he passed by the window and disappeared. They spent the next minute or so with their eyes lowered to the menus.

"So . . . ," Fanny finally said, drawing the word out. "What are you having?"

"I was thinking the turkey club."

"Me, too, except it has bacon."

"Get it without bacon."

She shook her head. "That seems a waste. Maybe I'll get a turkey sandwich on white toast and have them cut it like a club."

"But then it won't be a double-decker. Get the turkey club without bacon. It's the same price."

"It's not the price; it's the principle. Paying for something you're not getting. It's not fair."

"But it's the same price. You know he's just mad because he has to deal with us again."

Fanny put down the menu and picked up her phone. She pressed a button, and her new screen saver came up, with little icons surrounding the same photo of bleary-eyed Billy Strunk. She stared at it for about the fiftieth time since receiving it late last night. "So, were we being honest with him? Do we know something he doesn't?"

"We know that the murder is probably connected to Paisley MacGregor."

"Because of the 'if I die' envelope?"

"It would be a huge coincidence if the two weren't connected. Maybe the note said, 'If I die, Billy Strunk did it.'"

"Which it wouldn't, since that's not his real name."

"But if we find the note, we'll know his real name. Of course, the problem with this argument . . ."

"Strunk turned out to be the victim."

"We can't deny that." Marcus flipped his hands up on the table. "But the note is the one thing we have that the police don't. Not that we have it. But at least we know it exists."

"You're right, Marcus. We need to find the note."

"We?" Marcus violently shook his head. "No, there's no 'we.' There's not even a 'you.'"

"Why not? We caught a killer last time."

"Last time it was our business," said Marcus. "We need to give Rawlings the envelope."

"But that would officially connect Amy's Travel to another murder. Once is cute. Twice looks like we're hanging with a bad crowd."

"So we don't give him the envelope. The killer's a mugger. End of story."

"Or we could keep our little secret and do some investigating."

"Or we could burn the envelope. End of story."

"Maybe . . ." She stretched the word out. "Or maybe we—"

Marcus knew he was in trouble. Anyone who refused to order a turkey club without bacon on principle was not about to let a killer go free. "Oh, wait. I forgot," he interrupted, raising a finger for emphasis. "I have a business problem. Do you happen to know if Michael Bublé is afraid of heights?"

"Michael Bublé?"

"The singer. Of course the real question is, how do we get a piano up to the observation deck of the Empire State Building?" Marcus didn't elaborate. He sat there stone-faced and let his teasing, tempting words hang in the air.

"Are you trying to distract me, dear?"

"How's it working?"

CHAPTER 20

"**M**acGregor's doorman has a nicer uniform than yours."

Marcus had to agree. "Maybe."

They had just announced themselves at the front desk and were now in the center elevator of 142 Sutton Place, on their way up to the penthouse floor.

"Of course, I may not have that uniform much longer."

Fanny waved away his concern like she would a gnat. "Nonsense."

Marcus had spent the last day researching the proposed Bublé proposal and come to the conclusion that it was indeed impossible. The Empire State Building would not allow the private use of its most famous space, and Michael Bublé, according to his agent, was booked for the next eighteen months at venues slightly larger than an observation deck. Perhaps they could get away with a Bublé impersonator. Perhaps. But an Empire State Building impersonator was, well, impossible.

"No one's going to fire you," Fanny insisted.

"Whatever alternative I come up with is going to disappoint. He made that clear. And Gavin's just waiting for me to screw up."

"Nonsense." She had thought this through and saw a glimmer of hope. "You keep telling your billionaire that it's all set up and ready. Grand piano. Orchestra of fifty. And then you maneuver the situation so that he cancels it."

"He's not going to cancel. His fiancée has her heart set—"

"Cancel the wedding. Make him call it off."

"That's a bit harsh."

"The woman likes Michael Bublé. She has it coming."

"True." The elevator doors opened, and they stepped out. "How do we get him to call it off?"

Fanny slapped him on the arm. "Ingrate. I just changed your situation from impossible to annoyingly difficult. Try to meet me halfway."

When they arrived at the white penthouse door, they paused. Or rather, Marcus paused. "Our law firm?" he asked quickly as he watched one of Fanny's red fingernails hit the bell. They had gotten through the Ellis Eyewear incident in one piece, but it could have been easier. This time he had insisted on preparation. They had even printed a business card.

"Brummel, Brown, and Associates," answered Fanny. Brummel & Brown was Fanny's favorite margarine, and so it was easy for her to remember.

"And the firm's relationship to MacGregor?"

"Marcus, please. I'm better on the fly." Those words were barely out of her mouth when the door eased open.

Miss Archer stood in the doorway, looking both bored and formidable. "I suppose you're the lawyers."

"We are," said Marcus, employing his best concierge charm. The woman grudgingly stepped aside and let them in.

The first minute went smoothly enough. Amy had told them about Archer, so they were unfazed by the homey clutter of the maid's maid. Amy had failed to mention the cats, Fanny noted, so perhaps they were new. Out of the corner of her eye, she counted three, one scooting into the kitchen, one settled on a window seat, and a third, oblivious to their arrival, making long, deep claw marks on the arm of a white leather sofa. The general sheen of every surface was now dimmed by a thin, even layer of fur.

They had called ahead, lawyers representing the MacGregor estate, coming to take an inventory of the apartment and its contents. With the arrival of "lawyers," they had expected Archer to clean up her act. But Archer remained unapologetic. "I have every right to be here."

"Absolutely," Marcus agreed. He brandished his clipboard and pen and dazzling smile, trying to make her lift her eyes from their card. Why was Archer studying it so intently? And why in the world had he agreed to the name? Here was a woman undoubtedly familiar with margarine brands.

"We need to start listing the deceased's household possessions," Fanny said, pointing to the clipboard.

"Has the will gone into probate?" Archer's tone suggested she knew more about the legal system than they did.

"That depends." Instantly, Fanny knew it was the wrong thing to say. "I mean, the will hasn't officially been read, but that's a formality."

"This is just a kind of pre-probate inventory," Marcus suggested.

"Are you the executors?" Archer asked, checking the card again. "This isn't the firm Ms. MacGregor used before."

"They hired us for the inventory," said Marcus. "As a security measure."

"Security? Do they think I'm going to steal something?"

"No, no," Fanny said. "Actually, we don't know. We were just hired for the job. And the sooner you let us do it . . ."

"Go knock yourself out." Archer extended her right arm and used the business card to point. Marcus wanted to grab it back but didn't dare take the chance. They were lucky enough to gain access. Unsupervised access. Even better.

Marcus thought about it for a moment as they walked in—how uncharacteristic it seemed for the sour, suspicious Archer to leave them alone. Just like that. But he credited it to their natural good luck and breathed a sigh as he nudged the bedroom door so that it almost closed behind them.

"So," Fanny whispered, also accepting their luck. "If someone gave MacGregor an 'if I die' note, she'd open it. I don't know any self-respecting woman who wouldn't. The envelope somehow fell into the piano, which no one ever played until Peter came along. Then MacGregor read the note and, we assume, hid it someplace for safekeeping. She was a snoop, yes, but a loyal snoop."

"That's our theory," Marcus whispered back. He was already at the bookshelf, leafing through each volume, his eyes geared for anything bigger than a bookmark. The woman seemed to have the com-

plete collected works of Jackie Collins and Danielle
Steel, all in hardcover, with a few Barbara Cartland
paperbacks thrown in between.

"Marcus, come here."

Fanny was across the room, at a section of wall
that wasn't a wall at all but a door—not a secret
door, just a closet door for people who didn't like
the look of closet doors. She was standing in the
open doorway, fists on her hips, an upturned chin,
in a pose reminiscent of Columbus standing on the
shoreline of a new world. Marcus could see why.

It was a large walk-in, large even by millionaire
standards, although the lack of shelves and rods
and drawers made it look more like a storage unit—
a rather festive storage unit. Almost half the boxes
crammed in there were still in wrapping paper, with
fading ribbons and squashed bows, sitting on top of
each other like the remnants of a hundred lost
birthdays. The others appeared to be gift boxes, some
taped shut, some with the flaps folded.

They stepped inside the closet, and Marcus
reached down to a glossy Santa-wrapped parcel the
size of a shoe box. He read from the gift tag. "To
Paisley, Merry Christmas. The Pepper-Sands."

"What's a Pepper-Sand?" Fanny asked, bending
over to see.

"Don't know," Marcus replied. "But if the note is
somewhere in here, we've got our work cut out for us."

Fanny frowned. "We can't open all these."

"Yes siree. For one thing, it's illegal."

Fanny was shocked to hear these prudish words.
So was Marcus—because it wasn't he who had said
them.

Lieutenant Rawlings was leaning against the lid
of the bedroom's white piano, a broad, closed-mouth

grin replacing his usual open Midwestern smile. Directly behind him was Archer, arms folded across the front of her blousy pink cardigan.

"Lieutenant," Fanny chirped, even though it was a lost cause. "So good to see you."

"I thought you might show up," Rawlings said, not moving from the piano. "After our little talk, I came by to see Miss Archer."

"You gave her our photo," Marcus deduced. "From the diner."

So this had been Rawlings's plan all along: not just to warn them, but to goad them into leading him somewhere. It felt to Fanny like entrapment, although she didn't know exactly how.

"Worth a shot." His voice was brimming with false modesty. "If Amy is protecting someone from a murder charge in India, I figured it might have something to do with the woman who sent them to India. So I dropped by and asked Miss Archer to keep an eye out."

"Brummel and Brown?" snorted Archer, still clutching the business card. "I knew from the second you called."

"And at the risk of repeating myself . . ." Rawlings took a step toward them and the closet. "What evidence are you withholding? Was one of the tour members involved in Mr. Strunk's death?"

"We don't know," said Marcus.

"Then what are you looking for? Why are you here, rummaging through . . . ?" He grunted and turned to Archer, genuinely puzzled. "What are they rummaging through?"

"A closet of unopened presents," said Archer, making it sound almost normal.

Rawlings cocked his head, but that seemed as far

as his curiosity was willing to go. "Marcus, come on. This is your last chance. If you two don't cooperate, I can't help you."

Marcus had to ask. "Help us do what?"

"Get out of this mess. Impersonating officers of the court . . . That's what lawyers are, officers of the court. Plus, gaining entry under false pretenses and conspiracy to commit a felony. I'm not sure I can get that to stick, but I have to assume you came here to steal something." He glanced past them, into the closet of colorful wrapped boxes. "Or re-gift something, which isn't officially a crime, unless it's not yours."

"Lieutenant Rawlings!" Fanny pulled herself up to her full five-foot-one. "I need to speak to my daughter."

Rawlings nodded. "Fine with me. But I would suggest saving that phone call for a lawyer, a real lawyer. You're both under arrest."

"Under arrest?" Fanny didn't understand. For what? Telling little lies? Getting into places where she wasn't allowed? She did it all the time.

"I didn't bring the handcuffs," Rawlings said, finally stepping up to meet them at the closet door. "But I trust you'll come along peacefully."

CHAPTER 21

Barbara Corns had always been afraid of China, at least the idea of China. In her mind, it was this ancient third-world mystery that had morphed into a bureaucratic juggernaut nurturing untold billions of mysterious humans. Okay, maybe she had been "told" how many billions of humans there were, so it wasn't quite "untold," but she had a lot on her mind these days and couldn't be expected to remember little things like numbers. Somewhere in the billions.

China, at least so far, hadn't been all that daunting. True, Beijing Capital International Airport had been predictably shiny and monumental, with ceilings the height of European cathedrals and concrete posts the size of sequoias. And the drive from the airport into the countryside had been almost surreal, with their black limousines crawling painfully along a three-lane highway, wedged in between endless numbers of trucks, tractors, and buses, all spewing gray plumes of exhaust.

But once they'd left the highway and turned

onto the back roads, it had been quite pleasant. The countryside became suddenly, mercifully lonely, fragrant with the scent of pine and eucalyptus. When they turned off the road into the hotel property, they found it to be a sprawling enclave of hilly trails sprinkled with shockingly modern villas of stone and wood and glass. And the Great Wall. You couldn't miss the Great Wall. It was right there, visible from half the windows, snaking across the valley below, only a few minutes' walk from any of the far-flung villas. For that was the whole point of being here, wasn't it? The Great Wall of China.

This evening was to be devoted to recovery, with an undemanding buffet laid out on a pair of lazy Susans in the middle of a round table set for nine. It was the first time they had eaten family style as a group, and it was fascinating for Barbara to watch the dynamics unfold.

Some of them were considerate sharers, like Laila Steinberg. *Perhaps* timid *would be a better word,* Barbara thought as she watched her hesitate over the fried green beans with sesame seeds, not wanting to take too much or leave too little, her hands floating, always wary of the next turn of the turntable. Some were greedy, like Nicole Marconi and, she was embarrassed to note, her own husband. Evan and Nicole sat directly across from each other. The lazy Susans spun back and forth between them as each one tried to fish out the last prawn or clump of lobster meat or the nicest-looking tidbit of steak.

Barbara and Evan Corns stayed on after the bowls of lychee ice cream had been taken away, after their fellow travelers had all yawned their way back to their own villas. They were now thirteen hours ahead of New York. That was what Evan had said, although his math baffled Barbara. How could you be thirteen hours away from anything, if your clock contains only twenty-four hours? She preferred to think of them as eleven hours off—behind or ahead. What difference did it make?

From the next room, the estate's modest business center, Barbara could hear her husband on the phone, or at least his vocal tone. From twenty-plus years of listening through walls, she could distinguish the subtleties of his voice even when she couldn't make out the words—speaking to a subordinate, to a superior, to a client, to a call center, to a friend, to a female friend. They were all different. In this case, it was a hybrid tone, speaking to a subordinate whom he was pretending to treat like a friend.

Barbara sat by herself in the dimly lit dining room, listening and watching out of the corner of her eye a waiter doing something that obviously needed doing. It took her a while to finally focus and a while longer before she realized. He was standing at a table covered with red plastic chopsticks, the same ones they'd just used, rolling them between two napkins to remove the leftover oil and bits of rice, then placing them back in the same "hygienic" sleeves they'd come out of. She made a vow then and there never to use anything in this country without personally washing it first.

When Evan emerged from the business center, he was not looking happy. "Let's go," he said and grabbed his jacket from the back of a chair. "I have to pee and I want to do it back in the room."

"You always have to pee. What did Miss Archer say?"

"The police are interested in MacGregor's apartment," Evan whispered. They were making their way along the stone path between the main building and their villa. There was no need for whispering, given their isolation. But they kept whispering.

"The police? Why?" asked Barbara. The air had turned cold, but not crisp. In fact, the great outdoors felt a little musty. Another Chinese mystery.

"Archer didn't know," said Evan. "My best guess? I think they made some sort of connection between the murder in India and Paisley MacGregor."

"Oh." Both of them kept their flashlights aimed at the winding path, although Barbara wished she could see her husband's face right now. What was he thinking? "Did they search the apartment?" she asked. "Did they find . . ."

"They can't get a search warrant," Evan said, delivering the only good news of the night. "Not yet. Not without probable cause. Archer said something about two people disguised as lawyers trying to search the place, too."

"Disguised as lawyers? Is she sure they're not real lawyers?" A sign in Chinese and English—FOREST HOUSE—pointed their way up a smaller path. "What did Archer say about your offer?"

"My offer?" In the darkness, without looking, Barbara could tell her husband was annoyed. "You mean my kind offer to race over as soon as we get back, and search the place ourselves?"

"Not search. Help her pack things up for storage."

"Even Archer's not that dumb," he snapped. "People are coming out of the woodwork to search the place, and suddenly we're volunteering to help her pack?"

"So you didn't even mention it?"

"I did not mention it."

"So, what's your plan?"

There she went again, Evan thought, with "your" instead of "our." "Your" problem, not "our" problem. Why had he let her talk him out of the bomb? he wondered. If they'd done the bomb, this would all be over. They'd be dead and happy by now, off creating another life instead of facing more complications. Or worse. Horrible shame and a trial and years in prison.

"You need to have a plan," Barbara insisted. "Maybe Paisley named you her executor. You never know."

They had been through this before, fantasizing about the odd chance that, without telling him, MacGregor had chosen them to execute the terms of her will. "We would have heard by now," Evan argued.

"Not necessarily," said Barbara, maintaining some optimism. "Nothing's in play until the will is read. And if she made you the executor . . ." It was a soothing thought, for them to have the legal power to go through the dead woman's things. "You used to do legal work for her. Why not?"

"We'll see."

They had come to the top of a ridge. Below shone the lights of their villa, and beyond the big picture windows, beyond and below, lay the shadowy outline of the Great Wall. Much of this section was unrepaired. It was still so enormous, stretching in an uninterrupted line as far as the eye could see. But scrubby trees dotted the roadway on top, where once a team of four horses had pulled supplies and where sentries had kept guard against any barbarian hordes that might want to invade the Middle Kingdom.

Evan eyed the wall and for a moment became philosophical. He was certainly not the first person to wonder which way the wall actually worked. Did it keep trouble out or keep it in? Did it repel invaders or imprison a people? Evan wasn't even sure which side of the ancient wall they were on technically, Chinese or barbarian.

All he knew was that he was on one side of things and had to get to the other. With Barbara or without her. He could go either way.

CHAPTER 22

*O*kay, so maybe it wasn't the best idea, playing strip backgammon on the Trans-Siberian Express, barreling over the rails of an Arctic wasteland. But the two of us were snugly happy in my private compartment, decorated in the shabby red tassels of some bygone day, as we rolled the dice and moved our pieces across the board. The night was long and cold, my compartment was overheated, and the bottle of potato vodka was going down smooth.

The train was just grinding to a halt in Mariinsk. I wiped the steam off the small frosty window, and the scene outside was perfect—the cutest little whistle-stop, with the dim spring sun just beginning to melt the icicles over the station doorway. Think Dr. Zhivago, all cozy in the middle of the frozen white. But as much as I wanted to stay and keep playing with my boyish waiter, with his sandy blond hair and his Midwestern good looks . . . Well, my waiter had some "waiting" to do with the other passengers, he said. And I was ravenous. So I threw on my mink and my boots and tripped out into the cold.

The stop was just fifteen minutes, just long enough for me to grab a caviar blini from the blini wagon and duck into the Internet café, where I posted my last, breathless blog. Remember? No, wait. I guess it was more like twenty minutes. Fifteen wouldn't have given me enough time, would it? Anyway, it was a short stop. That's what I meant.

TrippyGirl was feeling pretty content right about then. I could hardly wait to get back into my cozy sleeper and ring for my waiter and get on with our backgammon game, which I was determined to lose. Little did I know that my playmate was a professional snitch.

When I returned and opened the door to my sleeper, there he was, Ivan, fully dressed and no longer smiling. Filling the rest of the compartment were two fat thugs from the station, ready to take me in for indecent behavior—or whatever it is they call it here.

Now I'm sitting on a rock-hard cot in a cell in downtown Mariinsk. They gave me raw cabbage, a whole head of it, and a sliver of soap that looks more appetizing than the cabbage. On the bright side, they accidentally left my bag, so I'm posting this—trying to post this—with a signal stolen from the police station's Wi-Fi down the hall.

I imagine they'll let me go as soon as I pay someone a bribe. That's how things work. But how can this be anything but entrapment? I had no idea it was even against the law. And the waiter came on to me in the first place. Entrapment, right?

Amy looked up from her mother's blog, pushed her hair back over her ears, and frowned. Fanny had an active imagination and absolutely no scruples about inventing facts. That was probably what had made the TrippyGirl blog so much fun. Hundreds of her fans, maybe thousands, were reading it not as a travel blog but as a kind of outrageous soap opera.

But Fanny was a self-involved woman, and her work always contained elements of autobiography. TrippyGirl's adventures were peppered with updated details from her honeymoon forty years ago or her last argument with Amy, or with glowing descriptions of a rakish, black-haired boyfriend whom she was always mistreating and who happened to resemble Marcus Alvarez to a T.

Amy scanned the next few paragraphs. Despite the typical, Fanny-like coincidence of having her smartphone, plus a Wi-Fi connection, in a Russian jail in the middle of nowhere, the descriptions had an unsettling ring of truth. The perpetual twilight of the cell. The noises coming from all directions at all hours. The routine and the food.

Plus, Amy noted Fanny's description of the waiter. It was different from a few days ago, when they had begun their little game of strip backgammon. Back then he was a young Daniel Craig, all craggy and cool. And an albino, if she remembered correctly. Now he was sandy haired, with a Midwestern smile. Fanny must have lifted his looks from someone. And what was this talk about entrapment?

All of this conspired to make Amy try her mother once again. It had been nearly two days since the woman had returned an e-mail or answered a phone. The lack of response was probably due to the time difference, bad phone connections, and China's limited Internet access. But Amy composed another quick, overly casual e-mail, just to be safe. Hey, Mom. Just checking in. What's new?

She was just about to press SEND when the goose-neck lamp staring down at her laptop flickered a few times and died, along with everything else in her villa. The view of the Great Wall outside her window had likewise fallen into darkness. The second blackout of the night.

Welcome to China.

Amy figured she would have the next morning to herself. The electricity was back on. And the service was not scheduled until 1:00 p.m., leaving her plenty of personal time, she thought, to hike the wall. To actually hike the wall was technically impossible in this section, not unless you were into climbing and jumping and maybe rappelling. But she had scoped out a nice four-mile circuit beside the crumbling stone, then back through the hills.

But her hike was destined to remain theoretical. That morning, when she arrived at the front desk in her hiking gear for a last-minute check, she found that no preparations at all had been made for the service. No plan was in place to bar other tourists from wandering onto the memorial scene. No chairs or table or champagne seemed to be available. And, she found out almost by accident, that the wall was scheduled to be closed today for repairs, starting at noon. Repairs? Really? Where would they even start?

It took her until 12:55 p.m. to straighten things out.

* * *

As the last speaker of the day got further and further into her story, the mourners were no longer concerned about their lukewarm champagne. They had all stopped thinking about the wobbly, uncomfortable folding chairs and the makeshift podium and the lopsided, well-worn photo of Paisley MacGregor staring out at them. Even their own precarious position on top of the slippery stones of the Great Wall had ceased to fill their minds. They were all too focused on Nicole Marconi, the woman at the podium.

"I was just a teenager and—you know kids—I could care less what my parents were fighting about that day. I was mad at them, anyway, for cutting short our vacation. But I remember all the way home on the plane, the two of them huddled in their seats in front of me. Angry whispers back and forth. You know, angry whispering . . ." Nicole adopted a guttural, choked-up voice. "What do you mean . . .? It's your fault. . . . If the IRS gets their hands on those records . . ."

Amy had no idea why Nicole was telling them this. It was not the usual feel-good reminiscence of Paisley MacGregor. It seemed to have very little to do with Paisley. Plus, it was way too personal, implying all sorts of illegal activity, even though her parents were dead now and the statute of limitations must be long past.

The Marconi family had owned a popular chain of pizza restaurants in the tristate area, a few dozen cash cows, back in a looser era when people didn't charge every three-dollar purchase on a credit card. As Nicole rambled on from her selective teenage memory, Amy and everyone else on the wall were silently jumping to conclusions. Tax evasion, certainly. And perhaps some other related crimes. The narrative came to a head when the Marconi family drove in the middle of the night directly from the airport to their accountant's tiny office in the suburbs, a few blocks from the Cross Bronx.

"As soon as we got off the expressway, you could tell something was wrong. There were sirens and fire engines and a street blocked off. When we finally got there, to the little storefront office, the place was totally engulfed in flames. And the IRS or the FBI was there, too. Some scary official men in suits. It turns out they had been following us from the airport that night, trying to see what Dad would do once we landed. Well, long story short . . ."

Long story short? No! Wait! Why? For once, everyone at the wake wanted the long story. They wanted details. But apparently, there was a limit to how much Nicole was willing to incriminate her late parents.

"The records, or whatever they were, got burned up, the fire got labeled accidental, and my parents were saved by what could only be described as some sort of miraculous intervention. It wasn't until a few weeks later, when Mother was going through the back of MacGregor's cleaning closet, that she found the can. It was smelly, like a paint can. I guess, looking back, I knew it was some kind of accelerant."

Nicole let the implication hang in the midday chill.

"MacGregor?" Laila Steinberg asked in a stunned voice. "How could she have known?"

"How did she know anything?" Nicole answered. "I suppose the authorities questioned her while we were away. After they found the can, Mother and Father never mentioned it to Paisley. And she never mentioned it, of course."

Laila was unconvinced. "You're saying that Paisley committed arson? On her own? Without telling them?"

"Would she really do that?" Peter asked.

"I'm not saying anything," Nicole shot back, her anger echoing over the hills. "I'm just stating what happened. Oh . . ." And here she grinned. "Two years later, when my parents died in a car crash, they left nearly their entire estate to MacGregor. But . . ." She added a smirk to the grin. "I'm sure that was just a coincidence."

Amy glanced around. All the others looked appropriately dumbfounded. And yet this was totally in keeping with what she knew about the maid—a woman who rearranged your files or redecorated your apartment for your mother's visit and then refused to ever discuss it. Except this time, with arson and an inheritance in play, her behavior seemed to have crossed the line into an unspoken, unacknowledged version of blackmail.

"To Paisley MacGregor . . ." Nicole toasted, but not with her flute. She toasted with her other hand, with a silver spoon of the chicken charcoal that was standing in for MacGregor. "Who so generously spent my family money in order to give us this trip around the world." And she sent the charcoal drifting over the Great Wall and into the land of barbarians.

Nicole had positioned herself to be last. Even if someone wanted to add a toast now, what could he or she say?

It's not just that she committed arson and risked arrest, Amy mused as she carefully led the silent mourners off the Great Wall and down the uneven stone steps. *These people are finally realizing how much power this woman had over them.*

Peter stepped down from the wall, and he hung back as the others passed.

"Did you know?" Amy whispered.

"Not a clue," he whispered back. "But I'm so glad I fired her."

CHAPTER 23

The Ohio billionaire pushed right past the French couple, with their maps and designer sunglasses and unending questions about shopping. He leaned across the antique concierge desk. "Alvarez," he shouted, as if the desk were as wide as the lobby. "All set for Monday? Bublé and the band and a camera crew? I want it private, don't forget. No gawkers."

"Excuse me," Marcus said calmly with a subservient smile. "This son of a bitch has no manners. Please wait a minute." He was addressing the French couple in French. Then he turned to the man from Columbus. "It's all set, Mr. George. And I asked them to make the spire pink for that night. I believe that's Calista's favorite color?"

"Pink?" Mr. Franklin George had to pause and think. "Yeah, I guess it is. How did you know?"

"That's my job," said Marcus. "Sunset is at seven-oh-two on Monday. So, we'll close the observation deck at six fifteen to give us time to set up."

Franklin George said, "Okay," which in his vocab-

ulary seemed to mean "wow." "Glad to see you're on
top of it, Alvarez."

The concierge desk was around the corner from
the elevators, and it was just at this moment that
Calista joined her soon-to-be fiancé in the lobby.
She was dressed for the weather, an Armani coat
with a pink scarf and a chilly expression. Franklin
went in for a kiss and got a peck.

"What's the matter?"

"Let's go," she answered with a snap. And without
looking back, the willowy blonde headed through the
lobby, followed closely by her substantially built
beau. "What were you doing last night?" she said into
the air of her wake.

"What?" Franklin asked, racing to catch up.

"While I was at the movies for three hours." A second later and they were swallowed up by the revolving doors.

Marcus spent five more minutes dealing with the
French shoppers—"Yes, it's possible to get good
prices in the Diamond District, but there's this
great little shop on Broome Street. Here's their
card. Mention my name"—then turned to deal with
someone new.

It was Fanny in disguise. She was dressed head to
foot in her rich-lady drag, a parody of wealth probably adapted from a dowager character in a Marx
Brothers movie. Marcus had noticed her following
Calista out of the elevator bank.

"Mission accomplished?" he asked.

"This was the easy part," Fanny said and modestly
snuggled her cheeks in her mink stole. "My penthouse suite—well, someone's penthouse suite—is

right next to theirs. That's what I told her. Most people will engage in elevator conversation if you seem rich enough and harmless enough."

Fanny's elevator icebreaker had been short, friendly, and provocative. "Are you friends with Mr. and Mrs. George?" she'd asked the willowy blonde. "I saw you leaving their suite just now. What a lovely couple."

"Mrs. George?" Calista had said, her brows furrowing for probably the first time in years. "You must be mistaken. Mr. George isn't married. Yet."

"Oops. I just assumed he was."

"What made you assume that?"

"Well, I was putting out my room service tray last night just as she came in. Around seven thirty. He was waiting at the door, so happy." Fanny clutched her pearls and mimed an embarrassed blush. "I shouldn't say this, but I could hear them through the wall." She tittered. "They were very, very glad to see each other."

For the remaining two dozen floors, Calista had asked Fanny the expected questions. Was this woman pretty? Did she have big breasts? Did she look like a hooker?

"Don't you feel bad about this?" Marcus asked, feeling just a little bad himself. "I mean, breaking up their engagement?"

"We're saving her from a ghastly mistake," Fanny reasoned. "And don't act so innocent. You're the one who talked her into going to that Italian movie last night. Alone."

"That wasn't hard. The girl is pretentious and loves Italy . . . blabbering on about Fashion Week in Milan, throwing around a few odd phrases. Of course, the more she tried to force him to go with her, the more he resisted."

"And of course you helped." Fanny lowered her voice and adopted a fawning, obsequious tone. "Mr. George, you'll love the movie too. Not movie, sir, a film. Three hours long, but the subtitles are marvelous."

Marcus chuckled at her re-creation, then instantly changed gears. "That particular musical is sold out, Mrs. Altengruber. But I'll see what I can do. Saturday night? Two on the center aisle?"

Fanny didn't blink or pause. She instinctively knew that the head concierge must be standing right behind her. "Marcus, dear, you are such a treasure."

"Is everything all right, Mrs . . . ?" Gavin paused for a split second. "Mrs. Altengruber."

"After all the times I've stayed here . . ," Fanny turned to face Gavin, pulled herself up to her full five-foot-one, and threw her stole back across her throat. "It's Altenstruder," she said huffily and marched off through the revolving doors, a Marx Brothers dowager to the hilt.

Gavin's expression turned from smug to crest-fallen. "Oh, my God."

Marcus kept a straight face. *What a woman.* "I'll fix it, Gavin," he said with reassuring softness and trotted out after Fanny. It was as good an excuse as any to leave and take the rest of the day off.

The house on Barrow Street, in the heart of the Village, had been in the Abel family for generations. The block was composed almost entirely of brownstones, many of them still single-family homes. But what made the block stand out wasn't the small-scale comfort of the street or the uniform row of shady ginkgoes. It was the communal garden.

It was a design still fairly common in London, but one that had almost died out in New York. In the center of the Barrow Street block, where one might expect to find small, dusty backyards or sheds or, more probably, home additions nestled right up to the property lines, was a manicured garden, surprisingly large, with benches and a play area and a fountain in the middle. It was accessible only through the houses, and every home owner gladly paid a share of the upkeep.

Fanny sat on the flagstone patio outside her kitchen, a Marlboro Light in one hand, a cordless phone in the other. Amy had called at an unsuspecting moment, just as Fanny had come racing through the front door. That had been five minutes ago, and Amy was still grilling her. "I'm sorry I'm not always here to answer the phone, dear. I do have a life."

"Mom, it was a simple question. Were you in jail?"

"Of course I'm not in jail. I'm out on the patio, enjoying . . . enjoying the air."

"Enjoying a cigarette? Mom, are you smoking again?"

"No." Fanny covered the mouthpiece and exhaled a lungful.

"You're smoking. Is that a habit you picked up in jail?"

"I wish. They don't let you smoke in jail."

"Aha. You were in jail."

And so the truth, which Fanny had been cagily avoiding for the past five minutes, fell out into the open. "All right, I was. But just overnight. Uncle Sol bailed me out the next morning."

Fanny went on to tell her the whole story, leaving out nothing, except the possibility that she and Marcus might have been in the wrong. "Don't worry. Charges were dropped. Rawlings isn't pursuing it," she said as she lit up a second Marlboro Light. "He was trying to force us to make a statement, say that the Billy Strunk murder might be connected to Paisley MacGregor."

"Why would he care about that?"

"He thought it would give him probable cause for a search warrant. He's dying to go through the apartment, but the maid's maid turned him down."

"So why did he drop the charges?"

"Your uncle Sol had a talk with an assistant DA. Rawlings had latched onto this case as a favor to the Indian police—and because he wants the glory. But when you come right down to it, it's just an unidentified body in India that may have connections to New York. I suspect Rawlings lost interest. I don't know whether to be insulted or not."

"Not," Amy shot back. "How many times did I tell you this kind of stuff would get you in trouble?"

"I was impersonating a lawyer. What's the harm in that? Your uncle Sol does it all the time."

"He's a lawyer."

"More or less. Dear, in a perfect world no one would have to impersonate anyone. But jail wasn't so very terrible. One night. And they were very sweet."

"So this wasn't like TrippyGirl?" Amy asked. "You didn't have to survive for two days on water and a head of cabbage?"

"I made that part up. At the time I was hungry for coleslaw."

"Is Marcus there with you?"

"No, dear." Actually, Fanny had just heard the front door open and close, so she knew Marcus was indeed there, technically. She pretended that Amy had asked the question ten seconds earlier, so it didn't feel like lying.

"Well, tell Marcus to stop it. The two of you to- gether . . . You're dangerous. This time you got ar- rested. Next time you could get killed."

A few seconds later Marcus appeared in the door- way, aimlessly flipping through a stack of the newly arrived mail. He stood on the cusp of the tiny patio and waited until Fanny had spoken her last insin- cere assurances, said good-bye, and hung up on her daughter. "So, that's the end?" he asked. "No more investigating?"

"Not by a long shot," she said, barely skipping a beat. "We can't go back to Paisley's apartment, obvi- ously, but there's another angle. Billy Strunk, or whoever he was. We have his picture, and we know he was connected to one of our mourners. Enough to get himself killed. I'm guessing that if we show his picture to the right people . . ."

"Why do we care?"

Fanny squinted. She seemed puzzled by the ques- tion, so he rephrased it. "If Rawlings doesn't think this case is worth pursuing, why do we care?"

"Because one of our clients is probably a killer."

"Not to be callous, Fanny, but there are plenty of uncaught killers in the world." Marcus was prepared to go on arguing, but he was stopped by a flash of bold red lettering. He shuffled the mail back be- tween his hands and found the envelope in question. It was addressed to Amy's Travel, Inc., and was marked COLLECTION DUE. FINAL NOTICE.

Fanny pushed herself up from the patio chair and reached for the mail. "Just junk," she said too casually and quickly.

Marcus held on. He didn't open the letter. He didn't have to. "How much do you owe?"

"It's just a misunderstanding," Fanny said. "Accounting error." Again, she tried to grab the mail.

"Really?" Marcus found himself mildly insulted. "Really, Fanny? We're lying to each other? Not that I object on any moral ground."

Fanny knew what he meant. If there was anyone whom she could confide in without the risk of judgment or a lecture, it was Marcus, who'd probably done everything she had and more. But she remained silent.

"I've had plenty of debts in my life," Marcus said, trying to prime the pump. No response. "I was arrested once for check kiting in Miami," he added, "but they couldn't prove it." That was, in fact, a lie. "Wound up spending two days in jail, until my mother bailed me out. And then I never paid her back." What would he have to confess to in order to make her open up? A Ponzi scheme?

For Marcus, her continued silence finally said it all. "My God," he whispered. His mind had leaped to the only possibility big enough. "Are you losing just the business? Or are you losing the business *and* the house?"

CHAPTER 24

Hawaii should have been the simplest location to arrange, but had turned out to be the hardest. Paisley MacGregor had stipulated the four other hotels by name, sometimes by room numbers. But for Hawaii, the Big Island, to be specific, she had left only instructions to find someplace exclusive and private—with at least one helicopter pad.

The helipad wouldn't be a problem, they'd discovered. Combining the exclusive and private aspects of their stay would be. Hawaii was part of the United States, almost home, and literally home to the Steinbergs, who lived just one island up the road. For all the previous stops, they had been this clique of Americans, united by a dead maid and separated from the local world by language and culture. But now, to be on the last leg, with fatigue setting in, with Americans on all sides, and with the atmosphere of everyday life seeping through the cracks . . . How would Amy and Peter keep their eight rich mourners united for two more nights?

Peter's knee-jerk solution had been the Four Seasons, having them occupy six suites in an ocean-side wing. Peter's solution to everything seemed to be the Four Seasons. But Amy had worked a little harder and had come up with a private home, one of several over-the-top residences for sale in the current real estate market. It had been vacant for a year, and the corporate manager was becoming flexible about short-term rentals. The buying price was set at forty million, but Amy was sure she could pick it up for thirty-eight, cash, if she wanted to buy a nice winter home.

The estate was spread out over several acres on the Kona coast, with eight Polynesian-themed guest cottages, in addition to the main house. The owner's identity was kept secret by the corporation, but the home went by the name No Mistakes, which Amy found a bit disconcerting. Shouldn't dream homes have carefree names, like No Worries or No Problems? No Mistakes sounded like way too much responsibility.

The Kona coast wasn't known for its sandy beaches but for its craggy, lava-laden shorelines. It was on just such a craggy promontory, under the shade of some architect's version of a native *hale*, that Paisley MacGregor's last will and testament was finally about to be read.

Amy was alone in the shade of the *hale*, except for the caretaker, who was helping arrange the chairs and the podium and was telling her what could and could not be done. For example, the landscaping lights could not be turned on; they were on a timer controlled from a computer in a warehouse in San Francisco. And if they weren't through by 6:15 p.m., the sprinkler system, controlled from the same warehouse, would make the act of leaving the *hale* a bit of a challenge.

When Amy looked around, she saw that the first three guests were arriving. Peter was in the middle, caught between David and Herb, the meat in a Pepper-Sands sandwich. The bickering couple had finally agreed in favor of their "fortieth" anniversary extravaganza. Now it was just a matter of the venue argument.

"I've done a bike tour through Provence," Peter said cheerily, siding with David for the moment. "Not all that strenuous. Maybe forty miles a day. Less."

"But there are hills," Herb protested.

"Yes, there are hills," Peter allowed. "It's Provence. But I can find you some great châteaus, and there will be a courtesy van following you, just in case of emergency. Flat tires, that sort of thing."

"You can ride in the van," David said with unrepressed glee. "Or better, we can put a little motor on your bike. I can just see it, the rest of us cycling away, working up a sweat, and you putt-putting like a motorized Queen of England, waving to the throngs."

"What's wrong with a private river cruise?" Herb countered. "A boat and a crew and a great chef. And we spend a few weeks on the Rhine or the Danube. Much more civilized."

"Yes, if all your friends are over sixty. Oh, I forgot. You're over sixty."

"Don't forget who's paying for this."

Amy couldn't decide if their bickering was real or a game, a way for them to pass the time and flirt with Peter. Of course, the proposed trip was real. Probably. But even more real was an attractive man's approval. Would Peter approve more of youth and adventure or money and ease?

"A river cruise is nice," Peter said, his high school stammer returning just at the edge of his voice. "And you can take bikes with you. That way, the younger people . . . I mean the more athletic . . . I didn't mean that, either. I mean the people who want to can take bike trips during the day, and the more sedentary . . . I mean the people who don't want to cycle . . ."

Peter seemed to have nailed it, the perfect lose-lose. David was incensed at the idea that Herb's river cruise might win the game, and Herb was incensed at being called sedentary.

By now, the Steinbergs were also maneuvering their way out to the *hale*. Maury was on his phone, dealing with someone or something back in Maui and ignoring Laila, who stumbled a few yards behind, trying to keep her footing on the shelves of black volcanic rock. Her leather-soled Manolos weren't helping.

Peter saw her on the rocks and grabbed at the excuse, any excuse, to leave the Pepper-Sands with a murmured "Excuse me." When Maury finally noticed his wife, her arm now securely around the waist of their tall, sure-footed guide, he reacted with an impatient sigh, then returned to his call. He seemed rather bipolar in regards to his wife, Amy concluded. Sometimes loving and protective, sometimes disdainful, with very little in between.

Nicole Marconi, in a much more sensible pair of white Top-Siders, was also making her way across the lava rock. Her demeanor was determined, almost solemn. Evan and Barbara were the last of the party to arrive, treading gingerly down a path of carved-out steps from one of the estate's manicured lawns. They, like Nicole, appeared solemn and nervous—eyes darting, mouths thin and straight.

For this particular ceremony, Peter joined the seven others on the bamboo folding chairs, facing Amy and the podium and the blue-green sea beyond. Amy had never read a will before, had never even heard one read. It felt like an outdated tradition, best left to the world of fiction. But Paisley MacGregor had requested it here, at their last stop.

Amy picked up the copy of a handwritten, notarized letter, the one Fanny and Marcus had examined that night over a week ago in her New York home office. She cleared her throat.

This wouldn't be Amy's first time reading Paisley MacGregor's notarized letter or Paisley's will, for that matter. After the murder in India, she had, very guiltily, sat in various hotel rooms, poring over both documents, hoping to find a connection, some little hint of a connection, between one of her tourists and the man who had called himself Billy Strunk. And although the letter and the will were in no way dull, they failed to shed any light—on anything. Amy cleared her throat again and began.

"My loved ones, thank you for coming. I know you're all here, in this beautiful Hawaiian setting, preparing to scatter the last of me into the sky. What a comfort to know that all my loving families cared enough to take time out of your busy lives and say farewell. You are very special to me. And I'd like to think that I had an influence over you, to make your worlds a little easier, to help guide you in my own small way."

This was vintage MacGregor, Amy thought as she

paused between the first and second paragraphs. *Now here comes the good part.*

"Even you, Peter, although I did have to lure you with a nice piece of business and a commission. Just teasing. I love you, too. Just don't skim more money than you should. The executors won't like it." It was meant as a joke, but . . .

"I never skimmed money," Peter mumbled, aware that he was arguing with a dead woman. Everyone avoided looking his way, and the temperature in the *hale* probably went up a degree. They could literally feel him steaming.

"You people were my life. It was a privilege to be a small part of yours and all your special moments. Nicole, I remember like yesterday you and your parents coming back from Europe, only to find all your records burned in that dreadful fire. I'm so glad I was able to be there to comfort you. The police can be so awfully rude to you. And for no reason.

"And sweet Herb. Was it really so long ago when you brought young, handsome David into our home? There were a lot of delicate moments in those first few years. At times it was almost like a French sex farce, the two of you and your secret friends, with doors slamming and naked strangers tiptoeing around and hiding in closets. But we were all discreet, and it all worked out for the best.

"And, of course, dear Evan and Barbara. I never knew how you could afford a full-time maid. Half the time it seemed you were just taking money from one account and throwing it into another. But I'm so glad you were able to afford me. Such fun-loving people. I don't think I ever laughed so much in my life.

"Last but not least, Laila and Maury. You found

me right after you found each other. Second mar-
riages are hard, so I've heard. It must have been especially hard for Maury, giving up his own gallery
and joining Laila's business. A lot of men would
have felt emasculated by it. But not you, Maury. I
don't want to keep rambling, but the memories are
golden. I wish I could be there to share a glass of
champagne, which I'm afraid I'm no longer allowed
to have in my situation.

"And now, if you'll indulge me, whoever is reading this is going to also read my will. All my love, my
dears. It's been grand."

Amy paused and peered up over the rims of her
glasses. Her audience sat frozen in place, too self-
conscious to even glance at their own partners, like
eight stone-faced mannequins displaying a line of expensive resort wear. She took a sip from her bottle of
Evian and flipped to the next document. "The Last
Will and Testament of Paisley Louise MacGregor,"
Amy read aloud to the mannequins. This document
was longer and much less dramatic.

It began by asserting Miss MacGregor's sound
mind and selecting the law firm of Corns and Associates to be her executor. At this news, Evan and
Barbara came back to life, looking relieved, almost
jubilant, then turning stone-faced again, embarrassed by their momentary enthusiasm.

There were a few small gifts mentioned first, for a
children's charity in New York, for Joy Archer, her
"loyal maid and friend," and for a few others. Amy
kept reading, although momentarily distracted by
the fact that MacGregor's humorless maid was
named Joy.

The will went on. "I request that all my remaining personal papers be destroyed without being

read or cataloged, and that the remainder of my possessions be publicly auctioned and the proceeds added to my estate. I hereby stipulate that this estate, including but not limited to all investments and accounts, be liquidated and divided evenly among the following individuals, provided that they are present, as requested, for the reading of this will." And here she went on to name her eight ex-bosses.

Amy had barely put down the will when Nicole spoke up, shouting into the whirl of motors and the wind, which had come out of nowhere and was starting to attack the *hale*. "Divided evenly?" she demanded over the din. "That's my money. And now you're saying the Steinbergs get twice as much as me because they're two people? And the Corns?" She probably also added the Pepper-Sands. But by this time the whirlwind of propeller blades was rendering her shouts inaudible.

Two waiters from the catering company approached the bamboo chairs, one on each side. They began to lead the guests to a pair of silver helicopters warming up at the twin helipads situated fifty yards inland, on either side of the black lava promontory. Above a row of coconut palms a third helicopter was just hovering into view.

CHAPTER 25

Amy knew better than to flirt on the job, especially with vendors.

Desmond Mansfield happened to be an Australian who had moved to the Big Island a few years back to buy a trio of Hughes 500s and start his own business. Aloha Jack, he'd named it. "Because," as he explained from between a set of perfectly dimpled cheeks, "no one wants to hire from a company called Aloha Desmond." His logo, emblazoned on each side of each of his helicopters, was a cartoon kangaroo in a bush hat.

In all their correspondence, Desmond had assured her that it would be no problem. The Volcanoes National Park allowed private helicopters to fly over the Kilauea volcano, and the rim of Halemaumau Crater was safe enough to permit the simultaneous landing of his choppers, which would be carrying three pilots, including him, and nine passengers, including her.

She had checked with him again in person hours after they arrived, and had found him just as cute as he was in the photo on his Web site. "This is more complicated than the usual tourist flyover, no doubt." He put on his work face, and his dimples disappeared, allowing Amy to pay more attention to the rest of him. Muscularly thin, a square jaw, with a sandy brown crew cut and an unlined face. *Why do small-craft pilots always look sixteen and adorable?* Amy had wondered, not for the first time.

"Have you tested the crater edge?" she'd had to ask. "Is it safe for three helicopters?"

"No worries," he drawled. "The park service wouldn't let us go if it weren't safe. My boys and me did a test run this morning. And conditions tomorrow will be even better. Of course, we won't be exactly on the rim. Sorry to disappoint."

"You're not disappointing me," Amy said. "The less danger, the better."

His dimples returned. "Good. I hate to disappoint."

"You probably don't get many requests for ashes to be dumped into a volcano."

"Seems a little redundant, eh? But rich blokes do all sorts of things, and no one calls it crazy."

"You're right." She decided not to mention that the ashes in the urn would be chicken and charcoal.

From the will reading, the mourners walked directly to the helicopters. Like a good guide, she made sure the first two were safely filled with clients. Then she and Peter and a simmeringly silent Nicole waited for the third. Amy found herself riding shotgun beside Desmond, although the one-way headphones made conversation impossible.

All three choppers landed on the upwind side of Halemaumau Crater, the only option, since the gas vents from the active volcano rendered the down-wind side nearly invisible in the white mist. This was vog, the pilots explained through the headphones, volcanic fog. The helicopters wound up fifty yards away from each other, lined up along the rim, rotors locked down. The guests slowly emerged, following their pilots, like aliens from their shiny spaceships.

As promised, they weren't all that close to the edge. But they could easily see down inside, down the perilous, rock-strewn slope and out to the red-orange glow of lava and the gas vents beyond. It was a breathtaking setting, just a shade windy, with bright blue skies above, an active volcano below, and white plumes shooting up and away into the vog.

Desmond led them to a two-ton basalt boulder that had been coughed out in some angry, unrecorded moment during the past million years. This became their podium. And this time no one insisted on telling any self-serving stories about long-lost vacations. The moment was simple, dramatic, and relatively short. Amy, for the first time, took part in the scattering and was glad to see the last of the chicken, several spoonfuls apiece, fly into the wind and down toward the lava.

No one had to encourage anyone to hurry back down the crater's side to the helicopters.

"This deceased one," Desmond said, looking back over his shoulder. "She had quite the sense of drama."

Amy had found herself walking beside Desmond again. "The woman led a quiet life. What's wrong with a little adventure after you're gone?"

"The ultimate example of living vicariously."

The air had turned surprisingly still, with their words echoing off the slope of the crater. Amy sighed and could feel the relief. It was a nice moment. A handsome man, an amazing setting. Her odyssey was nearing its end, with only one more night before their long flight back home. She probably wasn't paying quite as much attention as she should have.

On reaching their chopper, she turned to watch the stragglers. Out of habit she began counting. *The Steinbergs, walking together, one, two. Herb Sands, three. Nicole, four. Now to the left. David Pepper, five.* No, that was one of the pilots. And the woman she thought was Nicole was actually one of the pilots, too, the female pilot. By the time, Amy got to six, she had to start over.

And then came the echo of a shout. Or was it a scream? Whatever it was, it was followed by the grumbling, tumbling sound of a rock slide. Everyone heard it and stopped in their tracks. Amy paused, as well, then grabbed Desmond by the arm and began racing—gingerly—back up the slope.

When they reached the crater's edge, the real edge this time, a mini-avalanche of rocks was still pouring down the insides of the crater, on its way to being reheated by the red-orange lava swirling lazily at the mouth. Amy tried to get a better view, but Desmond held her back.

Everyone was coming now. The two other pilots, plus . . . She started counting again. *One, two, three . . .* She saw Barbara walking by herself at a nervous trot, coming faster than the others. Amy scanned the slope, not counting this time, but looking for one person in particular.

Evan Corns. Where the hell was Evan Corns?

* * *

Landing choppers on the crater rim had been totally illegal, despite Desmond's assurance to the contrary. That was the smallest of their newfound
problems, although Desmond would probably
argue otherwise.

Within two minutes of the rock slide, the Aussie
pilot was in the air, diving inside the crater as far as
he could, given the unpredictable air currents and
the heat and the vog. Aloha Jack's other pilots, a
best friend from Sydney and Desmond's wife, also
took to the air and flew in increasingly wider circles
around the crater.

Ten minutes later the park service responded
with their own battered helicopter. But there wasn't
much they could add to the situation, besides yell-
ing at Desmond and promising to start an investigation. The crater's interior was too dangerous for
climbers, not unless some trace of Evan Corns could
be found to justify their efforts. Then a few volun-
teers might try the descent.

The best friend and the pilot wife ferried the
other guests back to the estate, where the Hawaii
County police were waiting to question them, then
flew back out to join Desmond, Amy, Peter, and Barbara, who had refused to leave with the others.

An hour after sunset, when it was no longer safe
for anyone to be hovering over an active volcano,
they called off the search, with the promise of starting again tomorrow at sunrise.

The night was breezy and moist, with only a few
clouds flitting across the moon. Amy stood on her
veranda with a much-needed Campari and soda.

She watched the police cars pull out of the estate around 9:00 p.m., then gave Barbara a few minutes to settle in or pour herself a drink. At 9:05 p.m., Amy wandered over to the Corns cottage, prepared to knock. The door was open. Barbara was sitting on a brightly flowered bamboo sofa, hands clasped in her lap, head down, no drink. Amy left hers on a side table on the porch.

Evan's wife looked up and moaned. "Why did we even go there? An active volcano, for God's sake."

"Herb and David did this trip years ago. They had this volcano photo on MacGregor's piano." Amy stepped inside the cottage and settled into a bamboo chair facing the sofa. Barbara seemed to welcome the company.

"The police kept asking if Evan was depressed. That's ridiculous."

"Ridiculous," Amy agreed. "Seemed like he was in a wonderful mood."

The black basalt boulder had been perhaps ten yards from the actual rim, all uphill. The only reason for Evan to walk up to the rim might have been to get a slightly better view of the crater. But they had been warned not to, and no one had been seen attempting it. Also, Evan had been one of the few not to bring a camera, not even a phone camera.

Shortly after getting there, the park service had found the spot where the mini-avalanche had started. They had taken pictures of scuff marks that seemed to go over the rim and had placed a water bottle beside what might have been shoe prints in order to give scale to the photos.

"When did you last see Evan?" Amy asked, knowing this question had been asked a dozen times.

"Right after you threw the last of the ashes. After that, I was too busy watching out for my own footing. I think we all were. Those rocks are sharp."

"Can you think of any reason why he might have gone back up to the rim?"

"Maybe he had to pee," suggested Barbara.

Pee into the crater of an active volcano? Who would do such a thing? Go out of his way to walk up to the rim . . . ? "Actually, that kind of sounds like Evan," Amy had to admit.

Evan's tiny bladder had become something of a running joke with the group. He had been sighted by Nicole relieving himself in the river by the Taj Mahal, right before the ceremony began. She had been suitably disgusted and had told everyone. A similar incident occurred on the Great Wall of China just as Maury was concluding some endless Paisley story they'd all heard before. David and Peter had both seen Evan wander off to urinate over a crumbling edge of the wall, and both had gotten the giggles. The others noticed, too, even Maury. But far from being embarrassed, Evan seemed to enjoy the attention.

"I know," Barbara said, with the closest she'd come to a chuckle in the past five hours. "Evan could be like a big kid. He would totally pee into a volcano."

"Except he would want people to see," Amy added. "I mean, what's the point of doing something funny if no one sees it?"

"Maybe he did call out, 'Hey, everybody, look!' and no one heard him. Then he fell."

Amy tried to envision it, the burly, fun-loving man with his pants unzipped trying to get someone's attention, shouting, perhaps waving his arms, then falling backward, pants still unzipped, down the side of a crater. The whole scenario sounded comical, which was exactly why it struck her as so enormously tragic. "I think we would have heard him," she said softly.

"Well, it's more believable than what they're saying. My husband did not commit suicide."

"I'm sure it was an accident."

"He may not even be dead." Barbara's face brightened in a desperate, jittery smile. "He could have tripped and fallen the other direction. Away from the crater."

"It's possible." Amy had never been in this position, trading theories with a possible widow. She wasn't good at it, with too logical a mind to be of much comfort. "But wouldn't he have rolled past us?"

"It depends on the angle he fell."

"What about the helicopters? They circled around for hours. They would have seen him."

"Helicopters don't see everything. He could have been hiding. Under a ledge or behind a rock."

"Hiding?" Amy was taken aback. "Why would Evan be hiding?"

"I didn't mean hiding," Barbara said quickly. "Hidden."

"You think he started the avalanche, then ran away while the rest of us were looking over the edge?"

"I didn't say that."

"Do you think it's a possibility? But that would mean . . ." *Wow*, thought Amy. "Did Evan have any reason to fake his death?" She hadn't intended to say that out loud.

"Fake his death?" Barbara stood up, her ruddy face turning even ruddier. "How can you suggest such a thing?"

"Actually, you suggested it."

"I meant he could have fallen unconscious under a rock or a ledge. Hidden, not hiding."

"Right. Sorry." But there was something about Barbara's demeanor that left her troubled. Amy glanced through the open door and regretted having left her drink on the porch. She got up to leave. "I guess we'll take it day by day."

"Take what day by day?"

"The search. Not that it'll take more than a day to find him. Alive. Find him alive," she added. "But we'll have to book you into a hotel for the duration. Not that it'll be a duration. There's a lodge in the park with a nice view of the volcano. Not a nice view, but you can see the spot . . ." She was just digging herself in deeper.

"I understand," Barbara said. "We'll take it day by day."

When Amy stepped out the door, she veered slightly left and scooped up the Campari without missing a beat.

PART TWO
THE AFTER-WAKE

CHAPTER 26

"**I** know for a fact that Michael Bublé is performing in a casino in Macao."

"Do you even know where Macao is?"

"That's not the point." Gavin was determined not to fall for this distraction. "It's somewhere around China."

"Around China? That's a big perimeter."

"I think it's in China."

"You're kidding. China has casinos?"

Gavin shook his head in disgust. "You already know this, Alvarez. At least you should."

Marcus kept his smug smile in place, even though he figured his chances were about fifty-fifty. "I also know," he said, "that you can lease a Gulfstream V at Macao International and get to New York in just under eighteen hours." He was making it up, but it sounded good.

"A Gulfstream V?" Gavin choked. "Do you have any idea how much a Gulfstream V would cost?"

"I know exactly," Marcus lied. "To the penny."

The last time Marcus had seen Franklin George and his fiancée was ten minutes ago, as they were arguing their way across the lobby, batting insults back and forth in quietly explosive hisses. They had been coming in, not going out, and Marcus figured he had maybe another five minutes to see if his scheme had worked.

"And did you bother to okay this expenditure with Mr. George?"

"I think his exact phrase was, 'Whatever it costs.' "

"Yes, I can imagine. But even a billionaire might balk a little. . . ."

The knock on the door came two minutes later, toward the end of Gavin's lecture on the importance of communicating with guests and managing expectations, although Marcus knew Gavin would have come down on the other side of the argument if Marcus hadn't done everything possible to fulfill the customer's demands. There would be no winning. That was the whole idea.

Franklin George eased open the thick beige door, unlabeled on this side but clearly marked PRIVATE on the other. "Sorry. No one was at the desk." Marcus could tell by the man's sheepish demeanor that he'd won. "How are you guys doing?"

"Doing well, sir," said Gavin, slightly taken aback by the interruption. "Marcus and I were just discussing your big event."

"Yes." The tycoon drew out the word. "About the proposal . . ."

Franklin George went on to explain that he would not be proposing to Calista, after all. It seemed the woman was "crazy jealous" and delusional and, to top it off, had balked at the idea of a prenup. "So

I guess we'll have to cancel Bublé and the Empire State."

Gavin looked on in disbelief as Marcus graciously explained that it would be no problem. Two days was plenty of time, and he could probably talk the "Bube" into not suing him or charging anything.

"You call him the Bube?" asked Franklin.

"Well, after making all the arrangements, we got kind of close."

Franklin erupted into a grin, shook both their hands, said the Ritz-Carlton would be his only hotel from now on and, right before walking out, informed the head concierge that Marcus was "a keeper."

"I don't know how you did it," Gavin snarled as the door closed.

"Hundreds of hours of hard work," Marcus said.

"Don't bullshit me. You screwed up their engagement. Did you seduce her? Because if you did, it's going to come out, and I'll have your ass fired so fast. . . ."

"Seduce Calista?" Marcus mocked. "I've spoken to her twice. Now, if you'll excuse me, I have to get on the phone and cancel everything." And with that, Marcus took the rest of the day off.

An hour later he was at the travel agency, thanking Fanny with a couple of iced chais purchased from the trendy café down the street.

"We did them a favor," Fanny insisted. "It worked only because the girl is the jealous type, which is good for him to find out now. Besides, the bastard wanted a prenup. Destined for failure."

Marcus still felt a twinge of guilt. "So we didn't ruin two people's lives just to keep me from getting fired?"

"Nonsense." Fanny chugged the rest of her chai. "Manipulating people is like hypnotism. You can't make them do anything they wouldn't otherwise do."

"I suppose." Marcus thought, not for the first time, about how different mother and daughter were. He checked his Faux-lex. Still ticking away. "Where's Amy?"

"Can't stand to be away from her?" Fanny teased. "Now that she's finally home?

"No," Marcus lied. "Just curious."

"She went to visit Barbara Corns."

"Amy's been home for a week. When are you going to tell her about the money thing?"

The "money thing" was the fact that Fanny had lied to Amy about the money used to start up Amy's Travel. It had not come from the portfolio of Fanny's late husband Stan. That had all disappeared in the recession. It had come from a mortgage she'd taken out on the Barrow Street house, the first mortgage the house had seen in eighty years.

"Not in so many words," answered Fanny.

"You have to tell her. Amy wouldn't want you to lose the house just to keep her in business."

"That's not the problem. Unless a miracle happens, the business is already gone. As for the town house . . ." Her tone was almost cavalier. "Well, it's too big for me. And Amy needs an excuse to move on with her life."

"No." It was impossible for Marcus to imagine Fanny without her home. "There must be a way." He bit his lip and thought. "Did Amy sign a rental agreement for her half of the house? Because it's hard to evict a renter in New York City. The new owner would have to . . ."

"Of course not. What kind of mother do you think I am?"

"How about your credit cards? They can buy you a few months."

"Maxed out."

"Well, how about Uncle Joe and Sol? They're your brothers."

"They are Stan's brothers."

"Even more reason. This was their family home, right?"

"Now you're getting into the whole mess of family."

And, according to Fanny, it was a mess. Thirty-six years ago, neither Uncle Joe nor Uncle Sol had approved of Stan's marriage to the tiny, opinionated shiksa from Long Island. Relations had not improved a few years later, when Stan, the least successful of the Abel brothers, inherited the Barrow Street house. They felt their parents had always rewarded Stan for his unorthodox choices in life, which probably held an element of truth. He'd always been the squeaky, damaged wheel of the Abel family.

In the following decades, everyone had tried to heal the wounds. Fanny had done her part, transforming herself from a fifth-generation French Huguenot into someone more Jewish than Golda Meir. But Stan's death took its toll. And the brothers objected strongly to the idea of a travel agency. How would they react now, she asked Marcus, to finding out that she'd mortgaged the homestead to finance this pipe dream?

"But they still love Amy," Marcus protested. "They don't want to see her homeless. Talk to them."

"Remember what I said about manipulation and hypnotism?"

"This isn't the same." But he could see his argument was going nowhere. "Okay, but you have to tell Amy. Today."

Fanny was relieved when the office phone rang—anything to change the subject—until she checked the display.

"It's Amy," Marcus prodded.

"If you think I'm going to tell her over the phone, you're crazy."

Amy waited until the call went to voice mail, then hung up. Perhaps her mother was on the other line with a customer. That would be nice.

Barbara Corns and two paralegals from her firm wandered through MacGregor's white apartment with their clipboards, performing a real inventory this time. Amy was staying out of their way in the oval foyer.

Barbara joined her, seconds after Amy had put away her phone. "Sorry about this. I thought we could relax while my people did their thing, but it never works out that way." She led Amy into the kitchen, where the plates and stemware and salt-shakers had already been tallied up.

"Thanks for making the time." Amy had been concerned about Barbara and had made a point of reaching out. "Are you doing all right? If there's anything I can do . . ."

"I'm fine," Barbara assured her. "Keeping busy."

"I didn't realize you were a lawyer."

"I haven't worked in years. But since Evan's firm was named executor, I felt I had to come take his place."

The mention of Evan's name, as always, created an uncomfortable pause. "Have you talked to them lately?"

Barbara hadn't left Hawaii until the search was called off. Every post and bulletin board in the park was now plastered with Evan's photo and description, but the police held out little hope. "At this point finding his body would be something of a miracle. Don't worry. I'm not planning to sue."

"I appreciate it." It sounded so cold, put in those terms, but that had indeed been a concern. The money wasn't an issue. That was what business insurance was for. It was the publicity.

Peter had done a heroic job. There were no YouTube videos, a small miracle. Nicole and David had both shot portions of the ceremony and the aftermath but had agreed not to post. The authorities were labeling it an accident, which it undoubtedly was. And in every account, Peter had made sure it was his agency, not Amy's, that was listed as tour operator. But a suit by the victim's wife would open everything up.

They talked for another few minutes, staying in familiar territory, about the chances of Evan being alive and what in the world could have happened. Then Barbara excused herself and went back to work.

The probate inventory didn't take as long as Amy thought it would. MacGregor had not been fond of jewelry or art. Her financial files seemed to be in good order and were packed into cardboard boxes for their trip to the Corns and Associates offices downtown, in Murray Hill. The files marked PER-

SONAL PAPERS were set aside to be burned, as stipulated in the will.

Their primary focus was the walk-in closet, fabled repository of lost gifts. They had gone from one side to the other, unwrapping the wrapped ones, listing all the items. Amy noted four large bottles of Chanel No. 5, all from Peter Borg, and wondered why they were expending so much effort on cataloging long-forgotten birthday and Christmas presents.

"Miss Archer!" called Barbara, throwing her voice into the next room. The male paralegal had just whispered a few words in her ear. "Can you come in here, please?"

The maid's maid took her time. "Yes?" Joy Archer appeared, looming in the doorway.

"Did you happen to see a music box?" Barbara pointed to the newly cataloged and stacked boxes. "Did Paisley have a music box?"

"I don't remember one."

"Are you sure? Dark mahogany. There's a mother-of-pearl pattern on the lid, shaped like a diamond. Mr. Corns and I gave it to her as a birthday present."

"I didn't take it, if that's what you're insinuating."

"No," said Barbara. "I just thought you might have seen it."

"Because if I wanted to steal something, it'd be nicer than a music box."

"No, it's just personal. I was hoping to take it as a memento. The lid isn't made of diamonds, just shaped like a diamond. It was a little joke between the three of us."

"I never spend time in here except to dust, and I don't recall any music box. Maybe she sold it."

"Paisley didn't sell our presents."

"Maybe she gave it away."

"I guess that's possible," Barbara said without conviction. "It's no big deal."

But it was enough of a deal, Amy noted, to force Barbara and her paralegals to start from one end of the apartment and re-inventory their way to the other. Looking for a music box.

Amy quietly let herself out.

CHAPTER 27

As a rule, Lieutenant Rawlings didn't call in advance. This time he had, giving Amy and Fanny the hour between eight and nine to worry and wonder and drink—coffee for Amy, tea for Fanny—while pretending to read the *Times*. Rawlings was never the bearer of good news. Except for today, as it turned out.

"We found your Billy Strunk," he announced cheerily, settling onto a kitchen stool while Fanny brewed a fresh pot of coffee.

"And?" asked Fanny.

"He was an American from the Bronx, living in Istanbul. His real name was Bill Strohman."

"Why did he give us a fake name?" Amy asked. "And such a name?"

"The guy was a Columbia professor. Maybe he did it as a shout-out to the real Bill Strunk."

"There's a real Bill Strunk?"

"I thought you were an educated woman." His grin barely kept it from being an insult. "William Strunk and E. B. White. *The Elements of Style.*"

"Strunk and White." She had to resist smacking herself on the forehead. Back in freshman writing class, the famous little book of writing dos and don'ts had been her bible. "Was he an English professor?"

"Art professor," Rawlings said. "But he wrote a book, so I'm guessing he used Strunk and White." Amy was surprised that Rawlings knew the names, and was chagrined that she herself hadn't made the connection.

Bill Strohman, the detective told them, had married a Turkish woman, had given up tenure at Columbia, and had moved to Istanbul four years ago. Since then, he and his wife had separated, and he was living alone.

"His wife last saw him when he came over to celebrate her birthday."

"You see?" Amy took this as a victory.

"I never said you were lying," Rawlings countered. "She tried contacting him a few days later, but he wasn't home. Finally, she went to the police and gave them a photograph."

"And?" Fanny said, repeating her previous question.

"And . . ." The lieutenant drew it out, as if he were slowly pulling a puppy out from behind his back. "Bill Strohman had no connection to any of your tourists."

"Thank God," Fanny sighed, then rewarded him with a cup of coffee. Black, two sugars.

"We did a quick check. Strohman's first wife didn't recognize any of their names, and none of your tourists are in academia."

Given this information, the Indian authorities were sticking to their story. Strohman had taken a

last-minute vacation to India and had happened to
get killed by a mugger in the Protected Forest.

Amy moved her head up and down and wanted
to believe this, but . . . "Why did he use a fake name?
And isn't it a coincidence, him showing up at our
hotel?"

"He didn't show up at your hotel. He showed up
at the Taj Mahal. My in-laws went to the Taj Mahal.
Bill and Hillary went to the Taj Mahal."

And, just like that, the case was closed. Like it or
not.

It was an hour or so later, at the office, when
Fanny looked up from her computer and pointed
out that Amy was whistling.

"Am I? Sorry."

"Not that I mind," said Fanny. "I haven't heard
you whistle in some time."

"I didn't even realize."

Amy returned to her work, tallying up the last of
the wake's expenses in Hawaii, but her mind was
elsewhere. *It's finally over*, she told herself. And the
thought made her nearly giddy. Whatever trouble
had been brewing—from the note to the murder to
the loss of Evan Corns—had been dealt with, explained away to the satisfaction of the police on two
continents.

Across the office, Fanny had returned to her keyboard, and Amy couldn't resist skipping across and
planting a kiss on top of her henna-dyed head.

"What was that for?"

"No reason. What's TrippyGirl up to these days?"
She could see that her mother was working on yet
another posting.

"Right now she's sleeping in a yurt hotel in the Mongolian steppes."

"How'd she get to Mongolia?"

"There's a branch line from the Trans-Siberian Railway."

"And she's staying in a yurt hotel?" Amy was dubious.

"Motel? A yurt B and B? A yurt Airbnb?"

"How about . . . off the top of my head . . . Trippy has been rescued by a nomadic family who welcomes her into their yurt?"

"Doesn't sound as believable," said Fanny, but she gave it a moment's thought. "Does this Mongolian family have a cute son?"

"Yes. And he's a doctor."

"Ooh, I'll make him a vet. Trippy can help him deliver a baby yak."

"Perfect."

Fanny typed a few sentences, then looked up. "Is everything okay?" She wasn't used to seeing her daughter so relaxed.

"Perfect. I mean, business seems a little slow, but . . ."

"Business is fine," Fanny assured her. "I've been booking cruises on the Web site left and right."

It was exactly what Amy needed to hear, and she took it as an excuse for a long lunch and a pilgrimage to a thrift shop in SoHo. They might just have another pair of designer frames. She grabbed a collapsible umbrella from the stand by the door and headed out.

After walking just a few blocks south on Hudson, Amy stopped and looked back. It took her a few seconds to put a name to this sudden feeling. Was she being followed? The light rain had begun to get heavier, and people were sidestepping to stay under awnings, pausing in nearby doorways for the WALK lights rather than waiting at the corner. Maybe that was the source of her feeling, this rain-induced pedestrian shuffle all around her.

At the next corner she looked back again and noticed the mousy middle-aged woman in a brown dress and head scarf standing under a section of scaffolding. The woman glanced up and met Amy's eyes and instantly turned away. Maybe Amy was being followed.

Amy passed by a Starbucks, went another block, then pushed open the door of the next Starbucks and stood in line for a tall nonfat latte. She took it to a stool by the front window, and this time when the woman approached and caught her eye, Amy motioned with her head, as if to say, "Come join me." For some reason, Amy wasn't afraid.

The woman hesitated, then stepped inside, ordered a double espresso, and made her way to the stool next to Amy's. "I'm sorry," she said. Her voice was soft and lilting, with an accent Amy couldn't immediately place. "I didn't know what else to do."

"Do I know you?" Amy didn't, but it seemed like the right thing to ask.

"My name is Samime Strohman. I believe you knew my husband, Bill?"

Amy paused. *If, by "knew," you mean, did I chase him down in the woods and watch him bleed to death?* "Yes, I knew him."

The woman named Samime smiled with sad satisfaction, as if a goal had been reached. "The police say bandits attacked him at the Taj Mahal. Is that true?"

Yes, that's what the police say. "Yes."

Samime looked almost disappointed. "Bill was not the best man in the world. After we moved to Istanbul, he got sick with his hand tremors."

"I noticed he had trouble."

"The doctors could do nothing, and it absolutely ruined him. He loved to paint. When he could no longer do that, his world changed. I told him, 'Do another hobby. Photography.' But no. Finally, I had to leave and move back in with my family."

"I'm sorry. But why are you telling me this?"

"I'm not saying this to make you sorry. I'm saying . . ." She seemed to be thinking it through. "On my birthday, two weeks ago, he apologized for the small present. He said he was going to get money soon, that everything would be good. A few days later he was dead."

"Money? Where was he planning to get this money?"

"I asked, but he wouldn't say. That was his secret."

"Did Bill stay in touch with anyone in the U.S.? Any friends from his old days at Columbia?"

Samime sipped her espresso. "Bill was a sociable person back then. He took friends to restaurants and loved good clothing and wine. I was one of his students and was flattered when he started paying attention. I know he was not handsome. But he loved life so much. To me it was unbelievable that he would move to Turkey for me. I felt lucky. But after we got there, he changed. A lot of it was his hands, I think. But to answer your question . . . He did not stay in touch with old friends."

"If I told you some names . . ."

"The people on your tour?" Samime shook her head. "The Istanbul police told me those names. I didn't know any of them."

Amy was getting to the bottom of her tall and now wished she had ordered a venti. "And you came all the way to America to find me?" She didn't mean to make it sound ridiculous. "Why?"

"Bill was not a great man, just a sad, lonely man. But no one deserves to be stabbed to death and pushed aside." Samime drained the rest of her small paper cup. "Miss Abel, I looked you up on the Internet."

"Oh, God." Amy didn't mean to say it out loud.

"You have done this thing before, solving murders the police didn't want to."

"I did it once because my boyfriend was involved."

"My father is old and stingy, but he liked Bill. He gave me the money to come and try to get justice. I can pay you a little."

"Good God, no," Amy blurted out, then lowered her voice. "I'm not a private investigator."

Samime leaned in. "Imagine yourself like me, coming to a foreign country, trying to get answers. The police in Istanbul don't care. The police in India don't care."

"The police here don't care."

"But you do."

"He was killed thousands of miles away," Amy protested. "Even if I cared . . ." That didn't sound right. "Even if I tried to help, it's not an American crime."

"You think his killer was on your tour, don't you?"

"Don't tell me what I think." She had been feeling so good a few minutes ago. What right did this woman have to show up out of the blue and de-mand her help—even if she was right? Even if Amy had accidentally brought someone thousands of miles to India to kill this woman's husband? What gave her the right?

"Please help me, Miss Abel."

"Let me think about it."

CHAPTER 28

"**I** thought you were going to tell her."

"Marcus, she was whistling. She didn't even come back from lunch, which means either a great sale somewhere or a new Woody Allen movie. How could I ruin that?"

Marcus had taken off early and come by the Hudson Street shop in the hope of seeing Amy. Seeing Fanny was almost as good. On their walk home, they stopped by Morton Williams to buy the makings for dinner. Fanny complained about the chicken being too large for just her and Amy. That was her way of inviting Marcus. His way of accepting was to carry all the bags.

As soon as Fanny unlocked the door, she heard the two female voices drifting down from the upper half of the house. Amy was home, her door was open, and she had company.

"Yoo-hoo," Fanny shouted, giving everyone two flights of warning. Marcus took time to put the groceries away in Fanny's kitchen then followed her up the stairs.

Amy and Samime sat in matching red armchairs, huddled over a low, modern coffee table and luke-warm cups of Earl Grey. Amy made the introduc-tions, trying to keep it quick, although she knew that wouldn't be easy.

Samime was a typically shy Middle Eastern woman, probably halfway between Amy's age and Fanny's. Her height and girth also took a middle spot be-tween the mother and daughter. Her hair was curly brown, shoulder length, and a little frizzy, with a part down the middle. There was a grateful kind of helplessness to her, which Amy almost resented.

"She came all this way," Fanny gushed. "Of course we'll help." She spoke as if it were a matter of frequent-flier points. Five thousand miles and you earn a free murder investigation.

"Hold on," Amy shot back. "There's a lot to take into consideration. The police, for one thing. You don't want to go to jail again."

"Nonsense," Fanny said. "Did you go to the New York police? Samime?"

Samime seemed thrown. "I have not seen the po-lice. Do you think I should?"

"Absolutely not. And don't worry. My jail visit had nothing to do with your case."

"Yes it did," Amy countered. "If we're going to work together . . . *if*," she said with emphasis, "then we all have to be honest."

If Amy was hoping to douse the enthusiasm, she failed. The woman from Istanbul put down her tea and listened as Amy explained the whole situation, from the envelope in the piano to the man in the volcano.

"It's very confusing," Samime said at the end,

even though Amy thought she had done an admirable job of keeping it simple.

"What did your husband do?" Marcus asked. It was his first contribution.

"Bill had money when we moved. He spent it freely, buying a big house for my family, cars, a boat even. But money got tight. By the end he would go to fancy hotels and hire himself out as a guide. He was very good, but sometimes people objected to his tremors."

"That's dreadful," said Fanny, even though she could understand. The last thing a tourist wants is a guide who looks like he has some sort of plague. "So what's our strategy?"

Amy didn't want to argue. What was the use? "We need to find a connection between Bill and one of our people."

"His first wife would know more than me," Samime said.

"Then we'll have to question her," said Fanny.

"No impersonating lawyers," Amy warned her. "Or detectives or police officers or judges or doctors."

"Why don't you just bind and gag me?"

"Don't give me ideas."

"Does this mean you'll help?" Samime's tone was so perfectly plaintive, so vulnerable, that it would have taken a stronger woman than Amy to say no. Or a weaker one. She couldn't decide.

"Yes, of course," said Fanny with outstretched arms. Samime fell into them, and they were suddenly long-lost sisters. "So, where are you staying?"

"I don't have family here anymore. There is this guesthouse in the Bronx that helps out Turkish immigrants—"

"You're staying here," Fanny interrupted. And just like that, it was settled. Marcus would take the car and pick up her luggage from the Bronx. Amy would change the sheets in the guest bedroom on Fanny's level. And Fanny would call Aunt Madge in Chicago and tell her she would have to make other arrangements for her upcoming trip to see the family.

Later that evening, after the chores were done, after the chicken had been transformed into ke-babs and the bottle of raki had been dusted off and opened up and drained, Marcus found a moment, right before calling it a night and heading out the door, to take Fanny aside.

"I know what you're doing," he told her. "I figured it out. You're distracting yourself."

"Don't know what you mean," she said, knowing exactly what he meant.

"You're getting involved in this case so you won't have to think about the mortgage. Well, it's going to happen, whether you think about it or not."

"You don't want to help this woman?"

"Yes, I do. Someone helped me not too long ago. But you can't ignore—"

"I'm not ignoring anything," she shot back. "I've given it a lot of thought, and I came up with a plan."

"A plan?" Marcus cocked an eyebrow. "To pay off the mortgage? How?"

"You won't like it."

His other eyebrow went up. "That's saying a lot, because my bar is fairly low."

"Amy won't like it, either, which is the reason I haven't told her."

"You're scaring me now."

But that was all Fanny would say. A few minutes later Marcus said good night to the three housemates, grabbed his jacket from the hall coatrack, and headed out the door. He was halfway down Barrow Street when Amy caught up with him.

"So . . ." She was a little out of breath. "Are you okay with this?" They had never really discussed what had happened on the tour, and it seemed overdue.

"Seems like every time you travel, there's a murder."

"It's only twice. You need three to establish a pattern, although I shouldn't tempt fate."

"Fanny seems up for it," Marcus said. "I think she needs the distraction."

Amy smiled and swept off a spot on the Gregsons' stoop. Old man Gregson hated when people sat on his stoop, but Amy had been doing it since she was four. She cleared a spot beside her, and Marcus sat down. He reached out his hand and she laced her fingers between his. It felt good.

"Did you and Petey have fun?"

"We work well together," Amy said. "He's a better man than Mom gives him credit for."

"Are you going to enlist his help?"

"God, no!" They both chuckled. "You're a much superior murder buddy."

"Thanks. Hey, you never said anything about my job."

"Sorry. It's perfect," she confirmed. "You're great at solving problems and getting things. And you look dashing in a uniform."

"A Ritz-Carlton uniform."

"Twice as dashing. I won't even ask how you got the job."

"What?" Marcus frowned. "What is that supposed to mean?"

"People don't walk in off the street and become concierges at the best hotel in the city. I know you, Marcus. You did something sketchy."

"That shows a lot of trust. I thought you'd be pleased."

"I am pleased. But I know you." And with that, Amy took his face between her hands, planted a lingering kiss on his lips, then pushed herself to her feet. "See you tomorrow."

"I should be angry," he called down the street, at her swaying back.

"But you're not, because I'm right."

CHAPTER 29

The Zuck Studio was on the eighth floor of a red-brick apartment building in Washington Heights. Strictly speaking, the art studio, an extension of Colleen Zuck's one-bedroom condo, was a large terrace closed in like a greenhouse, with slanted panes of glass for the ceiling and three walls of half-length windows, the longest of the walls facing the Hudson River.

The space itself was laid out simply and neatly. A single easel and an adjustable chair dominated the center. Along all four walls were low shelves full of the tools of Ms. Zuck's trade: colorful jars of powdery pigment; oversize art books; jelly jars full of brushes, dozens of brushes; and a row of thin, deep drawers, the kind Amy knew from her favorite print shop on Greenwich Street.

"What a view," Amy said. They were in the living room, with the French doors to the studio firmly closed, but the vista of the river and the New Jersey Palisades still dominated.

"It's not the view. It's the light," Colleen replied.

"I'm working on a Copley now, and he painted with western light. I'd give you a tour, but I'm a little paranoid about keeping it clean."

"No problem," Amy said. "We're just grateful you could take the time to see us."

The ex-Mrs. Strohman hadn't offered them anything to drink. But she motioned Amy and Samime to the sofa and took a seat in a thinly padded armchair across from them. She was a short, slim woman with a gray bob. "I remember you," she told Samime in a flat tone. "You were one of Bill's students."

"No. I mean, yes." Samime swallowed hard. "I didn't really meet him until after your divorce."

"Doesn't matter. I divorced him for other reasons, not because of his girlfriends."

There was a substantial pause, which Amy felt obligated to fill. "Colleen, you're an art restorer."

"Conservator," she said. "We don't like to emphasize the restoring part. Our main job is conserving what's already there."

"Is that how you met Bill?" Amy asked. "Through your work?"

Bill's ex-wife nodded. "I taught a winter studies course in art authentication. Bill was an adjunct professor and was auditing the course. This was close to fifteen years ago. We met for coffee after that first class, and one thing led to another. My studio at the time was at Columbia, and he used to drop by after the light faded with a bottle of wine." Her voice was warming to the memory. "He showed such an interest. We would sit by the easels, discussing brushstrokes and the pigments the masters used. I know that doesn't sound romantic."

"His work was a strong part of his being," Samime said. "I know."

"I was just starting out," Colleen explained. "Bill was an expert in the Postimpressionists. At the time a lot of private collectors were bringing them in for cleaning and touch-ups. Pissarro was a favorite. A lot of Pissarros, especially his late English period, when he was so prolific."

"That's a Pissarro, isn't it?" Samime was focused on a small landscape, perhaps nine by twelve inches, on the wall above Colleen's armchair. It was a bucolic vision of a haystack in a field, with a trio of cows grazing under an olive tree. All the possible shades of green and brown.

Colleen turned to look. "Good eye," she said. "Pissarro, yes. But that's a copy. I could never afford a real one, not from that period."

Samime got up to take a closer look. "It's a very good copy."

"Yes, I have talented friends. Mrs. Strohman, I'm sure you didn't come here to renew your studies in art history."

Samime looked down at the hands folded in her lap.

"That was rude of me," Colleen admitted and turned her attention back to Amy. "I'm glad you called. What can you tell me about Bill's death? The police didn't say much, other than he was murdered while visiting the Taj Mahal."

"It was actually outside the grounds, in a park." Amy didn't know why she was being so precise. Something about Colleen brought it out in her. "I'm the one who discovered the body. He'd been stabbed. I don't think he suffered much."

"You weren't with him?" Colleen asked, turning to Samime. "Taking separate vacations?"

"No. I mean, yes. We'd been separated for over a year."

"Oh, I see," Colleen said with the hint of a smile. "What's her name?"

"Her name? No, it wasn't another woman. It was more about the money."

"Bill had plenty of money."

"Not toward the end. And there was his sickness."

"Sickness?"

Samime gently explained about the tremors. She had one of those soft, lilting voices that could be annoying in normal conversations but were very comforting at moments like this. Colleen seemed both surprised and saddened.

"Poor Bill," she said with what seemed like real emotion. "I can't think of a worse affliction for an artist. Although there is a kind of poetic justice, I suppose."

"Poetic justice?" Amy asked.

"I'm just being cruel. Ex-wives are allowed that." Colleen stood up. "Well, it was very nice seeing you again, Samime. And, Ms. Abel . . . , I wish I could help. But the police have already been here."

"No, wait," Amy said. "We need to ask you about his friends."

"The police already did. And I'm afraid I can't spare any more light." She tilted her head toward her greenhouse studio. "I'm already behind for the day."

"Don't you want the police to catch Bill's murderer?"

"I don't see how. He was killed thousands of miles away."

"Perhaps by someone he knew," Amy suggested.

"Someone from the old days. If we can just ask a few more questions . . ."

"I'm sorry, no. Now, if you'll please leave . . ."

Meanwhile, Samime was of no help. She didn't plead her case at all but just kept staring at the painting on the wall above Colleen's chair.

CHAPTER 30

They'd been home five days now, and Amy hadn't called. She had e-mailed him twice, both times in response to some work-related matters. He had always been more into her than she was into him. He accepted this, although he'd hoped that eleven days together, with no Fanny and no Marcus in sight, might help change things. While still on the plane going home, he had promised himself not to be the first to call.

Peter broke the promise in the middle of day one and left a message. But having been the first to call, he absolutely refused to be the second. So far, this promise was holding. He knew how much he missed her, because just now, as he was glancing out his street-level window, he could swear he saw her mother waddling by on East Sixty-Fourth. Good Lord, things were bad. He was even missing Fanny.

"There's a woman here," Claire said, easing open the door to his inner office. He was both reassured that he hadn't been imagining Fanny on the street and distressed that she'd shown up out of the blue. This couldn't be good.

"I was in the neighborhood," Fanny said as she sneaked under Claire's outstretched arm. "You can leave us alone, dear. Petey and I are old friends."

"Mrs. Abel." It was the only thing he could think of to say.

She waited until the door was firmly closed. "Actually, I wasn't in the neighborhood. I came to apologize for my daughter. She hasn't treated you well, not at all." Without being asked, she seated herself in the brown leather chair opposite his desk.

"Would you like some coffee? No, I forgot. You and TrippyGirl switched over to tea. Claire!" he yelled through the door. "Two cups of Earl Grey."

"You see?" Fanny said with a soothing nod. "So thoughtful. And she didn't even send you a thank-you note, I'll bet. Go on. Sit down. Make yourself comfortable."

Peter sat, but it took several minutes for him to start to relax. Meanwhile, Fanny swooped into her monologue, one that he interrupted with a syllable every now and then, when he had the chance. It seemed that Amy's Travel was grateful for everything he'd done, whether or not Amy admitted it. He had given them a nice influx of cash, given Amy a much-needed trip, and absorbed much of the PR fallout from the volcano incident. Fanny only wished that all the men in Amy's life could be so mature and considerate.

"Frankly, just between us . . ." And here she leaned forward, so sincere that it was almost a parody. "Marcus has become a real pain."

"I thought you liked Marcus."

"Whatever gave you that impression?" Fanny

seemed befuddled. Of course, Marcus was irreverent and fun and easy to talk to. He was also proactive and knew how to get things done. Oh, and he was dashingly handsome in an adorable, roguish way. Great hair, too. But—and it seemed to take her forever to get to the "but"—Marcus was an irresponsible liar and not at all the man she would wish for her brilliant and gorgeous and lovable daughter.

"I couldn't agree more," Peter said. "When it's just Amy and me, we get along perfectly."

"I think it's a matter of proximity." Fanny pretended to give it some thought. "Marcus lives a few blocks away, and he's always at the house. We should figure out a way for you and Amy to spend more time together."

"We spent eleven days together," Peter pointed out.

"I know. But there was a murder and a volcano. Amy finds those things distracting." Her eyes fell on his darkly polished desk, which led her seamlessly to her next objective. "By the way, I just love your offices. I've never been here before."

Peter preened. "I'll have to give you a tour. Did you notice the interactive display on the Madison Ave. side?"

"I noticed it, yes."

"I'll show it to you before you leave."

The display, he said, had been his innovation. Rather than relying on window cards to entice the would-be traveler, Peter had installed a state-of-the-art video system. All the curious passerby had to do was type in a destination and the screen would come alive with a virtual tour of the world's most exotic travel experiences.

"We do get some homeless usage," he had to admit.

"But that's generally at night. They think we're like the Travel Channel."

"You see?" Fanny gushed and laughed. "We could learn so much from you. Your Web site, by the way, is amazing."

"Thanks. But the shop is crucial. I find that folks at a certain level are reassured by a brick-and-mortar presence. Or, in my case, a mahogany-and-marble presence." He brayed at his clever turn of phrase, and Fanny brayed along.

After Claire delivered and poured and sweetened the tea, Fanny reminded Peter about the tour, and he eagerly took her around. There wasn't much to see, just the reception area, the front desks, and Peter's inner sanctum. But Fanny made the experience last, oohing and aahing over the rugs and the crown molding and whatever fancy booking system that had just been installed.

"I'm so glad you're not opening a branch in the Village," Fanny said in mock horror. "You'd put us out of business." They had finished their second round of tea and were lingering by the door. Behind them, Claire was dealing with a pair of walk-ins interested in taking their five dogs to London on the *Queen Mary 2.*

"I've actually thought about expanding," Peter said. "Either the Village or SoHo."

"Oh, no," said Fanny. "That would break Amy's heart."

"Just a thought," Peter said quickly. "It would be nice to have a presence. . . ."

Five minutes later Peter brought up the subject of a merger. "It would solve so many problems," he said, warming to his own idea. He and Amy would get to work together on a daily basis. He would gain a ready-made presence in the Village, with three more years on the lease. And Marcus would be gradually elbowed out of the picture. "Why did it take me so long to think of this?" Peter asked himself out loud.

Fanny had exactly the same question. She had suffered and smiled her way through two cups of over-sugared tea in order to maneuver Peter to the place he should have been in the middle of cup one. "What a fabulous idea!"

"Well, it's just an idea."

"Of course," she said, moderating her enthusiasm. "Amy may not be in favor, and the finances may not work out. But it's definitely worth thinking about."

"You think she'll be against it? Against partnering with me?"

Fanny had forgotten how easy he was to manipulate. "We'll have to plan it carefully. Have a nice dinner with several bottles of wine and then all look at the finances together. I think we might talk her into it."

CHAPTER 31

The gas fireplace in the bedroom gave off more heat than Joy Archer had expected. She stood back and absorbed the warmth on her outstretched hands. To her, the idea of a roaring fire in a Manhattan penthouse was the epitome of luxury. And a chilly, overcast morning like this provided her with the perfect excuse.

She returned to the kitchen and put her cereal bowl in the overcrowded mess of a sink. Then she got to work, continuing her project from last night, searching for the music box. She had no idea what it was or why Barbara Corns wanted it. But the fact that she wanted it made it worth finding. Was it antique? Did it hold diamonds or a gold bar? That was unlikely, since it had been a present from the Corns, people not known for their generosity.

For the most part, she was treading well-trodden ground. The paralegals had already scoured the apartment. But Paisley MacGregor had kept a few special places. Archer had run across them over the

years, when the maid was off cleaning houses and
she was supposed to be doing the same. There was
the old dumbwaiter behind a cabinet in the pantry,
left over from when the penthouse had been a two-
story affair. There were various cubbyholes, like the
empty panel box in the library and the attic-like
storage space in the hallway ceiling, with an almost
invisible handle to pull down the trapdoor. These
big prewar apartments were filled with such oddi-
ties.

Archer had left the most promising for last—the
floor safe hidden under a parquet trapdoor under a
rug in the big bedroom. The square, shallow safe
had been part of the original 1920s structure. The
apartment's current owners probably had no idea it
was there, but MacGregor had found it shortly after
moving in. An old locksmith had spent two hours
opening the iron door, only to find the safe empty.
MacGregor had had him reset the combination before he left.

Settling in with a fresh cup of coffee and a few
pillows, Joy Archer hovered over the floor safe and,
by the flickering of the fire, tried various numerical
combinations: MacGregor's birthday, backward and
forward and European style; the woman's e-mail
password; all the possible variations of her Social Security number.

Crinkles brushed up against her leg, distracting
her. "Not now." The old dear chose about one hour
a week to be affectionate and always at the worst
time. The maid banished her favorite cat to the living room, topped off her coffee, and started again.

She was beginning to fear that it might just be a
random number when, on a whim, Archer input

her own birthday. It was a silly time waster of an idea, but . . .

"Why would she set it to my birthday?" she muttered. That was her first thought as the gears clicked into place and the handle turned. "That's weird." And the weirdness of it kept her from enjoying the moment as much as she might have. "It's like she knew I would try to open it."

On top of the pile preserved in the hollow iron square were old documents and photos. "MacGregor used to be a child?" she mused as she leafed through the ancient pictures: a flaxen-haired girl on a swing, the same girl staring stone-faced at the camera with her parents. Archer placed to one side a cheap gold-plated broach dangling from a black ribbon.

Directly under a batch of legal-looking papers she found it: a rectangular box of dark mahogany. Inlaid on the lid was a marquetry panel, the image of a diamond made from pieces of mother-of-pearl.

Archer opened the lid. Four slow musical notes played from the mechanism. *To our diamond in the rough. Happy birthday. Evan and Barbara.* This was handwritten on an engraved card, sitting lonely in the empty box.

"I don't get it," Archer mumbled. She would have to take it in to an appraiser to see if it was really as worthless as it looked.

The maid removed the music box and was about to close the safe. Then it occurred to her that everything in this black hole must be priceless in some way, and that made her continue rummaging through.

The photos and love letters held no more than sentimental value, of course, although Archer was surprised to see a photo of a young suitor who was not as homely as she might have expected.

*If you are reading this, then I am dead, and there
are certain things the police need to know.*

The letter was handwritten on three pages of a
yellow legal pad, stapled in the top left corner.
Archer had to read the entire thing—well, skim the
entire thing—several times before she realized what
was being said. Luckily, she had paid just enough attention to Paisley's ex-employers over the years to
be able to put a face to the name signed at the bottom of page three.

This next time she read the letter slowly. The
facts were stated clearly, as if the writer were addressing a rather slow and literal-minded cop. She
was amazed that someone would actually put all this
in writing. Well, Paisley had that kind of power over
people. She made you trust her. Paisley would take
care of everything.

Archer treated herself to two healthy slugs of
whiskey in her coffee, then returned to the glowing
warmth of the bedroom, where she sat in a Louis
XV chair, toasted her own cleverness and, in light of
this new information, tried to devise the most lucrative course of action.

Paisley's cell phone was still at the bedside, still
attached to its charger. It didn't take her long to figure out how to access the directory and scroll down
the numbers to the one she wanted. She was just
about to press CALL when the doorbell rang. With a
sigh, the maid put down the phone and lumbered
out toward the foyer. Who the hell could it be? The
police again, maybe this time with a search warrant?
Barbara, making up another excuse to paw through
the apartment?

"Who is it?" Archer peered through the peephole. She recognized the face, although it took several seconds to accept the reality of the fish-eye distortion peering back at her, smiling and looking so ingratiating. Well, speak of the devil . . .

"Just a minute," she said. "Give me a minute."

It took her closer to three minutes to dump the music box and the letter back inside, close the safe, lower the parquet trapdoor and slip the area rug back on top.

Then she returned to the door and removed the chain.

Javier Martinez had been the maintenance engineer at 142 Sutton Place for almost two decades and didn't appreciate his judgment being questioned, especially not by a young, gum-chewing Con Ed worker who had probably gotten his cushy job through some highly placed relative in the union.

The problem had begun around noon, when Mrs. Daniels in penthouse 1 called the front desk, complaining of a gas smell. Javier had arrived within three minutes, no more. He had checked all the fittings—stove, both fireplaces, clothes dryer—then gone out into the hall, where he'd discovered the smell was stronger. When no one answered the door at the only other penthouse, Javier tried the penthouse 2 phone. No answer. Finally, he'd telephoned Con Ed.

"The minute she said 'gas,' you should have called," the muscle-bound Guido scolded between snaps of his gum. "That's Safety one-oh-one."

Javier didn't respond. But it crossed his mind that no one ever made an argument by talking about course 102. Everything seemed to be taught in 101.

He himself had never been to college, but he imagined that all the things people said were a part of blah-blah-blah 101 would probably fill up more than a year's worth of classes, even at a good school.

When the elevator doors opened on the penthouse floor, the smell was stronger than before. Luckily, Mrs. Daniels, a cautious woman, had already taken her poodle out for a walk.

"I'm calling the police," Javier said, pulling a cell phone from his jacket.

"No," the Guido scolded again. "Even the current from a cell phone . . . Does this floor have a shutoff valve?"

Javier led him from the elevator toward the utility closet, which had been transformed into a storeroom for the residents' recyclables. The valve was still there, behind the bin for plastics, cans, and glass.

"There," the Guido said after he'd turned the gas valve tightly shut. "We'll give it five minutes, then go in and open some windows."

"What if someone's in there?" Javier protested.

"Not my problem. I gotta follow protocol."

"To hell with your protocol," Javier said.

At least that was what he later told the *Daily News* reporter he said. He actually said nothing. But he did take the keys from his belt, did find the right one, and did place a handkerchief over his face before approaching the door to penthouse 2.

It wouldn't have mattered one way or the other.

CHAPTER 32

Normally, Fanny and her daughter would have their coffee, tea, and croissants in the garden. But the blustery morning forced them to stay huddled in the cozy eat-in kitchen. The only sound to break their groggy reverie, besides their soft sips and the occasional car horn from Seventh Avenue, was the sound of the TV from Fanny's guest room one floor up.

It bothered Fanny more than she was willing to admit. "She spends so much time in her room. This is not what I expected."

"It's not her fault," Amy replied. "That's the chance you take when you invite strangers into your home." Her tone said, "I told you so," although she purposely avoided using those words.

"I thought it would be nice. We would have adventures and talk about the case, then exchange eggplant recipes for dinner."

"Mom, this isn't a Lifetime movie. Some people are shy."

"Did you say something to insult her? Ever since

you girls went to visit the first wife, Samime's been even quieter."

Well, that's understandable, Amy thought. There had to be something empowering to flying across two continents to try to get justice for a dead man you still loved. It had to be equally empowering to track down Amy and enlist her in the cause. But then came reality: being far from home, with no idea how to find a killer; sitting down with your husband's first wife, who couldn't help you and didn't seem to care.

"I think she was expecting more help from Colleen," Amy said.

A commercial had just begun to blare on the upstairs TV—"In troubled times like these, gold is a crucial part of your investment portfolio"—and both Abel women paused to take a bite of croissant.

"What's the plan now?" Fanny asked.

"Archer, the maid. She's our only lead. And no, you can't come along."

"Why not?" Fanny asked, without an ounce of irony. "Archer and I already met. I can introduce you."

"Mom, she had you arrested."

"And I'm sure she feels guilty. Come on. I can work her."

"No. Besides, three visitors would be too many." Damn. Amy caught herself a second after saying it. You couldn't leave Fanny an opening, no matter how small. It was like a drop of water seeping into a crack in a ten-ton statue. Good-bye, statue.

"Then we'll just leave Samime here." Fanny clapped her hands. "That was simple."

"That's not what I'm saying. I'm saying you can't come."

"Because there'd be three. Understood. I don't know why you're even thinking of bringing Samime. She's a lovely woman." Fanny lowered her voice. "But English is not her first language."

"I'll go by myself."

"Without backup? What if Archer says something incriminating? You'll need a witness."

"She won't open up to you. She won't. I'll bet you anything." Damn. Another crack.

"It's a bet," Fanny crowed. "We can open up the office a little late." And with that she got up, placed the cups and plates in the sink and headed for the coat closet by the front door. "Come on, dear. Time's a wasting."

Fanny Abel didn't do public transportation, and parking on the Upper East Side would be nearly impossible. So they cabbed it up to 142 Sutton Place.

Amy was puzzled when she told the desk man their names and told him the apartment number—penthouse 2—and he didn't bother to call up, just motioned them toward the elevators. That should have been a warning.

Two minutes later the faint smell of gas in the hall as they stepped off the elevator also should have been a warning. And the open, tempting door to penthouse 2. There was no yellow tape stretched across the doorway, although there should have been.

"Well, if it's not my two favorite detectives." Lieutenant Rawlings was just passing by the white oval foyer. He was accessorized with white plastic gloves and blue booties over his shoes. There was a microrecorder in his right hand, and he had just pressed STOP. "Don't come in," he added. "Life is simpler when you girls don't contaminate a crime scene."

"Crime scene?" Fanny said with some excitement. This would be her first actual crime scene. She turned to Amy. "I told you time was a wasting."

"We have three dead cats and an asphyxiation." Rawlings joined them in the hall but left the door open. "And what, may I ask, are you doing here?"

"We dropped by to see Miss Archer," Fanny said.

"Yes, but why? I thought we'd agreed there was no case."

"We did. But is there a case now?" Amy tried not to sound callous. "Is she dead?"

"Yes, she's dead."

"And it was a murder?" asked Fanny.

Rawlings lifted the corners of his mouth and resembled even more a patient, boyish waiter ready to recite today's specials. "Ms. Archer was found an hour ago, lying fully clothed on her bed. There were empty pill bottles in her late employer's bathroom— painkillers, sedatives— and a funky smell in her coffee mug. Samples have been taken back to the lab. The front door was dead bolted from the inside, and the chain was on. Cause of death, pending an autopsy, was gas from an unlit fireplace in the main bedroom. That's also what killed the three cats."

"Was there a suicide note?" Amy asked.

"No note."

"It seems pretty selfish to take your cats with you," Fanny offered.

"So, you're thinking accident?" Amy guessed. "Either way, it's not murder."

Rawlings smirked. "You see? This is where us dumb cops start asking our questions, like, who would take sedatives mixed in with her caffeine? No one planning on killing herself. And no one trying to relax and get back to sleep."

"You're confusing me, dear," Fanny said sweetly.

"We checked the kitchen," Rawlings went on. "From the grounds in the waste can, we know she made two pots of coffee this morning. In the cupboard we found a mug that was slightly damp. On the coffee table there were fresh rings on two of the coasters. When my guys dusted, they found that the empty pill bottles had been wiped clean. Is any of this sinking in?"

Amy knew this scenario from some half-forgotten novel or a long-forgotten episode of *Law & Order*. "Your conclusion is that Archer had a visitor, who touched the pill bottles, had coffee with her, then tried to eliminate all evidence of his or her presence."

"Very good."

"So it *is* murder," Fanny said.

Rawlings confirmed it with a nod.

"How did the killer dead bolt the door from the inside?" Amy asked.

"He didn't. The vic's prints were on the dead bolt. She did it herself—after the killer left."

"I'm confused, too," Amy admitted, which was all Rawlings wanted to hear.

"Good. Remember that the next time you think you're smarter than me." And with that, the lieutenant turned and led them down the hallway, speaking over his shoulder as he went. "Like you said, she had a visitor. Since the doorman didn't let anybody up, we're guessing he gained entry through the basement garage. We're checking the security tapes, but we're not holding out much hope.

"Ms. Archer made a fresh pot of coffee, meaning the two of them had something to discuss. At some point, I figure the visitor used the bathroom and laced her coffee with the pills. When our mystery guest left, Ms. Archer was probably a little woozy but still together enough to lock the door and wander back to her bedroom."

"How did the killer turn on the gas?" Fanny asked.

"He didn't," Rawlings said. "Miss Archer's prints are on the gas key. That's probably what gave him the idea, seeing that she already had a fire going. It's a chilly day."

The homicide detective brought them to the open door of the utility closet. A young female technician was squeezed into a corner, taking samples of something or other, slipping them into little clear vials and labeling them. She didn't look up or say hello.

Rawlings pointed past her to the gas main and the valve six inches off the concrete. "The Con Ed guy said something to me. He was the one who turned off the valve. He said he had expected it to be rusty. These things are turned maybe once every five years. Often he has to whack the damned things with a wrench. But this one was easy to turn. When he said that, it got me to thinking." The lieutenant stood back and folded his arms across his chest. He was showing off to his audience, so proud of himself.

Whoever did this, he explained, left MacGregor's apartment and simply waited in the hall. The penthouse floor had just two apartments, so there wasn't much chance of being seen. When he figured the drugs had done their job and Archer was unconscious, he forced this gas valve closed, effectively dousing the flaming fireplace. A minute or so later he turned the knob again, and the bedroom in the locked apartment began filling with natural gas.

"And it looks like an accident or suicide. Take your pick. Locked door, pills, gas turned on . . ." Rawlings shrugged. "I'll know more when the reports start coming in."

"Very clever," said Fanny.

"Thanks."

"I meant the killer. But you, too, for figuring it out."

"Your killer knew a lot about this building," Amy suggested. "How to get in through the garage, where the gas valves are located . . ."

Rawlings nodded. "We're checking frequent visitors, any friends she may have had in the building."

"Who would kill an unemployed maid?" Fanny asked.

"That I don't know," Rawlings said. "All I know is I drew a murder this morning. Could be a big one. And you two are involved again."

"We're not involved," Amy protested.

"So let me get back to my question. Why did you come to pay Joy Archer a visit?"

CHAPTER 33

Amy was growing tired of memorials. She had spent the past month planning and attending six of them for Paisley MacGregor, including the first in New York. And now number seven. Evan Corns's memorial, it so happened, was being held in the same reposing room that his deceased maid had used, on the third floor of Frank E. Campbell's.

Although there was no body to repose, the Corns clan had pressed Barbara to hold a service. They wanted to hold some sort of event before summer came and the families all headed off on vacation.

Amy had wound up telling Rawlings everything. The homicide detective had asked for custody of the manila envelope, and she had gladly turned it over.

"So this is it," Rawlings had said that day at the station as he placed the envelope in an evidence bag. "This is what you were hiding from me." He'd sounded disappointed.

"That's it."

Forensics had confirmed his suspicions about a

visitor to Archer's penthouse on the morning of her
death. But the scene had produced no usable DNA
or prints. And Rawlings's superiors at One Police
Plaza were accepting his theory, but only for the
time being. They would need more in order to officially rule it a homicide.

Rawlings had volunteered to be Amy's plus-one
for the Saturday afternoon memorial, and for the
first time she learned his full name. Rory Rawlings.
What a tongue-twister. She understood why he'd
never mentioned it.

It was a measure of the detective's desperation
that he was taking this "if I die" note half seriously.
"You're making a lot of assumptions," he told Amy
as his eyes swept over the reposing room. "You're as-
suming this note was still in the apartment, that
Archer had found it, and that it was something worth
killing her for."

"Why else would anyone want to kill Joy Archer?
I'm waiting for a better theory."

"So am I," said Rawlings. His gaze rested on the
framed photo of Evan Corns, looking ruddy and
full of life. "I'm not even going to guess about this
guy's death."

"Me neither."

In addition to the Corns and a few close friends,
Barbara had invited her fellow tour members. The
Hawaii-based Steinbergs were the only ones not to
accept, giving Lieutenant Rawlings a chance to meet
most of the cast of characters. Earlier Amy had
given him a briefing. Now she was just adding faces
to the names.

Peter didn't seem pleased by the idea of Amy
showing up with another man, but he said nothing.
Neither did he blink an eye when Fanny and Samime

dropped in to pay their respects and also ogle the suspects.

"That's Nicole Marconi," Amy whispered to Rawlings.

"Is she stealing food?" he whispered back.

"Um, yes." Amy couldn't deny it. Nicole was once again at the buffet table, stuffing a row of mushroom tartlets into her purse. "She likes the food."

"And she's the one who felt cheated by the will."

"According to her, MacGregor had quasiblackmailed her parents into giving MacGregor their money. She expected the will to rectify this situation, but it didn't."

And those, I take it, are the Pepper-Sands?" He tilted his head toward the May-September pairing, who were silently critiquing an exotic-looking floral tribute sent by the Steinbergs in lieu of their attendance. It was in the center of a long table of flowers, set up where the casket would normally be. "The boys look pretty harmless."

"Either one could have given MacGregor the note," Amy said. But she agreed that it was unlikely.

"Herb Sands's money is mostly inherited?" Rawlings asked.

"His grandfather founded an investment house back in the twenties. Sands and Sons. The blond, gorgeous one, David Pepper, moved here from Oklahoma. I don't think he's kept any contact with his family."

"What about the widow, Barbara? Any dirt there?"

The woman in question was across the room, talking to a few teenage nieces. "She and Evan used to do some legal work for MacGregor."

"Lawyers, huh? Any chance that Evan wrote the note and Barbara pushed him into the volcano?"

Amy gave it a moment's thought. "It's possible. Oh." She'd just remembered. "Barbara has been asking about a music box."

"Music box?"

"It was a birthday present she and Evan gave to MacGregor years ago. She was looking for it in the apartment. Maybe that's where MacGregor kept the note. It's possible."

"Anything's possible when you don't have any pesky facts to deal with."

"I wish the Steinbergs were around," Amy said. "If there's one person I think capable of murder, it's Maury Steinberg."

"Because he fought with his wife and encouraged her to eat an entrée with chestnuts?"

"Pretty much."

"Well, I'm glad he's not. One less suspect in the Archer case, which is the only angle I'm interested in. Speaking of suspects . . ." The lieutenant cocked his head toward Peter Borg. The East Side travel agent had once again found himself trapped between Pepper and Sands. By this point he'd given up any hope of booking an anniversary tour and was just hoping to get out alive.

"You mean Peter?" Amy asked. She had to laugh.

"If we're suspecting Miss MacGregor's employers, he's on the list."

"Technically."

"And he was in the forest by the Taj Mahal. You weren't together when Bill Strohman was stabbed. He could have done it."

She laughed again. "First off, Peter's too big a wuss to stab anyone. Second, he would never entrust anything important to MacGregor. And third, he's the one who found the envelope. He showed it to me."

"I'm keeping him on the list."

As Amy and the lieutenant continued discussing suspects, Fanny and Samime hovered around the buffet, making small talk with the Corns's relatives. Fanny had created a backstory for them, in case anybody asked. They were, she had decided, a lesbian couple, happily bonded for the past thirty years. They'd met Evan when he'd drawn up a living will for them six months ago.

Fanny hadn't informed Samime of this backstory. It made no difference, since the Turkish woman barely spoke to a soul. But Fanny felt this sort of detail, even if left unsaid, would help her own performance.

"We should pay our respects," she informed her partner. She took Samime by the hand and led her toward Barbara, who was standing beside the easeled photo of her husband. An angular middle-aged man in a cheap suit was in front of them, talking with the widow, and they waited their turn. Fanny let go of Samime's hand. No need to overplay it.

"I don't mean to talk business on a day like today," the man whispered.

"Brendon, don't be silly," Barbara replied. "You're family."

"It's just that you're not returning my calls—not that I'm worried."

"Of course," Barbara assured him. "I'm sorry I haven't been more responsive. But . . ." And here her voice caught. "That was always Evan's project, and it's taking me some time to get up to speed,"

"No problem," Brendon said before she'd even

finished. "Just sometime soon I hope we can get an accounting. Maybe a small check. Jennifer is starting college in the fall."

"Yes, yes. How is Jennifer?"

"She's great. She's fine." Brendon looked around the room, a little sheepish. "She's in Connecticut with some friends. Couldn't get away."

"I understand," said Barbara and patted his hand. The angular man in the cheap suit made his final apology and fled, letting himself be replaced by Fanny and Samime.

Fanny did all the talking, expressing sorrow at Barbara's loss while simultaneously expressing hope that her husband might still be alive. At the end of her condolence speech, she asked if she could refresh Barbara's glass of white wine.

Fanny held the glass by the stem and, as they took the long way around to the bar, placed it in a Baggie that Samime had taken out of her purse. Fanny sealed the Baggie, wrote something on it with a Magic Marker, and placed it gingerly in Samime's oversize purse.

"Is your mother stealing from the buffet, too?" Rawlings asked.

Amy had seen it. She sighed. "She's taking fingerprints."

"I realize that," said Rawlings. "But why?"

"I don't know why. I have no idea what my mother does."

CHAPTER 34

Amy opened up the shop after the service and worked the rest of the day alone. It was a decent afternoon, with two walk-in inquiries and a deposit from Lou Halpern, the co-owner of a nearby diner who had won a few million in the New York Lottery and was using some of the proceeds to take his extended family on a cruise.

On arriving back at the brownstone, she was surprised to find the door to Fanny's apartment closed. This was rare. Even when her mother was out, she almost always left it wide open, trusting in the exterior lock and the safeness of the neighborhood. It was her way of telling her daughter, "My door's always open." Except today it was closed.

Maybe it's reverse psychology, Amy thought. *Pretending to keep me out so I'll want to come in. Then bam! An hour spent discussing Uncle Sol's upcoming divorce. Well, it's working.* "Mom?" She knocked softly, then turned the knob.

"Amy, darling. How was work?"

She found her mother at the small kitchen table,

hurriedly stuffing papers back into a file folder. Across from her sat Peter Borg, who was even worse at covering up his embarrassment. "What's going on?"

"Nothing," Peter replied. "Well, not nothing, obviously."

"Come and sit down," Fanny said and patted the top of the third chair. Her expression was serious.

The truth came out quickly enough. Peter was there to discuss a merger. "It'll be great for all of us," he explained with his nervous, ingratiating grin. "I need to open an office downtown, near all the SoHo and Tribeca lofts. Your place could use my connections. And face it, the two of us work well together."

"You do," said Fanny, her grin equally as nervous.

Amy said as little as possible, trying to wrap her mind around it. It wasn't the idea that she found so shocking. It was the implication.

The inescapable fact was that Fanny hated Peter. And Peter was scared of Fanny. There was no way Peter would have proposed this merger on his own. That meant that it had to be Fanny's idea, even if Peter somehow thought it was his. And that meant that Amy's Travel was dead broke. There was no other possibility.

As Peter continued his sales pitch, Amy threw her mother a slightly raised eyebrow. She responded with an apologetic nod, confirming her daughter's deduction. Not the nicest way to learn bad news, but that was Fanny.

And then, as if the moment wasn't awkward enough, they heard the front door open. Marcus's voice boomed down the hallway. "How are my girls? Anyone in the mood for cheesecake?"

* * *

Half an hour later Amy was walking Peter along Barrow Street, looking for a cab. He had been planning to take them out for a celebratory dinner. He'd even made a reservation at One if by Land, Two if by Sea, Amy's favorite restaurant, just down on Barrow. But the scene with Marcus had put an end to that notion.

As soon as Marcus was informed of the news, he'd flown into a rage. "So this is how you solve your problems?" he'd shouted at Fanny. "Selling your daughter to get out of debt?" Amy had never seen him this angry.

Fanny had shouted back. How dare he? This was none of his business. And it was business, not personal. No one was selling anyone. Peter and Amy had had the good sense to fade back into the living room. The argument had ended with the cheesecake being thrown into the garbage and Marcus storming out.

"He shouldn't be jealous," Peter said as they strolled past the polished, upscale restaurant, where tonight there would be one empty table for three. "It's business. It makes sense."

"I don't know what makes sense," Amy said.

"We won't do it if you don't want to."

Amy knew in her heart that this was probably the best solution, the only solution, to a problem she hadn't even known existed until this evening. "No. It makes sense," she said. "I'm just a little overwhelmed."

"I'll bet." A cab flew by. Neither had reached out to flag it.

Amy and Fanny would discuss it later, of course. But Fanny, despite her flaky view on life, was smart about things. If she had to make a pact with Peter in order to save the company, then there was probably no other option.

"Let me think about it, Peter."

"My lawyer will draft a document. We can fold Amy's Travel into my corporation. And you don't have to change the name right away."

"I have to change the name?" She tried not to gasp. "No."

It seemed like such a betrayal of her dreams. A betrayal of Eddie. The founding of her company had been a tribute to her adventurous fiancé, who had never lived to see it. Now it would just be the downtown office of Peter Borg Travel. *Our finances must really be desperate,* she thought.

"Not at first," Peter said. "But at some point . . . I mean, that's the whole idea, to make a cohesive product. We'll merge our business plans and our Web sites. Fanny can keep writing TrippyGirl. I wouldn't take that away from her."

"I don't know if I can change the name."

"We'll talk later. I shouldn't have brought it up."

"You can change your name instead."

"I wish I could." He actually seemed sincere. "But I've got a lot of equity in the Peter Borg brand. It's a known commodity."

"Whereas Amy's Travel is known only for killing off customers. I wonder if merging with me is such a good idea. You should reconsider. I'm like an albatross."

"Don't be hard on yourself. No one was murdered on this trip."

"Peter, we found a body."

"He had nothing to do with our tour."

"We were just at a memorial."

"That one was an accident."

Amy shook her head, either in annoyance or admiration; she couldn't quite decide. "I wish I could accept all of this as easily as you. I'd probably be much happier and healthier."

"Hey." Peter shook his head back at her. "Don't make me out as some heartless jerk. I feel bad. I feel bad about that guy dying at the Taj Mahal. I feel bad about Evan falling into the volcano. I feel bad about Paisley's maid. What's her name? Archer? I feel bad for Maury and Laila Steinberg trying to sell that place after such a terrible accident or suicide or whatever."

"Maury and Laila?"

"The resale value. I mean, even if they try to rent it again instead of selling . . . people at the high end of the market don't like messes. If I were them, I'd take out the fireplaces. Rip them out, so there's no question. No reminder, you know?"

They'd stopped at the corner of Hudson, in the light of a streetlamp. Amy was confused. "Are you saying the Steinbergs own the MacGregor penthouse?"

"Yeah. Laila mentioned it on the trip. They bought it at the bottom of the market as an investment property. They never lived there. But they figured they'd rent it out to MacGregor until prices turned around. Laila was worried they'd have some trouble getting MacGregor's maid out of there. But that's not a problem now."

"You never mentioned they owned the apartment."

Peter considered this. "The subject never came up."

"For eleven days we did little else but talk about Paisley MacGregor, and the subject of her apartment never came up?"

"I don't think it did. Why are you suddenly interested in who owns her apartment?"

"Because that's where Archer died."

"Yes . . ." He drew the word out. "And what does Archer's death have to do with Maury and Laila?"

"Because the Steinbergs would know the building. They would have access."

"Access to what? To the apartment?" Peter cocked his head. He inhaled and exhaled forcefully through his nose. Not a good sign. "I hope you're not saying what I think you're saying."

"Her death wasn't an accident or a suicide. Joy Archer was murdered. My theory? Someone was trying to get back MacGregor's 'if I die' letter."

"The 'if I die' letter? I thought we settled that weeks ago." Peter groaned, and his hands flew up to hold in place his exploding head. "Amy, you cannot keep doing this."

"I'm not doing anything. The guy who came with me to Evan's service—he's a homicide detective. He's investigating."

"You brought a homicide detective to a memorial? Why? To spy on our clients? You are out of control."

"Well, the police agree. And the fact that the Steinbergs actually own that apartment . . ."

"Are you saying Maury and Laila killed Archer? That's ridiculous. For one thing, they're in Hawaii. I talked to Maury the other day."

"His landline or his cell?"

"I don't know."

"The police eliminated the Steinbergs because they weren't around. But, of course, we don't know that. Let me borrow your phone."

"No." Peter laid a protective hand on his jacket

pocket. "Amy, this is not your business, and it's not mine. If we're going to be partners, you have to promise. No more involvement in murder."

"But we're already involved."

"No we're not. Damn you. Clients come to us to forget their problems, not to get dragged into police stations."

"Fine." Amy turned on her heel and headed back up Barrow Street, stewing every step of the way.

"Amy!" he shouted, but she didn't stop.

Was this really the man she wanted to be in business with? she wondered. Even if it meant saving the business?

Meanwhile, there was a cheesecake in her garbage can and another man out there, a man who wouldn't hesitate to get dragged into a police station for her. Any day of the week.

CHAPTER 35

The painting hung above eye level, but she could still make out the masterful details—thick layers of short, self-assured brushstrokes, each stroke a slightly different shade. A multitude of browns shifted gently into greens here or grays there, given form mainly by the angle of the strokes and by the eye's distance from the canvas.

Samime thought back to their early days in Istanbul. Bill would spend every morning in the studio on the top floor, working on some project or other, happy in his self-imposed isolation. Once a week or so, an art dealer friend would drop by. They would all have tea in the sun-dappled courtyard, under the lemon tree, before the men retired up to the studio to talk. Afterward, he would take her out to her favorite restaurant, the one with the French wines and the endless view of the Bosphorus.

And then slowly that changed. The friend stopped by less and less. Bill became more and more withdrawn, angrier, and more sullen. And finally, one winter day she came home from the meat market to find her husband at the living room hearth, burning a canvas in the fire, cracking pieces of the frame and tossing them on top of the pungent, acidic flames.

"Bill painted this, didn't he?"

Samime had never been this assertive. But today was different. She had planned it perfectly: arriving after the light had faded, so Colleen wouldn't have an excuse to say no; finding a way to sneak through the building's outer door, so Colleen couldn't turn her away on the street; charming her way into the apartment on the pretext of needing to talk about Bill, which wasn't really a pretext.

"A friend painted it," Colleen said, walking back into the living room with two small glasses of red wine.

"It is very much Bill's style."

"It's Pissarro's style." Colleen approached and handed over a glass. "I suppose if Bill imitated Pissarro, it would be his style, too."

Samime had known she would say this. "It's not just his brushwork. It's the frame. I remember Bill bringing a lot of old molding pieces on the plane with us to Turkey. We brought them as carry-ons, and he was very careful. He made me keep them under my seat the whole way."

"A lot of old moldings are similar. Even then they were mass-produced."

"You must have a lot of them lying around here. Old frames. Old canvases. Authentic pigments and brushes."

Colleen began to look a little wary. "Yes. That's my job."

"Of course. People want them reframed, so you keep the old frames. You re-stretch a big painting, and there's a nice piece of nineteenth-century canvas left over. Can I keep this?" Samime put down her glass then lifted the small painting off the wall. She heard Colleen's thin gasp behind her. "As a memento from Bill?"

"I told you. He didn't paint it."

"It's good enough to be real," Samime said, examining it from just a few inches away. "It's even signed Pissarro, which a normal copier wouldn't do."

"What exactly are you saying?"

Samime wrapped her arms around the painting and clutched it to the front of her coat. "As soon as I saw this, I knew. Suddenly it made sense—why Bill's money dried up, why he became so depressed over a few shakes of the hand." She turned it around and ran her fingers over a sticker from a gallery on the back. "Bill used to visit this gallery."

"Go ahead. Take it." Colleen downed her wine in two quick gulps. "I don't know why I kept it in the first place."

The Turkish woman didn't thank her but just nodded. "Is that what ruined your marriage? Some fight about what he was doing?"

"I never knew." Colleen reconsidered her reply, then reached over to Samime's untouched glass. Two more gulps and she was feeling better. "Not at first. But I had a pigment, a rare Naples yellow. It's toxic and not used anymore, except for restorations. One day I noticed about a third of my jar was missing."

"You weren't helping him do it?"

"Heavens no." Colleen's anger seemed genuine. "When I found out how he was using me . . . not just my supplies, but my expertise . . . There's always inside information floating around—which paintings are in private hands, which have been lost over the decades. You need that to help establish the provenance of any good fake. Where has it supposedly been all these years?"

"But you didn't call the police."

"No." Was that a note of regret in her voice? "Reputation is a delicate thing. The work I do is based on judgment—how much to strip away, how much to paint over. A bad restoration can cut the value of a piece in half, so my clients have to trust me. The idea of an art conservator being involved in any way with a forger, even innocently . . . When you told me about his tremors, I felt both happy and sad." Colleen allowed herself a tiny smile. "I cared for Bill, yes. But there was a certain justice to it. God's way of putting an end to the travesty."

"Meanwhile, he stayed in business. Millions of dollars' worth of his fakes are now in galleries and private collections. If they knew the truth . . ."

"I don't think anyone wants that kind of scandal," said Colleen.

Samime didn't answer her.

"Don't be so high and mighty, Mrs. Strohman."

"Me? I never suspected."

Colleen's laugh was both wounded and cruel. "Want to know an interesting fact? Istanbul is a world center of art fraud. It's always been hard to trace forgeries through that corner of the world. When I heard that Bill was moving there, it made perfect sense. Things start getting hot in New York, and you marry a starry-eyed Turkish girl. Move your operations offshore."

"That's not true."

"What part isn't true, dear? That he suddenly married you? That he wound up with dual citizenship? Or that he continued in Istanbul with a dealer who was even more unscrupulous than his man in New York?"

Samime exhaled, as if the wind had just been punched out of her. "You're a bitter, lonely woman. Good-bye."

"Are you going to sell it? I mean, as a Pissarro?"

"Maybe I will," Samime said, without bothering to look back. "Why not? Bill would want me to be provided for."

"One word of caution." Colleen kept her distance. "What I said about things getting hot, that's true. One of Bill's paintings was declared a fake. The buyer, some broker or hedge-fund manager, was trying to get insurance. He happened to find a very smart and diligent appraiser. The gallery owner managed to smooth things over. He bought the piece back, a small, lovely oil with a haystack and some cows."

Samime pursed her lips and shrugged her shoulders. "Why do you tell me this?"

"Because that piece"—Colleen pointed—"is on record as a forgery. The Interpol art division has a photo on file."

"You forget I live in Istanbul, the forgery capital," said Samime as she opened the door and walked out.

CHAPTER 36

Marcus had invited Amy to lunch, and she'd accepted. This was their standard way of apologizing. If one of them wasn't ready to make up, that person would be too busy. If the rift was only one person's fault, it would become a dinner date, with the offender paying the tab. But this was scheduled as a lunch—Dutch treat—and they met on the corner out in front of the Ritz-Carlton.

Since the day was nice and the lilies were in bloom—and no one had bothered to make a reservation—lunch was purchased from the gourmet food trucks that had recently emerged from their winter hibernation. Amy went with a coriander-braised duck burger from Le Camion, parked by the fire hydrant on Fifty-Eighth Street, while Marcus chose a lobster and orange salad from See Food, near the crosswalk on Sixth Avenue. They found an empty bench overlooking the Central Park Pond and talked as if nothing had happened.

This was the best part of a relationship, Amy thought. *Well, maybe the second-best part. To have someone you*

*could talk to about anything, to not have to struggle to
make conversation or be on your best behavior.*

The one sore subject in their repertoire came up
only afterward, when Amy was walking Marcus back
to the Ritz. "So you knew about our finances." She
tried to keep the accusing tone out of her voice.
"And you didn't tell me."

"Fanny made me promise."

"Since when do you keep promises?"

"Now you're blaming me for keeping a promise?"
He had to smile. "There's no winning."

"Okay, you're right. It's Mom's fault, not yours."

"As long as we're on the subject . . ." His voice
turned serious. "I think you should be wary of Peter
Borg. Personal feelings aside."

"He should be wary of Mom and me. Have you
seen our bank account?"

"That's my point. Why would Peter want to
merge and assume your debts? It's not like you have
a great business model or the only available storefront in Lower Manhattan." He tilted his head in
her direction. "I'm just being honest."

"You know what he wants," Amy said, giving her
butt a sexy little shake.

"I do," Marcus admitted. "I also think Peter's
smarter than he lets on. He wants you to think it's
personal, that he's giving himself a bad deal just for
you. But the guy's a pro. There's got to be a reason."

"You don't think I'm reason enough?"

"Seriously, Amy." He put on his serious face.
"You're sexy and smart and worth everything. But
that's not how Peter thinks. There's something
we're not seeing. That's all I'm saying. It's a warning."

Could Marcus be right? Amy thought about it as they began to jaywalk gingerly across Central Park South. When Marcus looked over a few seconds later, she was gone. He found her back on the curb, standing behind a parked bus.

"Amy, I'm sorry. But I can smell a con job. . . ."

"It's Maury," she whispered and nodded toward the other side of the bus.

Marcus glanced across the six lanes of traffic. Sure enough, Maury Steinberg was on the sidewalk in front of the Ritz-Carlton, waiting as the doorman hailed him a taxi.

"If we can see him, he can see us," Amy said and pulled him back behind the bus.

"So? You knew Maury was staying at the Ritz."

That was true. After Amy had found out about the Steinbergs owning the penthouse, she had called Lieutenant Rawlings, who had in turn called Maury's cell phone. After some hemming and hawing, Maury had admitted to being in New York for a few days.

"I was hoping to slip in and out," he'd told the detective. "As much as I liked Evan, I didn't want to have to spend an afternoon at another memorial service. You understand."

The lieutenant did. He asked Maury where he was staying and how long he would be in town, but somehow neglected to ask where he'd been at the time of Joy Archer's death.

"I don't want him to see me," Amy said, still on the other side of the bus. "He'll think I'm following him, which will be awkward if I ever do intend to follow him and he catches me."

"He's your suspect? Maury?"

"Only because he knows the building and probably has keys to everything."

"Do you want to search his room? I can get us into any room in the Ritz-Carlton."

"You would do that for me?" It was so much nicer having someone like Marcus on her side. "I'm not sure what we'd be looking for. But thanks."

He seemed disappointed. "Well, think about it."

They were still behind the bus when Amy's phone rang. "Amy?" It was Fanny, and she wasn't in the mood for chitchat. "Samime's leaving. I came home and found a note. What did you say to the woman?"

"Nothing. What did *you* say to her?"

"Nothing. The note says, 'Thank you for all your help and friendship. I'm forever indebted.' Blah, blah . . . 'No more we can do. Have to go home.'"

"Really? It says, 'Blah, blah . . . '?"

"Amy, don't be a jerk. Something's wrong."

In the taxi on the way to JFK, Amy checked her phone. There was a nonstop Turkish Airlines flight leaving in about two hours. She told her cabbie to take her to Terminal One, then sat back, buckled up, and wondered what could have happened. She tried Samime's cell phone every few minutes but saw that it was going directly to voice mail.

There wasn't much hope of catching her, Amy knew, but she didn't have a choice. If Samime left, there would be no contacting her again, short of Amy making her own trip to Istanbul. It was early afternoon on a Wednesday. Grand Central Parkway was clear, and the airport nearly empty.

Once inside the terminal, she followed the overhead signs, half running toward the security gate. She was hoping to see the usual rats' maze, with hun-

dreds of fliers snaking their way through the endless
nylon ropes. Instead, there was only one chaotic family and a few silent couples and business travelers.

At the front was a modestly dressed woman in a
brown head scarf, just placing her shoes on the belt.
There was no way to get to her, Amy saw, not without going through the ID and ticket control. She
considered shouting out Samime's name but didn't
want to risk having her disappear completely.

Amy scanned the edges of the hall, looking for
another way to get to the woman. And that was
when she saw the other modestly dressed woman in
a head scarf. This one was seated in a nearby row of
plastic chairs, rearranging the contents of a plastic
shopping bag.

"Why are you leaving?"

Samime looked up from her shopping bag and
frowned. "Amy?"

"I know it's not working out like we wanted, but
we have to give it time." She settled into the third
plastic seat, with the shopping bag between them.
"You knew I wasn't a real detective."

"Sweet girl, I have imposed enough on your kindness."

"It's not about kindness. It's about getting justice
for Bill. It's about . . . Is that a painting?" Amy stared
down into the shopping bag, where Samime had
been in the process of wrapping the familiar scene
in a cocoon of silk scarves. "Is that from Colleen's
apartment?" She dug down among the scarves and
gently pulled it out. "It is."

"She gave it to me," Samime explained.

"You went back to see her, and she gave you a
painting?" Amy didn't know which half of the sentence was odder. Why would Samime go back to see

Colleen without mentioning it? And why would Colleen give this woman, whom she didn't much like, a painting from her wall?

"Bill painted it," said Samime. Okay, that sentence was the oddest. "Sometimes he would paint copies of impressionist paintings. As an exercise."

Amy recalled Samime's reaction on seeing it and Colleen's claim that it had been painted by a friend. "You recognized it as Bill's work."

"Correct. And she was nice enough to make me a present of it."

"Are you sure you didn't just steal it?" Amy blurted out. She had a pretty good thought filter, but every now and then she found herself speaking like her mother.

"I did not," said Samime, then proceeded to remove it from Amy's hands. The small painting was halfway back in the cushion of scarves when Amy noticed the pale green label glued to the back. The label held only five words, but they were enough: THE STEINBERG GALLERY, NEW YORK.

It took Amy a few seconds of blinking silence to make the connection. "That's Maury Steinberg," she said, pointing to the label. Yes, of course. Bill had been an art professor and a painter. And, according to Paisley's postmortem speech, Maury had owned a gallery before teaming up with Laila. "That's the connection." Amy was still pointing. "We were looking for a connection to someone on the tour. Here it is. Maury Steinberg and Bill."

"I have to go," said Samime. She covered up the label with the edge of a red scarf, then stood up with her shopping bag and headed toward the security desk.

"No, you can't." Amy tried grabbing her by the

arm but was too slow. "We can take this to the police. They can check out Maury's old gallery. Who
knows what they'll find."

"Police?" The Turkish woman shook her head.
"No. I have to leave. I'll be late for my flight."

"What?" Amy couldn't believe it. "Samime, you
can't go now. This is why you came, to track down
your husband's killer."

"I don't think it will help." She was moving faster
now, stepping up to the nylon rope and the little
podium and the stern-looking TSA agent who was
checking tickets and passports. "I shouldn't have
come and bothered you."

"It's no bother. Okay, maybe at first I was reluc-
tant. Sorry about that. I didn't want to put myself in
the middle of another murder." Amy found herself
speaking faster than an auctioneer. "But you were
right. There is a connection. Maury Steinberg.
Don't you owe it to Bill's memory to stay?"

"Boarding pass and ID." The TSA agent was a
bulky woman in blue who was interested only in
doing her job with as little physical movement as
possible.

Samime produced the two documents out of the
folds of her dress. "I'm sorry. I changed my mind."

"But that doesn't make sense," Amy countered.
"We're closer now than ever."

The TSA agent waved Samime through, then repeated her demand to Amy. "Boarding pass and ID."

"You can't go." But Amy found herself speaking
into thin air as the woman scurried through the
nearly empty maze, toward the next TSA agent and
the walk-through metal detector.

CHAPTER 37

It took Amy over an hour to get Rawlings on the phone. In the past she had always found herself avoiding the homicide detective or having him pop up at the most inconvenient time. The idea of not being able to contact him was new and unsettling and probably should have been a hint.

"Abel, I'm busy."

"I found a connection." She was at work on her big-screen Mac, toggling through several open windows.

"That's nice. Between what and what?"

"Between Bill Strohman and Maury Steinberg."

"The guy who isn't in Hawaii."

"It's more than that," she insisted. "Maury ran a Manhattan art gallery before he married Laila. You think everyone's life is an open book these days, with the Internet, but you still have to know where to look. Anyway, he sold at least one painting by Strohman. So there's a connection."

"I suggest you call Inspector Badlani in India. It's his case."

"But it's also connected to yours." She couldn't understand why the lieutenant was suddenly so cool. "You yourself said—"

"My case is officially an accident."

"Accident? What about the gas valves and the pill bottles?"

"The DA's office disagrees. They placed a call to my captain. Told him to stop wasting their time and our resources on some 'grandstanding lieutenant trying to make headlines.' I believe those were their exact words."

"But Joy Archer was killed. You can't just let it drop."

"Amy . . ." He adopted a patient tone, which let her know his patience was gone. "I am not some amateur sticking my nose into things. My boss gives me cases, and I investigate."

"But you can argue with them. Make your case."

"Hey, I'm not Bruce Willis, either. I can't say, 'Damn it, Chief. I won't let you close this one.' It doesn't work that way. You want to know where I am now?" He didn't wait for a guess. "I'm in a loft in the Meatpacking District, playing second officer in a drug dispute turned homicide. Thanks to you."

"Thanks to me?"

"I trusted your instincts."

Amy was outraged. "I didn't ask you to. You hounded me. You arrested my mother."

"Well, I guess the joke's on me."

For several minutes after the call, Amy was steaming, pacing the floor. How dare he blame her? How dare he give up, now that she finally had a suspect? And how dare he hang up . . . ? When the phone rang right in the middle of her mental tirade, she picked up without thinking. "This had better be an apology."

"Actually, it's not."

"Mom, I'm sorry. I thought it was someone else."

"So who owes you an apology? Never mind. I need you to go to the Sutton Place apartment."

"Paisley MacGregor's apartment? Why?"

"Arthur, the sweetheart at the front desk. I asked him to let me know if anyone takes the elevator to the penthouse floor, other than the police or the staff or the neighbor. Anyway, someone is there now."

"Who?"

"Arthur didn't see, but his monitor recorded it. Whoever it is has been on that floor for nearly an hour. Oh, and bring a hundred bucks in cash. Give it to Arthur."

"What are you doing?"

"Obviously, someone's searching her place. Dear, I can't talk. I just stepped into the elevator."

"Elevator? You're there now?" But the line had already filled with static and gone dead.

Fanny Abel put away her phone and watched the lights blink their way up to the top of the Sutton Place building. She wasn't worried. At the worst she could knock on the door and say it was a mistake. She was looking for Margery Daniels, she'd say, the woman in the other penthouse. She was more curious than anything—about whoever was there and whatever she could worm out of them.

The door to penthouse 2 was ajar a fraction of an inch. Fanny knocked lightly, then pushed it open a crack and called, "Yoo-hoo, Margery." After waiting a few seconds, she called again, even as she pushed the door all the way open.

Fanny tiptoed through the white oval foyer and into the living room, with its tall, stunning view of the Fifty-Ninth Street Bridge. The evening shadows revealed two lanes of taillights on the upper level moving slowly into Queens and two lanes of headlights crawling at the same pace into Manhattan.

From here, she softly yoo-hooed her way into the master bedroom and was finally stopped by the sight of a parquet-topped trapdoor, angled back to reveal an open floor safe, approximately two feet square. "Yoo-hoo," Fanny whispered, not really wanting an answer at the moment.

Amy had mentioned Barbara's inquiry about the music box, but Fanny really didn't understand what the problem was. The music box was right here.

The dark rectangular box lay on top of the satin bedspread, its diamond-patterned lid now open. The box's false bottom had been removed, she noticed, revealing a bundle of folded certificates stuffed inside. Fanny was old enough to recognize stock certificates. *Do they even make them anymore?* She unfolded the bundle, saw the company title, and vaguely recalled some CNN segment from about a month ago.

The flush of a toilet alerted Fanny and gave her nearly a minute's warning. She could have left right then. But she had a good sense of who the flusher was and how she could play this to her advantage.

A white door, nearly seamless in the white wall, opened, and Barbara Corns emerged. Fanny had the element of surprise and used it.

"I see you found the stock."

Barbara saw the woman standing by the bed and froze. "Who are you?"

"Barbara, Barbara," Fanny said, sounding a little

disappointed. "Who do you think I am?" It might be better not to actively impersonate anyone this time around.

"I don't . . ." Barbara focused on the face and the red hair. "You were at Evan's memorial service, asking questions. Are you the police? You don't look like police."

"Why? Because I'm a woman? Because I'm older? The mandatory retirement age is sixty-five." She was guessing. "Do I look sixty-five?"

"No, no, you look great. Look, ma'am, I have every right to be here. The crime-scene tape is down, and I'm the executor of the will. I have a key."

"Let's not waste time, Barbara. My partner will be here any minute, and she's not as understanding."

"I've done nothing wrong," Barbara sputtered. "I found the floor safe. It was unlocked. I was doing an inventory."

"We know about the music box," Fanny announced. "And we know why you want it back." That was an easy deduction. The certificates, according to her memory of the CNN story, were probably worth millions.

"How much do you know?"

Bingo, Fanny thought. *Home free.* "Why don't you start from the beginning? It'll go easier. Don't worry. I'm not recording. It's just you and me—for the next few minutes. After my partner arrives, however . . ." She raised her hands in a helpless gesture.

The clock was ticking, at least in Barbara's mind. And although Fanny continued to ask leading questions, the story more or less poured out. First and foremost, it was all Evan's fault.

Evan had been born into a long line of stockbrokers. Jerome Corns, Evan's great-grandfather, had been noteworthy as the only person to actually jump out of a window on Black Thursday in 1929. The other jumpers, according to family lore, were mere imitators and started doing it days later. Over the subsequent decades, Corns and Associates managed to stay afloat and eke out their meager profits, which was the reason why Evan decided on law school instead.

When the stock market boom finally hit and his brothers raked in the dough, Evan and his wife were still writing wills and paying off college loans. "Evan felt left out," Barbara confessed. "He tried to keep up. But mostly that meant living above our means and hiring a maid we could barely afford."

Evan's solution to his embarrassing state was to lasso a group of investors of his own, using his family name as a lure, and create a REIT, a real estate investment trust. The housing market was at a low point at the time and, he assured his partners, it had nowhere to go but up.

At some point, Fanny began to zone out. She had no affinity for finance. But she maintained a sympathetic expression, eyes wide and unmoving. Barbara obviously needed to tell someone. Fanny knew the syndrome. When you were used to having a husband to talk things over with, it became hard. Before you knew it, you were pouring out your secrets to the homeless guy cashing in bottle deposits at the grocery.

"Evan couldn't let his brothers see him fail. That would be the worst. So he started throwing good money after bad and cooking the books when he had to."

"Why did he give the stock to your maid?" Fanny didn't mean to skip ahead, but she felt there was a window here, one that would slam shut. As soon as Amy walked through the door, it would be apparent that Fanny was not a police detective on the cusp of retirement.

"It was a joke." Barbara unfolded the ancient certificates and spread them flat on the bedspread. The elaborate print across the top said it all. *Senosha Diamond Mines, Northwest Territories.*

"Great-grandfather Jerome left a lot of worthless stock lying around after the crash. Evan found these in the back of a desk he inherited. We did our due diligence. I mean, we're not idiots. The mines are still incorporated in Canada. But in the thirties, they went dry—or whatever mines do. The certificates were worth a few bucks apiece, for their historical value."

"So you gave them to your maid."

Barbara sighed. "You know how it is. There's a birthday coming, and you don't feel like shopping or spending. We re-gifted a tacky music box with a diamond pattern and wrote a cutesy little card. 'To our diamond in the rough.' That's what we used to call her."

Evan and Barbara had no way of knowing that a few years after they handed over their gift, a new hydro-mining technique would be developed and that the Senosha Mines would reopen and enjoy amazing success. A share from 1925 would split twenty-four times. When they read the news in *Forbes,* the couple was floored. And angry. And embarrassed.

"Well, that must have rankled," said Fanny with a straight face. "You're in desperate need of money, and then your little gag gift to your ex-maid . . ."

"Yes," said Barbara. "Evan and I spent many

drunken nights discussing this and blaming each other. We wanted to talk to Paisley, but by the time we got up the nerve, she was dead."

"You probably thought she'd already cashed them in and made millions."

"We thought so, yes. How else could she afford a life like this? But then we found out that she had never opened her gifts. Eight million dollars at the bottom of a music box. A few pieces of paper that could solve all our problems."

"Eight million. Is that how much you owe?"

"We owe more. But eight would cover us for now."

"My, my." Fanny cocked her head to one side and scrunched her eyebrows. "I hate to bring up a delicate subject, but thinking about your financial hole and your dearly departed husband . . ." She paused. "You know what I'm getting at, right?"

"Did Evan kill himself? Is that what you're asking? Is that why the police were at his memorial?"

"That's not an answer."

Barbara raised both shoulders and let them fall. "I've thought about that. No, I don't think so. There was still hope. Evan would cling to any hope."

"And you think this would solve your problems?" Fanny asked, tapping the top certificate.

"Who would I be hurting?" Barbara demanded. "It was worthless at the time. She never even looked inside."

"Would this solve your problems?" Fanny asked. She liked solving problems.

"Hello?" came a hesitant voice, echoing in from the living room.

"That's my partner. I must have left the door open."

"I'll split it with you," Barbara said, her eyes almost devouring the old pieces of paper on the bed. "Your partner doesn't need to know."

"I'm not fond of re-gifting," said Fanny.

"Please! If it becomes part of the estate, I'll get just a fraction. And it'll be months. Much too late."

"Okay, just take it," Fanny whispered. "No one needs to find out."

"Really?" For a moment Barbara was stunned. "God bless you." And she slipped the wad of certificates into the music box just a few seconds before Amy walked through the door.

CHAPTER 38

"**M**om?" Amy breathed a sigh of relief. Fanny and Barbara were sitting on the edge of the bed, smiling, looking like old friends. "Are you okay?"

"Your partner calls you Mom?"

"We're very informal," Fanny explained.

The room was dim from the fading light. Amy's hair was up under a gray wool newsboy cap, and it took Barbara a second to recognize her. "Amy? I didn't know your mother was a cop."

"I never said I was," Fanny protested. "She made an assumption that I neglected to correct. Is that a crime?"

"You never said you were a cop?"

Amy sighed again. "Barbara, I'm so sorry. Mom likes to stick her nose into things. I asked her to meet me here, but obviously, she took it upon herself . . ." As she rambled on, doing her best to explain, she couldn't help noticing the furtive glances going back and forth between Barbara and her mother. Noticing them—and trying to ignore them. "I hope she wasn't too much of a bother."

"No. We were just . . ." Barbara pointed to the open safe in the middle of the parquet floor. "Finishing up the inventory."

Amy looked down into the shallow steel square. "Who would imagine a floor safe in a penthouse apartment? That's wild."

"The rug was off-kilter," said Barbara. "When I went to straighten it, I happened to notice the edge of the trapdoor. The safe itself was unlocked."

"Anything important?"

"Nothing," said Fanny with some conviction. "Just a bunch of papers."

"Must be important papers." She glanced inside. From the second she'd seen the well-hidden safe, Amy had hoped that it might hold the document she'd been puzzling over ever since Peter Borg hit a wrong note all those weeks ago. But she hadn't expected it to be so easy. She'd almost looked right past it. "Oh, my . . ."

"Oh, your what?" asked Fanny.

"You didn't see this?" Amy asked, pointing.

"No. We were preoccupied." Fanny finally looked. "Oh, my . . ."

There it was, right on top, three handwritten pages from a yellow legal pad, stapled together. Fanny bent over for a closer look. The writing was clear and precise, on paper wrinkled only slightly by the years and humidity. *If you are reading this . . .*

"Mom?" said Amy, leaving the rest of her statement to be relayed telepathically.

"Barbara was just leaving," said Fanny, straightening up and standing up.

"Leaving?" Barbara shook her head, feeling emboldened. "I'm not leaving. I'm the executor. I have every right to be here, while, unless I'm mistaken, neither of you do."

"Well, if you have a right to be here, then you won't mind coming back later." Fanny smiled.

"Why should I? And why are you even here in the first place?"

"Because . . ." Amy was hoping an answer, any answer, would just come out, but none did. "Because . . ."

"We're here because we want to snoop around MacGregor's apartment," said Fanny. "And you're leaving because you found the music box you were looking for and you have no reason to stick around. Am I right? Enjoy your day, dear."

Amy was used to her mother's logic. Usually, it left you with your mouth hanging open and no good response. But this argument had been a little weak and disjointed even for Fanny.

"Yes, the music box," said Barbara. It was lying, lid shut, on the bed between them. "That's a good point. I should go." And she took the music box, placing it under her arm like a purse, and headed out of the bedroom. "Just close the door behind you," she added meekly. "Take your time."

"You're welcome," said Fanny and watched her go.

Amy waited until she heard the front door close. "What was that about?"

"Nothing," said Fanny. "Oh, she found the music box."

"I saw that. What was in it?"

"Nothing. Sentimental value. Look, dear heart, are you going to read the damn note or not?" Fanny switched on the nearest bedside lamp, three clicks to high, while her daughter pulled the pages out of the floor safe and started reading aloud.

"If you are reading this, then I am dead, and there are certain things the police need to know."

"An intriguing way to begin," said Fanny. "Keep reading."

"My name is Maurice David Steinberg. For over a decade, I owned the Steinberg Gallery in New York City, and I knowingly sold art forgeries to the public. I make this confession at this time in the hope of rectifying some of the wrong I have done and of establishing once and for all the facts that many of my victimized collectors may have suspected throughout the years.

"First, let me say that no one else at the Steinberg Gallery knew of the forgeries or had any reason to question their authenticity. What I did, I did on my own, with the sole collusion of Professor William Strohman of Columbia University, who created the forged artworks and provided me with them.

"I became acquainted with Bill Strohman during a New School course he taught in the summer of 2000 on the subject of art authentication. During our conversations after class, he more than once brought up the subject of forgery and how the art world unknowingly colludes to make this crime easier than it should be.

"Our first effort to prove his point began as an experiment. One afternoon he drew a small Salvador Dali sketch, ink on paper, like a hundred others of that period. Without consulting Strohman, I framed the piece and put it on display in my gallery. I told myself at the time that I had no intention of selling it and just wanted to gauge the reaction, but of course that was a lie.

"The next day a surrealist expert and collector saw the Dali sketch and demanded that I sell it to her. I should have had the ethical strength to tell her the truth, but I didn't. It sold for eight thousand dollars.

"From that moment on, Strohman and I became partners in defrauding the New York art world. Not to use this as a defense or an excuse, but it was surprisingly easy. Through his wife at the time, Strohman had access to old canvases and paints, while I personally forged the provenance documents."

Below this last sentence came a list naming every forged work of art: its title, size, attributed artist, and buyer, and the price paid. Nearly two dozen pieces in all, taking up a full page and a half. In the final paragraph of the note, Maury apologized to his wife, to Colleen Strohman, and to the collectors they'd cheated over the years.

"So this is the 'if I die' note," said Fanny after her daughter had finished reading every word. The moment wasn't quite as fulfilling as she had expected. "Not written by a victim."

"Written by a bad guy."

"Why the hell would he put that down in words?" asked Fanny, shaking her head. "In his own handwriting?"

"Paisley MacGregor," said Amy, without hesitation. "She was a very maternal, moralistic woman. No one could talk him into going to jail. But she must have convinced him to try to set the record straight after his death. As luck would have it, she died first."

"So what does this mean?" asked Fanny. She had taken the pages and was rereading the first. "Maury flew to Istanbul to kill his old partner?"

"I think their meeting in Istanbul was accidental," said Amy as she started to piece it together. "Strohman's forgery career was at an end, thanks to his tremors. He'd been reduced to hanging around the high-end hotels, renting himself out as a guide. That's where he saw Maury, looking prosperous and happy. Well, as happy as Maury was capable of looking."

"And he followed Maury to India," said Fanny, continuing the train of thought. "To blackmail him. Maury was rich and respectable. The last thing Maury needed was a call being placed to the Manhattan bunco squad, outlining his role in all this."

"Bunco squad?" Amy asked. "I don't think anybody's had a bunco squad since the nineteen forties."

"You know what I mean," said Fanny.

"I think Dick Tracy had a bunco squad."

"Art forgery squad. Don't get snooty, girl of mine. If it wasn't for me, you never would have found this."

Amy focused on the three yellow sheets. "And if we weren't dealing with a cold-blooded killer, I might even thank you."

"A two-time killer," Fanny reminded her. "He must have killed Joy Archer while trying to get this back."

"Right." Their mood turned more serious than ever. "This not only connects him to the forgeries," said Amy. "It connects him to Bill Strohman. We need to get this to the police."

"It's not going to prove murder."

Amy thought it over. "Not exactly," she had to admit. "The death in India's been ruled a mugging. And the one here was an accident."

"So, what good would it do, handing this over to the police?" Fanny's tone was rhetorical, as if her question were some incomplete thought.

Amy's eyes flew open. "Oh, no, no, no. You're not going there."

"Going where?" No one could feign innocence better than Fanny.

"We are not keeping that." Amy leaned away from her mother and the toxic three pages. "Two people have died for this secret."

"And their killer's getting away with it."

"He's not getting away." Even as Amy said the words, she realized the truth. "Okay, he's getting away with murder. But once we give this to the bunco squad, his life will be ruined."

"What do you think he'll get? A few years? Plus, the embarrassment, of course. I believe it could be quite embarrassing. Poor man."

"Mother!"

"Don't 'mother' me."

"It's punishment enough, from his point of view. It drove him to murder."

"Lucky for us. That's the only advantage we have."

"Advantage?" Amy didn't like the sound of this. "What do you mean?"

"The fact that he's been willing to kill for three pieces of paper." Fanny flattened them smoothly on the bed. "That's how we're going to catch him."

"We? Oh, no. There's no 'we.' In fact, there's no 'you' or 'me' or anyone."

"It won't be that hard."

"Won't be hard? What are you saying? Are you saying you have a plan?"

"No. But between you, me, and Marcus, I'm sure we'll come up with one."

CHAPTER 39

For the past few days, Maury had been living in a kind of nightmarish limbo.

His plan, concocted on his flight in from Maui, had been simple: to take back the Sutton Place penthouse. There was still a month left on Paisley MacGregor's lease. Until then the place would be managed by the executor, Corns and Associates, who would see to the sale and disposal of all the late maid's tacky white furniture and lifetime possessions. There was no stipulation for the late maid's maid to continue squatting, no legal right, even by the lax New York City housing code. His plan had been to nicely but firmly evict Joy Archer and give her some cash for her cooperation, maybe five thousand dollars. He and Laila had agreed on that part.

Somewhere along the way, Maury figured, he would have the time, the keys, and the excuse of being the landlord to enter and search for that damned letter. Why, oh why, had he written it in the first place?

It had all been Paisley's fault. She must have eavesdropped on one of his conversations with Strohman; or jimmied open the locked file cabinet in his home office; or pieced together tidbits from the scare, when an appraiser labeled the little haystack Pissarro a forgery and the buyer demanded his money back. Knowing Paisley, it had probably been all three.

The scare had been enough to make him quit. He had always been squeamish about the forgeries, criminally and morally. And now he was married to Laila—generous, clueless Laila—so money was not an issue. He could give up his business and devote himself to meddling in hers. But he had continued to feel guilty about defrauding his customers, many of whom had been good, longtime friends.

Paisley MacGregor had observed his loss of appetite, irritability, and erratic sleep and took him aside one evening, right before cocktail hour, his most vulnerable moment of the day. She seemed to know everything. "Would it make you feel better to confess, Maury, dear, like the Roman Catholics do? They say it's good for the soul."

"And ruin my marriage and go to jail? Not in my lifetime!"

Not in my lifetime. A choice, unfortunate turn of phrase. "Well, what about after?" Paisley had asked in her soulful, maternal way.

That was how the idea had come about, three handwritten pages meant to help cleanse his soul. Paisley had agreed to protect his secrets, the way she always had. In the unlikely event that she died first—she was younger, after all, and had an air of invinc-ibility about her—she would leave the pages in a safe place. But she'd never told him where the safe place was, and the next time he'd heard, she was already dead. "Too soon, too soon," he'd muttered, tears in his eyes, at more than one of the worldwide wakes. And he'd meant it.

As for the murders, they were just flukes, little more than accidents, moments when he'd been backed into a corner and had to protect his interests.

He hadn't recognized Billy Strohman at first, just another English-speaking guide hanging out in front of the luxury hotels. When Billy came up to him, Maury was startled by the palsy and the tattered suit. He felt sorry for his old partner—until the subject of money reared its ugly head. The man was greedy and desperate and, worst of all, persistent, showing up not once, but twice, in different cities. What else could Maury do?

Joy Archer reacted in much the same way. Maury had knocked on the penthouse door, fully prepared to charm his way back into an apartment that was rightfully his. But he could tell from the second she greeted him with that superior, canary-eating grin that she'd found it. She practically admitted that it was there in the apartment with her. Again, wrong place, wrong time. He was just unlucky, he told himself.

After the police removed the crime-scene tape, he'd taken his time searching the place from top to bottom, between the pages of every book, behind every painting and photo. Two long, frustrating afternoons with no results. Wherever the maid's maid had slipped it, it remained hidden. Perhaps, if he was lucky for once, it would stay hidden forever.

Maury stood in the elevator of the Ritz-Carlton,

on his way to the nineteenth floor, checking his phone app for possible flights back to Maui. When the doors dinged his arrival, he barely looked up.

"Sorry, sir," someone mumbled.

The doors had opened, and he was facing a sleek, youngish man in a black hotel uniform. The man lowered his head and stepped aside to let Maury off before getting on himself and pressing a button. The man with the sharp nose and wavy black hair didn't look up as the doors closed, but he seemed familiar. Of course he looked familiar, Maury chided himself. A hotel worker in the hotel where he was staying. Why wouldn't he look familiar?

Maury was still checking flights—a once-a-day nonstop from Newark to Maui on United, which would be nice—when he used his other hand to swipe his key card and open the door to his junior suite. He switched on the lights, distracted, still waiting to see if there might be another, even more convenient nonstop, perhaps out of LaGuardia.

He paid no attention to the object that had been slipped under his door, walking straight over it. Probably some hotel promotion or an accounting of his purchases from the minibar last night, when he hadn't felt like going down to the Auden Bistro & Bar for his pre-bedtime drink and had made do with a mini-bottle of pinot grigio and a bag of cashews.

He was considering another purchase from the minibar right now, perhaps a bag of peanut M&M'S as an antidote to that too-healthy vegan salad he'd had for lunch. Laila would never let him eat M&M'S at home. And then the object caught his eye again, a manila envelope, blank and thin, definitely not anything official from the Ritz. He bent down to pick it up.

At first he didn't recognize the contents. The three stapled pages were photostats, black on white, not the black on legal-pad yellow that he recalled writing all those years ago. Even his own handwriting seemed unfamiliar. And then came the icy chill. *How in the world? Again?* Why was everyone trying to blackmail him? You'd think after two murders they would start to get the idea.

On the last page of the copy was a green Post-it note with a phone number, ten digits written in bold. Nothing more needed to be said.

His first thoughts went to Barbara Corns. She was the only other person with access to the penthouse. But it didn't feel like Barbara. Evan Corns, yes, but not meek and mild Barbara. Not without her husband to goad her on.

But if not Barbara, who? Maury sat down on the bed and stared at the pages between his hands. Could this new blackmailer be someone from the tour? Someone who had seen him and Billy together in Istanbul or maybe in India? That seemed far-fetched. It was a long way from connecting Billy and Maury to finding an old letter outlining their past life together. And yet . . .

And yet Amy Abel had a track record with this sort of thing, didn't she? Just last year she'd been responsible for the arrest of someone on one of her tours. Maury didn't recall the details, but like almost everyone, he knew how to get the answers to most of life's questions. He opened the laptop on his hotel desk and typed in three words: *Amy Abel crime.* That should do it. Within .34 seconds, the

Google results came up, including "Images for Amy Abel." Of the seven thumbnail images, two were from newspaper articles, one showing Amy arm in arm with a sharp-featured, good-looking man about her own age, with black, wavy hair and a dangerous smile. Maury double clicked on the image, and it expanded.

Maury couldn't be sure, but this looked like the man he'd seen getting into the elevator, the same man in the same uniform—he remembered now—he'd seen with Amy on the edge of Central Park a few days ago, when the Ritz doorman was hailing him a taxi. That was why he'd looked so familiar.

For his last confrontation with a blackmailer, Maury had left his Walther P22 in his hotel room, in his luggage, undisturbed since he'd packed it in Maui, just in case. He would not be making that mistake again.

Fanny studied her hand, then glanced at the six cards turned up in the dummy hand, then at the seven turned-down cards, then at the cell phone in the middle of the small round table, then back at her hand. "Two clubs," she announced to Marcus and her daughter, the two other players at the table.

"You don't mean that," sighed Amy.

"I think I know what I mean, dear. I've been playing bridge since before you were born—while you were being born, if I'm not mistaken. It was a long, very annoying labor."

"Then you must know that two clubs is an artificial bid. It means you're looking for a response from your partner. But you don't have a partner in

three-handed bridge, which is what we're playing.
Our partner's the dummy."

Fanny was unfazed. "Well, maybe I'm psychic and
I'm asking the cards to tell me what they are."

"You're not psychic."

"Maybe it's not artificial. I happen to have a lot of
clubs."

"You don't have a lot of clubs," said Amy, checking her own hand. "Not unless they doubled the
number in a deck."

Fanny released a theatrical groan and threw
down her hand. "This is ridiculous."

Amy had to agree. "Maury may not call today. He
may not call at all."

"If he calls, it'll be soon," said Marcus. "This isn't
the kind of thing you put off."

They had bought the prepaid, disposable phone
with cash at the Duane Reade on Seventh Avenue,
and according to their plan, Fanny would be the
one to pick it up when it rang. Amy certainly couldn't
answer it. And Maury Steinberg had heard Marcus's
voice, just a few words as they'd passed in the elevator. They'd decided to err on the side of caution. So
it would be Fanny.

"About the call . . ." Fanny picked up her cards
again and pretended to study them. "I still think
fifty thousand is too low."

"Mom." They'd been over this again and again.
"Fifty thousand is probably the most he can get out
of his bank on short notice."

"But he's not going to go to his bank, dear. He's
going to try to kill us—Marcus and you, to be precise. I was voted out. God forbid I should be around
for the fun part."

"The fact that you refer to a murder attempt as fun is the reason you were voted out," said Amy.

Fanny waved away her concern. "Yes, murder isn't fun. Got it. But the police will be there, so it's not like he's going to get a clear shot. Who knows if he even has a gun?"

"He's done pretty well without a gun," Marcus pointed out.

"No gun? Then why can't I come along?"

"Let's all assume he has a gun," Amy said, not wanting to lose any of her hard-won concessions. "And fifty thousand is the right number. Any more and he'll want to delay the payoff."

"Why would he delay, since he's not going to the bank in the first place?"

"Fanny, dear." Marcus leaned across the table and stared into her eyes. "If we ask for half a million and tell him the payoff is tomorrow, he'll smell a rat. He'll know that we know that no normal person can get that much cash in a day. He'll know that we know that he's going to double-cross us. And he'll know that we must be laying a trap for him. Fifty thousand is reasonable."

Fanny shrugged. "I think we can get more."

"Get more what? He's not bringing money." Amy used the same tone of voice she would use on a dense and stubborn two-year-old. "He's bringing a gun."

"I know he's not bringing money," said Fanny. "But it still feels like we're selling ourselves cheap. Especially since he killed two people."

"Yes, but he doesn't know that we know that he killed two people," Amy said in the same tone. "As far as he knows, it's just art forgery."

"Well, maybe we should let him know that we know about the murders. We can get him up to half a million, easy."

"Why do you care about the money he's not bringing?"

"It's not the money, dear. It's the principle. He should have to pay, even if it's just symbolic."

They could go on like this for hours, Amy knew. And, honestly, there were worse ways to while away a late afternoon. But then the phone in the middle of the table rang shrilly, like a cheap, cheery alarm clock, bringing them back to the moment.

Amy reached over to an old oak sideboard, retrieved a digital micro-recorder, and placed it next to the cell phone. A second later Fanny slid open the phone and pressed the speaker button.

"Hello, Mr. Steinberg." She tuned her voice half an octave lower, even though he'd never heard her voice before.

"Who is this?" Maury Steinberg's words filled the small wood-paneled dining room.

"That's not important," said Fanny in her best baritone, "which isn't to say I'm not important personally. I have a lot of friends who think very highly of me. But my identity isn't important right now, for the purpose of this conversation. That's what I meant to say. What *is* important is that I have something you want."

"I know that. How did you get it?"

"Again, not important. But it will cost you one hundred—" Amy had been trying to kick her mother under the table for the past ten seconds. Finally she connected. "Ow! Okay, fifty. Fifty thousand. You have to admit that's a bargain, considering what's in your little note. Normally, I would demand a hundred thousand, you understand. Even that's a bargain. . . . Ow!"

"You sent me a copy. How do I know it's the only one?"

"I don't want this getting out any more than you do, dear. That would defeat the whole purpose of blackmail. You'll get the handwritten original. No copies. I want this to happen quickly."

"So do I."

"Good. So I'm thinking, since it's late in the day . . . tomorrow? Tomorrow should give you the time to get the money together."

"I can get it tonight."

"Tonight?" Fanny threw the other two a worried glance. "Are you sure that gives you enough time? Fifty thousand?"

"My bank has already authorized the withdrawal. There's a branch staying open late, so I can get it in cash."

"Really? Which bank do you use, if you don't mind my asking? Mine closes at five p.m. sharp. I'd love to switch."

"Let's get this over with, all right?"

Amy and Marcus had picked out several possible places for the exchange, locations that seemed to have the right mix of private and public, places where Maury would feel safe to talk but that would still afford Lieutenant Rawlings and his men access and good sight lines. Fanny started with the first one on the list.

"Do you know the Irish Hunger Memorial? Down in Battery Park City? It's kind of a park. Not used much in the evenings."

"I can find it."

They had expected this to be an involved negotiation, with Maury rejecting certain locations or making suggestions of his own. But he'd accepted the first one on their list. Just like that.

"Nine p.m.?" Fanny asked.

"Nine p.m.," Maury agreed and hung up.

Fanny, Amy, and Marcus continued to sit around the little table, staring at the disposable phone and the playing cards, now scattered in meaningless clumps.

Marcus cleared his throat and said what everyone was thinking. "I think Maury found a gun."

CHAPTER 40

The Hunger Memorial was a perfect little Irish hillside re-created on a half-acre lot in Lower Manhattan. The mossy hill began at street level and meandered up a rocky path, through the roofless ruins of a stone cottage imported from Ireland, through a field of wildflowers and vines, also imported from Ireland, to a fieldstone wall that looked out over the thin edge of a city park and the Hudson River beyond. It had been built to honor those who died in the Irish Potato Famine of the 1840s, in the same way that another, much larger, more famous memorial a few blocks to the south honored those who died in the attacks of 9/11.

This was one of Amy's favorite spots in the city, one that felt remarkably isolated in the midst of all the office towers and apartment buildings. Even at the height of the summer, few tourists took the time to wander up the stony, weedy path—which was why the memorial had been at the top of Amy's list of blackmail spots.

Marcus stood beside her on the crest of the artifi-

cial hill, leaning on the stone wall three stories above
the occasional car passing by on the far end of Vesey
Street or the late evening jogger running through
the narrow riverside park. He watched as she shrugged
uncomfortably and scanned the tinted windows in
the offices facing them from three sides. "None of
those windows can open," he reassured her. "Plus, I
don't think Maury has a long-range rifle."

"Good to hear."

"You picked a great spot."

Even Lieutenant Rawlings had been impressed
by the site selection. If Maury Steinberg was intent
on killing his blackmailer, he would either have to
expose himself on the street or try to do it at close
quarters, which would mean entering the memorial
from the single entrance directly under the fake hill
and making his way up the path.

A chilly breeze blew in off the river. Amy felt
grateful for the Kevlar vest under her cotton blouse
and light cardigan. True, it was uncomfortably tight
and pinched under the arms, but it kept her
warm—and safe. Presumably safe.

"Thanks for being here."

"Hey." His crooked smile got her every time. "We
have a history of this."

It seemed odd, maybe a little sad, that they got
along better when they were facing the prospect of
a killer with a gun than they did in normal life. He
was supportive, adventurous, and instinctively knew
how to control her mother's crazier impulses. In
normal life, Peter Borg was a much better fit—pre-
dictable, honest, less exciting, but also less infuriating.
And most of life, she had to admit, was the normal
part. You couldn't always count on a murder popping up just to rescue your love life.

The phone in her left pocket startled her back to reality. It wasn't the throwaway but her regular phone, which she should have turned off but had forgotten to. Amy checked the display, scrunched her face into a frown, and pressed IGNORE.

"If that's Fanny, you should pick up."

"It was Peter."

"Oh." Marcus let the dead air between them grow. By the time Amy had counted to eleven . . . "How are the negotiations going? Does he still want to merge?"

"I haven't had much time to think about it, to be honest."

"You should watch out for him."

"Why? Because he wants to work with me and make my business a success?"

"The way you phrased it, I don't think that's a serious question."

It was Amy's turn to let the dead air grow. At the end of twenty seconds, she checked her phone again. "Maury's late." It was 9:17 p.m.

"What if he doesn't show?"

"He's got to show. Or do something. Even if he just walks by and tries to see who we are, Rawlings and his men will spot him."

"But what if he doesn't?" asked Marcus. "Worst-case scenario."

"Okay, let's say he somehow spotted us without us spotting him. Or he saw the cops and ran. We still have his confession."

Amy had taken a copy of the confession to Lieutenant Rawlings at One Police Plaza at approximately the same time that Marcus had slipped the other copy under Maury's door at the Ritz-Carlton. The lieutenant had demanded to see the original, but Amy had refused. It was the only leverage she had. "It's someplace safe," she'd assured him.

"That's a criminal confession you're withholding, Ms. Abel."

"I'm not withholding. You have a copy in your hands."

"That's not the same, and you know it."

"I know." She would deliver the original, she explained, after the lieutenant came through with a police presence at her proposed blackmail exchange. Rawlings was suitably outraged.

"Do you honestly think you can plan a police operation and just have me go along with it? First, you're not an officer. You're not trained."

"You can say it was your idea. Plenty of civilians cooperate with the police in operations like this. I know that for a fact."

"And if it goes south? What then? I would be in a mess of trouble, endangering a civilian, not following protocol. Not informing my superiors, which I couldn't do, because they would never approve in a million years. Meanwhile, you'd probably just be dead."

"But if it works . . . then you'd have a killer behind bars, in a case your superiors say was an accident. Don't you want that?"

Rawlings looked tempted. "It's a very long shot, Ms. Abel."

"Can you think of any other way?" she asked, trying to sound braver than she felt. "The man committed two murders. All this note does is connect him to art fraud."

"So you want to goad him into a murder attempt?"

"Basically, yes," she said, sounding braver than she felt. "Although you're making it sound scary."

"It is scary, Ms. Abel."

"Look, I'm not a district attorney, but if Maury shows himself willing to kill, it might be enough to change their minds about Joy Archer's death."

Amy had expected the lieutenant to put up more of a fight. But she could see what was going through his mind as he continued to shake his head and think it out. If he stuck to protocol, the note would be turned over to a white-collar unit, and he would have nothing. But if he bent the rules a little . . . if he went out on a limb . . . if he could finagle some equipment and manpower for an hour or two . . . then he would be making front-page headlines not only in New York but also on the subcontinent of India.

"Remember the last time you didn't listen to me," she reminded him.

Rawlings continued to shake his head, only the shakes were getting smaller. Toward the end, some of them began to take on a vertical aspect.

"The lieutenant's going to be furious," said Marcus, standing by the Irish wall, squirming in his own Kevlar. "If Maury doesn't show? After all this?"

It was now 9:19. "If you were Maury, what would you do? You'd have to do something."

"I'm not worried about him," said Marcus. "I'm worried about Rawlings. What's he got? Five plain-clothes officers? Three on the street, one in the park, one at the entrance? Plus him?"

"We played him the audio. It was his decision."

"And what if Steinberg is already on his way back to Hawaii?"

"So, we gave it a shot. What's the lieutenant going to do?"

"Technically, we did withhold evidence. Isn't there something called 'interfering in an ongoing investigation'?"

Amy snorted. "Is that a real charge?"

"This is the guy who threw your mom and me in jail for impersonating lawyers."

"You're aware that I can hear you, right?" crackled an unamused voice embedded in each of their left ears.

The clock on Fanny's old stove clicked to 9:10. She sat facing it, a cup of coffee warming her hands, then turned her focus to the beige phone hanging on the wall. Amy had said she would call the second Maury was in custody, but that should have happened ten minutes ago. Weren't blackmail victims always punctual when they came to a drop-off? You'd think they would be.

She had put on an old Henry Mancini CD, thinking the music might calm her down. This was some collection of his old movie themes—"Moon River," "The Pink Panther Theme," "Charade." She hadn't listened to it in years, not since Stan's death. Her late husband had hated Henry Mancini, had sighed deeply every time she put the CD on the stereo, which was probably why she didn't play it anymore. What would be the point? The CD had just finished the final track, "Two for the Road," replacing the sea of soaring violins with an ocean of silence, wave after wave of silence.

Fanny didn't like a quiet house. She wondered

what she would do when Amy and Marcus finally got married and moved out, or just moved in together somewhere else, which was more likely these days. She loved the muffled sound of life in the house's upper half. Perhaps she could rent it out, she mused, perhaps to some young, single career woman who might need some judicious guidance in her life. And then she remembered. *Oh, yes. Good.* The bank would foreclose on the house soon enough, so she wouldn't have to worry about any of that.

She was only a few minutes into her musings when she heard the noises from upstairs. A muffled bump every now and then, like someone trying unsuccessfully to be quiet. For how long had that been going on? Had Amy come home without dropping by? Without calling, as she had promised to do? Here she was, sitting alone in the dark, worrying her heart out and staring at the clock—9:13—while her daughter didn't have the simple decency . . . Fanny headed for the door.

Well, Miss Amy Josephine Abel, you are about to get a piece of my mind.

Eight thirty-two p.m.

Maury Steinberg stood in the shadows, half hidden by the broad trunk of a ginkgo, and watched from across the street as Amy and her concierge boyfriend walked to the end of Barrow Street and disappeared around the corner.

He waited another ten minutes, wandering up and down the nearly deserted block, just in case they might have forgotten something and turned back. He was in no hurry. It wasn't a bad evening for this time of year, perhaps a little breezy, and he figured he had plenty of time. Their appointment wasn't until nine. And they would probably wait a good half hour before giving up and heading home.

From the moment he'd seen the search results for "Amy Abel crime," Maury knew he had options. It couldn't have been a coincidence, seeing Amy's boyfriend just before finding the blackmail note shoved under his door. And the more he read the online articles—the *New York Times*, the *Daily News*, a feature in *New York* magazine—the more it made sense.

This couldn't be a real extortion attempt. For one thing, Amy didn't seem greedy, not like his old partner or MacGregor's maid. But she and her boyfriend did have a history of playing amateur detectives. From what Maury could tell, the police hadn't been involved in their previous escapade, not until the end at least. The fact that the blackmail amount was pitifully low served to confirm his suspicion. Amy and Marcus would be showing up at the meeting point with a video camera or a voice recorder, trying to force him to incriminate himself. The one thing they would not be showing up with, he knew, was the actual note. That damned note.

Maury remained in the shadows while a middle-aged couple loudly argued their way down the block. The woman hated it, she said, when he drank too much at cocktail parties. Why did he always do that? He drank, he said, only because she refused to leave after two hours, which was the time limit they'd agreed on beforehand. What was he supposed to do? They were her boring friends. Maury realized that he didn't have all the facts, but still he sided with the husband.

The couple talked their way up the steps to their

brownstone and let themselves in. Maury waited an extra two minutes, then crossed the street to Amy's front door. At some point during the tour, she had described her beloved block of Barrow Street, with the rare communal garden in the center. It hadn't been hard to find.

As with many New York town houses, the door at the top of the stoop was unlocked. Inside the small vestibule, Maury found a pair of mailboxes embedded in a wall of red brick, a small mirror gracing the opposite wall, and two buzzers right next to the inner door. The lower buzzer had no name tag, as if everyone should automatically know whoever it was who lived here. The upper buzzer's label said A. ABEL. There seemed to be no cameras, which was just what he was hoping for. From somewhere behind the mailboxes came the faint strains of "Moon River" being sung by a wistful Audrey Hepburn. Laila had always loved that song.

Maury took a pair of plastic gloves from one of his jacket pockets and put them on. Next out were a carbon steel chisel and a small ball-peen hammer, both newly purchased at a Village hardware store for cash. After checking one final time for anyone nearby—inside the door and out—he began to slowly, quietly attack the section of ancient wood between the doorknob and the doorjamb.

CHAPTER 41

The lock on the third-floor door proved to be more problematic than the lock on the front door. Maury spent quite a few minutes—at least two full Henry Mancinis by his calculation—on his knees, quietly chiseling one flake at a time, before the bolt by the lock mechanism was exposed enough. Then it was simply a matter of forcing the small chisel into place and easing back the bolt. It was the first time he'd ever done anything like this, and he was proud of himself.

By the time he was ten minutes into his search, both his pride and his confidence had fallen. That damned letter, those haunting three pages torn from a yellow legal pad, was nowhere. He'd emptied the file cabinet, taken every book off the bookshelves, and rifled the pages. Amy's bedroom had been fairly neat when he walked in. Now it was strewn over with clothes thrown angrily from the drawers and the closet. The only things he had left in place were the two drawers full of eyeglasses, dozens of pairs. Maury considered it a professional courtesy, respect for the woman's collection. Two of the frames, he noted, were classic Ellis pieces, designed by his wife.

Had he been wrong? he wondered. Where else could she have hidden it? Only at the edges of his mind did he notice the end of Henry Mancini and the lapse of the house into silence. For the second time, he made the trip from the top floor down to the third, and he was standing by the door in the main stairwell when he heard the determined pattern of footfalls coming up toward him.

"Amy Josephine Abel!"

Maury put aside his chisel and reached for his Walther P22.

The woman who arrived on the landing was short and sturdy and energetic, with hair the color of old rust. Her pink slippers and lack of a jacket told him that she was the nameless downstairs neighbor. At probably the same moment, the wood shavings by the door frame and the handgun informed her that he was up to no good.

"Who are you?" she said. There was something about her attitude. She already knew who he was. But how? There was also something about her voice.

"Who are you?" he asked.

"This is my house, Mr. Breaking and Entering. But if you turn around and leave right now, I won't call the police."

"You're the woman on the phone," he guessed and saw from her startled reaction that he was right.

She shrugged. "I'm Amy's mother, Mr. Steinberg. I'm sure Amy's mentioned me."

"She hasn't."

Her head tilted quizzically. "Are you sure? It's

hard to believe she wouldn't mention her own mother. We're very close."

"Come inside." Maury stepped back and waved the P22 inward, like an invitation. The woman's eyes flitted from the gun to the mess of books and papers and the shredded pillows from the sofa. "Where is it?" he demanded. "Where's the letter?"

"What letter?"

"The letter you were blackmailing me about on the phone."

"Oh, that letter. I'm sure I have no idea."

"I think you do."

"I don't. And I'm not the woman on the phone. Her voice was much lower." And she demonstrated. "Hello, Mr. Steinberg. Like that," she growled. "Not like my voice at all."

Maury couldn't decide if the woman was really so dense or if this was some ploy. "Give me the letter, or you're dead," he said, leveling the P22 straight at her heart. "I mean it."

"I know you do," the woman agreed. "Amy said you had a gun. We were debating that just this afternoon. My theory was that since you killed twice before without using a gun, you might not. Looks like the joke's on me." *Oops!* She immediately bit her lower lip. "I wasn't supposed to know that, was I?"

"You know?"

"What do I know?" Her attitude was suddenly all innocence.

"About India. About the other one."

"You mean the maid's suicide?"

Maury's mind was swimming. They knew. It wasn't just about the forgeries anymore. He shook his head, trying to clear it, and when he focused again, she was gone, tripping down the stairs at full speed.

Fanny was aware of her effect on people, even on relatives, who were used to her and should know better, the disoriented, almost glazed look that gathered in their eyes when she hit her rhythm, the amount of energy it took to try to follow her arcane logic. She'd been anticipating another minute or two of hard-fought conversation with Maury Steinberg. But when the man's pupils began to twitch from behind the frames of his thin tortoiseshell glasses, she knew she had to take her chance.

From nearly forty years of taking these stairs, she knew them perfectly, every uneven step. Without looking back, she tore down from the third floor to the second, then around the safety of the bend and down one more flight.

In a few seconds she would be facing another decision—out the front door to Barrow Street, into her own half of the house, or back into the communal garden? The first held the promise of freedom, but the threat of being in the open and being shot from a distance. The second held the reassurance of home and a dozen hiding places, but also the terror of being cornered, with no way out. The third seemed to be a combination. The hollowed-out block was large but familiar, with nooks everywhere. And it was semipublic, with a dozen curious neighbors attuned to every sound, looking out through their curtains, willing to open their back doors perhaps to give her sanctuary from a killer with a gun.

Her mind immediately went to Douglas What's-

His-Name, across the garden and down two houses. He was brand new to the block but as nosy as the Westons, the previous owners, who had moved away last year in order to be closer to their children in California.

Lieutenant Rawlings had arrived at the Irish Hunger Memorial with the rest of his team in two unmarked vans. He left on foot with Amy and Marcus after they handed back the vests and the earpieces and the microphones. It was a mostly silent process, with a female officer packing the equipment into the empty baby carriage she'd been pushing around for the last half hour. They signed again, acknowledging the return of the items, then joined the lieutenant on Vesey Street. The three of them walked east through the corridor of darkened office towers toward West Street.

All three kept silent until after they rounded the corner and saw the taxi stand. A single cab stood idling, its hood light illuminated.

"Why didn't he show?" Amy asked, her inflection making it sound like an apology. She'd been fighting the urge to apologize ever since Rawlings had made the call to "scrub the action." The only thing stopping her had been the professional way the officers had dealt with it, like it was just part of their job. Sometimes things worked; sometimes they didn't.

"He's probably on the run," said the lieutenant.

"Then we have to stop him," insisted Amy. "Alert the airports. Put a tag on his credit cards, or whatever you call it."

"Did it five minutes ago." Rawlings shook his head.

"I would have done it earlier, but that would have en-
tailed telling my captain. Instead, I got talked into a
sting operation with a couple of civilians."

"Oh. So you told your captain five minutes ago? I
take it from your tone he wasn't happy."

"He wasn't."

"But it was worth it," said Amy. Again making it
sound like an apology. "We had to give it a shot."

"I'm going to need the original of that letter,"
said Rawlings.

"Absolutely," said Marcus, raising his hand to hail
the cab. "We can get it for you right now."

The homicide detective shrugged. "Morning's
good enough. Unlike us, the fraud division rarely
works overtime."

"I'm sorry." There. She finally said it. "I pres-
sured you into this, and it was all for nothing."

"I'll handle my captain." Lieutenant Rory Rawlings displayed a wistful version of his midwestern
smile, and suddenly he looked older, perhaps no
older than his actual age, but no longer the arro-
gant teenage waiter. "There'll be some questions
about manpower and equipment. I can't hide that.
But it just reminds me why I got into this business.
You were right about not wanting him to get away
with murder."

"Thanks for saying that," said Amy. But what she
was thinking was, *Aw, that's not fair. Don't make me like
you. It was hard enough five minutes ago, when I thought
you were a total jerk.*

"You guys have a good night," said the lieutenant
and opened up the cab door for them, just to rub it
in. And when he closed the door, he didn't slam it.

Amy gave the driver the Barrow Street address
and then, for the third time, dialed her mother's

number. "No answer," she said, hanging up before it could go to voice mail.

"You tried her cell?" asked Marcus.

"Cell and house." And she tried the cell phone again, just to make sure.

By the time the yellow cab stopped in front of her stoop, Amy had talked herself into a comforting explanation. Fanny was upset because she hadn't called precisely at 9:01, or whatever time her unreasonable mother thought reasonable. In retaliation, she wanted to make Amy worry the same way. Well, Amy wasn't about to fall for it, even though she had a feeling in the pit of her stomach that there was no such strategy and that something was actually wrong.

While Marcus paid the driver, Amy made her way up the stairs. Her first glimpse through the glass of the door into the vestibule made her stop, frozen in place with her hand on the knob. "Marcus?" The word came out as a choked whisper.

Only after he had joined her did she feel brave enough to open the door and step inside. Wordlessly, they bent down to examine the chiseled-out section of doorjamb and the fresh chips of mangled wood on the tattered welcome mat.

Just inside the hall, they saw the open door leading into Fanny's living room. Amy wanted to call out, but Marcus grabbed her elbow with one hand and put his other to his lips. Of course. Odds were that if Fanny was around to answer her, she wouldn't be alone.

The two of them did not split up but went from room to room as quietly as possible, then up the interior stairs to the next floor, then out to the landing and up again. Amy took small comfort in the fact that there'd been nothing unusual in her mother's half, no blood or signs of a struggle. All that comfort vanished when she saw the condition of her own door and, beyond the crippled door, the chaotic mess that was her own half. Amy felt like screaming. But she forced herself to stay silent as they tiptoed throughout the third floor, then up to the fourth.

Her bedroom was in the same decorative state as her living room and kitchen—furniture overturned, books scattered, pillows shredded, and drawers torn out. Amy didn't realize she had so many drawers. Her greenhouse office at the rear of the house was in even worse condition, with every folder from her file cabinet opened, the contents scattered across the floor like an uneven rug. She was just making her way into the bathroom when her phone rang. It was her phone, not the throwaway, and the name on the display was Mom.

It was not Mom.

"Amy, hello."

"Who is this?" She knew, obviously. But it took her a few seconds to process what he must know now and what he knew that she knew.

"Let's keep it simple," advised the voice, "just in case you're preserving this for posterity." He spoke with a calm, casual smugness that made Amy want to reach through the phone and strangle him.

"I'm not recording it."

"Forgive me if I'm unconvinced. I would like my letter back now, the one you stole from my apartment."

Despite her predicament, Amy couldn't help feeling a little pride. *Good.* He hadn't found it.

"Do you have the fifty thousand?" asked Amy, playing along with the evening's premise.

"I have something even better," said Maury. "A mutual acquaintance. Would you like to speak to her? Just for a second."

There were some muffled noises on the other end, then softly . . . "Hello, dear. This is your mother speaking." Fanny had feigned fear on many occasions: seeing her daughter go into the pool right after a meal, backseat driving as Amy tried to merge onto the Henry Hudson without slowing down. But this was the first time Amy had heard actual fear in Fanny's voice. It was perhaps the most unsettling moment of the night.

"Mom, are you all right?"

"He has that gun we were wondering about, just for your information."

"That's enough." It was Maury, back on the line. "Is your concierge friend with you? Marcus? Yes, of course he is. I need you to listen carefully to what I have to say."

Amy listened carefully. After Maury hung up, she went into her bathroom. Could it still be here? She reached down into her wicker wastebasket, past a thick layer of balled-up tissues, and pulled out the three folded pages from the yellow pad. This had always been the perfect hiding place for her. The combination of disposable (who would hide something in a wastebasket?) and disgusting (who would reach into a moist bathroom wastebasket?) had preserved many a girlhood secret from her mother's prying eyes.

CHAPTER 42

The three yellow pages, a Zippo lighter confiscated from Fanny in a failed effort to keep her from smoking, her smartphone, a flashlight, and Marcus. In accordance with Maury Steinberg's instructions, Amy brought all of these down with her to the picturesquely disused fountain in the center of the garden. It was after ten when they put on their jackets and stepped out the rear door. For some reason, Amy took the precaution of locking it behind her, both the lock and the bolt.

For being technically part of the city that doesn't sleep, the Abels' little block of New York got to bed fairly early, at least tonight. There was no one else in the communal area, and the majority of the windows facing out onto it were dark. Here and there were just a few illuminated rectangles, lit by the flicker of TVs or the soft, steady glow of reading lamps, all of them behind curtains or blinds.

"Why here?" asked Marcus as they checked once again for any movement among the bushes and trees.

"What?" Amy was distracted, almost catatonic, unable to even process his simple question. She almost always froze at moments like this, not the best trait for a woman who kept getting herself involved in murder.

"Why here?" Marcus repeated. "Is he in one of the houses? Looking out a window?"

Amy thought for a moment, then pivoted in a slow circle, taking in the shadowy expanse of brick walls and dark glass. "That makes sense."

"Should we call Rawlings? His men can surround the block."

"And have my mother be a hostage in the middle of a shoot-out? I don't think so."

"It won't come to that. Maury's not the type."

Before Amy could reply, her phone rang. This time it didn't play its usual snatch of Mozart. It played a chirpy conga beat, the screen lighting up in a sky blue. There was a *woosh*, a *pop*, and a circle in the middle of the screen with an image of Fanny's smiling face, lifted from the woman's Facebook page. Amy was being Skyped.

She had installed the video app a month ago on both their phones, hoping they'd get in the habit of speaking face-to-face during Paisley MacGregor's worldwide wake. But Fanny had never been enthusiastic about the video phone and had feigned ignorance of how to answer a call, even though it was no more complicated than answering her phone.

"Mom?" Amy asked the screen so tentatively.

The image was not Fanny's, but Maury's, staring back at her through expensive frames, with his thin face and short gray hair and unnerving scowl. "I want to see Marcus."

Amy looked to Marcus, who was busy texting on his own phone. *What the hell?* But she was in no position to quibble. "Why do you want to see Marcus?" she vamped, speaking slowly, trying to look calm for the camera. Marcus sped up his texting.

"Don't argue. Do it."

She didn't answer but held the phone at arm's length. She spun it around the garden, and finally, when she aligned it to include Marcus, his phone was securely back in his pocket.

"Good," said Maury. "I need to keep track of you both."

Maury's face took up most of the screen, but Amy scanned the room behind him, searching for anything, any clue to his whereabouts. The walls were white and well lit, as if from an unshaded overhead bulb. She glanced up from her phone and could see no brightly lit windows facing the garden. "I want to talk to my mother."

Maury considered the request. A second later the phone jerked away, then refocused on a close-up of Fanny, a white gag, perhaps torn from a bedsheet, tied through her open mouth and around the back of her head. Her eyes were bright with fear, or with anger. It was hard to tell. "Sorry, Amy. But your mother can be quite the chatterbox."

"Don't hurt her," said Marcus.

"I won't, if we do this quickly. Marcus, hold the phone. Amy, show me the pages. Up close. I'll know if they're the originals."

"Release her first," said Marcus, trying to sound as if he was the one in control.

"Harming Mrs. Abel would do me no good—if I get what I want."

The process would be a simple one, he explained. Marcus would focus the phone and the flashlight, making use of both hands. Amy would hold the lighter and the letter, again using two hands, poising them over the dry basin of the stone fountain. After Maury was satisfied that this was his handwritten confession, Amy would light it up with the Zippo, and all three of them would watch his problems go up in smoke.

Amy had to cock the Zippo three times before she had fire. But the pages caught quickly and evenly, with Amy lighting them on two corners, then dropping them into the stone basin. Marcus seemed to take forever, several seconds at least, to readjust the phone and the flashlight. Spiderlike lines of black ink turned gray through the orange flames. The paper crinkled into black, and the wisps of smoke reminded Amy of crisp burning leaves. It was almost mesmerizing.

"Excellent," said Maury after the last little edge turned to ash. "Thank you." And then another quick blast of tropical bongos signaled the end of the call.

"Maury? No. Don't hang up."

Amy turned to the phone. But instead of it being in Marcus's right hand, with the flashlight in his left, the phone was balanced horizontally, precariously, on the rim of the fountain. The flashlight was balanced on its side on the same rim. And Marcus—*Damn you, Marcus!*—was hunched over and tiptoeing away, vanishing from view around a row of trimmed boxwoods. "Marcus?" she hissed. "Marcus?"

Almost as soon as the Skype call began, he had noticed it. Out of the corner of one eye, Marcus had seen it go on, a naked ceiling light flashing from the narrow ventilation window in one of the basements across the garden from the Barrow Street side. Three slowish beats, on and off, then three even slower ones, none of them timed particularly well. But he had managed to get the message.

When the time came to adjust, to visually follow the burning pages into the fountain, Marcus tried his Hail Mary shot. Miraculously, the phone kept its balance on the rim, and so did the flashlight. As he sneaked off toward the flashing light, he could hear Amy calling his name, but he didn't stop. He didn't have the time.

The brick row house was one of the more modest ones, probably worth only a few million in the current market. The door to the small kitchen was hanging open, but no one was in view. The basement window was a few yards to the left of the door, and Marcus did his best not to approach it directly. Instead, he knelt on the patio's cold slate tile and moved his head slowly into view.

The space was a typical city basement—steep wooden stairs, old cardboard boxes piled in a corner, a water heater with foam insulation, and water pipes that trailed overhead and up the walls. But wrapped around a trio of vertical pipes were long strips of white bedsheets, holding in place a tall, thin middle-aged man, with more bedsheets around his body and across his mouth. He was extended full length, his head nestled awkwardly on one of the lower stairs, his torso securely bound to the pipes but twisted, his left leg on the floor, half flexed, pushing him up, while his shoeless right foot attacked the light switch on the wall. He must have been working on this for some time, Marcus thought with admiration. As soon as he saw Marcus through the window, he stopped.

Their eyes met, and Marcus concentrated on the man's craggy face. Several expressions played over the sunken eyes, one after the other—relief, exhaustion, then suddenly a renewed tension, perhaps fear. Did he assume Marcus was another bad guy? Was that it? Maury's unseen partner in crime, catching him trying to signal for help? Or was he perhaps fearful for Marcus? Was Maury still lurking nearby? And where the hell was Fanny?

Marcus took a deep breath. He had a choice to make. He could return to Amy and the fountain and work out a sensible plan. Perhaps Maury had already let Fanny go. Or Marcus could rush inside now, when every moment might make a difference, even though there might be a desperate man still in there with his hostages and his gun.

It wasn't really a choice.

CHAPTER 43

At nearly the same moment, Amy was facing nearly the same choice. Should she stay frozen in place, following Maury's orders, hoping for Marcus to return? That was her usual way of dealing with danger. Marcus had been texting someone. Was it the police? Should she just wait for things to work out? Or should she force herself to do . . . she didn't know what, but something to help get her mother, wherever she was, back to safety, wherever that was?

Just like Marcus, she knew it wasn't really a choice.

She took her first steps, baby steps, gaining confidence with every extra foot away from the fountain. She didn't dare call out his name, but Marcus had gone in this direction. There must have been a reason. He'd seen something or heard something. Her hearing and eyesight were as good as his, at least with her glasses on. If he could notice a clue, so could she. She took a deep breath now and tried to focus.

The night air was still. The wind that had gusted off the river an hour before was gone. The usual staccato blare of taxis from Hudson Street might have distracted a non–New Yorker, but to her ear they were barely audible, like soft city crickets. Amy began to take the meandering path from the Grove Street side around to the Bleecker side. This backyard park was her childhood playground, a safe haven where she'd played cops and robbers with Billy and Juan and Heather from across the way. Now she was tracking down a real killer in the same shadowy darkness, listening for any soft footfall or . . .

She actually saw Maury, at least a glimpse of him, before she heard him.

There were two iron gates that opened into the garden, one on the Barrow side, one on the Grove side, each eight feet tall, with ornamental spikes on top. They'd been designed to give entry to the gardeners and the maintenance crew. Each was at the end of a narrow alley between two of the row houses. Amy was still on the path, just passing the alley on her own street, when her eye caught a movement, a silhouette at the alley's end, flickering in the light of a streetlamp. She stopped in her tracks.

The silhouette was facing the iron bars and the street beyond, bent over at the waist. The wise thing for Amy would have been to stay put, maybe take a secluded position behind one of the boxwoods, and wait it out. No way could anyone get in or out without the four-digit combination. Either Marcus or the police would arrive soon and take control. But the thought of a killer invading the safety of her garden, of Fanny in that room with the gag in her mouth . . . It was enough to lead her to the entrance of the dark alley.

"Where is she?" Amy kept her voice low. No reason to disturb the neighbors. Mrs. Montague, the home owner on the left, was a particularly light sleeper. "I kept my part of the bargain, Maury. Where's my mother?"

The figure straightened and turned. Maury saw her and let out a long, rueful chuckle, which took her by surprise. "I've had the damnedest time. Your house is locked. His front door is locked—on the inside, no less. I thought this would be easier."

"Whose front door? Is Fanny with someone? Is she safe?"

Maury ignored the questions. "Be a sweetheart and tell me the combination." His silhouette adjusted its right shoulder, taking the handgun from a jacket pocket and leveling it in her direction. "Better yet, come here. Unlock it for me."

Amy stood her ground. "The police are on their way. There's no way out." When Maury didn't respond, she continued, her voice filling the narrow alley. "Too many people know. They have a copy of the note."

The silhouette seemed thrown, but for only a second. "A copy? So what? Any good defense attorney—"

"Too late, Maury. You kidnapped my mother. That's kidnapping."

The five-second pause that followed took forever. "So what?" he finally said. "It's my word against yours."

Amy couldn't believe his gall. "And my mother's word. You didn't shoot her. I would have heard. The whole block would have heard." *Please let this be true*, she silently begged.

"Maybe I should have," he replied with a shoulder shrug, and Amy's heart skipped a beat. *Still alive.* "Unlock the gate, and I'll tell you where she is."

"Why should I trust you? Give up before it gets worse."

"Worse? I don't see how. Goddamn MacGregor. 'Confession is good,'" he chirped in a prim, thin voice. "'No harm writing it down, Mr. S. For your own peace of mind.' Well, guess what, MacGregor? There was harm."

"There's a statute of limitations on art fraud," Amy said, trying to sound sincere. "If you give yourself up . . ."

"Who are you kidding? You know about the murders. Your mother said . . ."

"My mother says a lot of things."

Maury's groan reverberated off the walls. "You meddling bitch. You knew about the letter from the beginning. And everything else. I don't know how you knew, but . . ."

"I don't mean to meddle," Amy apologized. Why was she apologizing? "I honestly don't. Things just happen."

"Luckily, I took out cash. Plus, I have accounts from the old days. All I need is to get out of this damn yard." He tossed his head back against the bars, banging them in frustration.

"What about Laila? What about your life?"

"I won't have a life unless I get out of this yard."

"You have to give yourself up."

The gunshot took her by surprise, loud as a cannon, ricocheting off the bricks in two bright sparks. Amy fell to her knees, her ears ringing, her heart racing. "Nine-two-eight-seven. Nine-two-eight-seven."

She couldn't hear a thing she was saying—no, shouting. "Nine-two-eight-seven."

Maury might have said something in reply. Or not. His silhouette turned to the gate and bent again at the waist.

If Amy had been braver or more reckless or hadn't been battling instant deafness and a heart rate of two hundred beats, she might have pounced to her feet and done something, like a superhero. She might have run the alley, the length of a house, and propelled herself onto Maury's back, slamming him into the gate and knocking him unconscious. Instead, she stayed on her knees and watched as the gate opened. Only then did she get up and follow him through the tunnel-like alley.

By the time Amy emerged onto Barrow, Maury was nearly to the corner of Houston, turning left. When Amy turned the corner onto Houston, she saw him in the middle of the block, standing in the bus lane, hand raised to hail a taxi. He looked perfectly normal and relaxed now, not even bothering to look behind him.

Amy didn't know what she was prepared to do. The gun was in his jacket, she supposed. She could tackle him right there. Or she could shout to the trickle of passersby, "Stop that man! He's a killer!" But would anyone pay attention? How about just, "Stop that man!" Or would they pay too much attention? Would Maury panic and pull out the gun? He was irrational enough. Would she be responsible for more people getting killed?

A taxi arrived in the next wave of traffic, its sign lighting up as it slowed and pulled past Maury to

the corner of Barrow. He followed it back and
stopped for just a second as he noticed Amy, twenty
feet away, staring at him. Their eyes locked, and
precious seconds ticked away.

The passenger exiting the cab was in an incredible hurry. The youngish man paid the driver, left
the door open, and began heading toward the one-
way neck of Barrow Street. Maury grabbed the cab
door and was just stepping in when Amy finally
mustered up the courage.

"Stop him! Before he gets away!" She was shouting at the passenger, no one else. "He's got a gun!"

The youngish man skidded to a halt, looked
down Barrow Street, then back at Amy, then back at
the cab, just about to pull off. He seemed to understand exactly what Amy had meant. Without even
checking to see who had taken his place in the
backseat, he raced to the front of the taxi, blocking
its path, and lowered his palm down onto the hood
with a thud.

The taxi driver slammed on his brakes, honked
loud and long, and let out a string of curses in some
unknowable language. He only stopped cursing
when the passenger reached under his arm and
pulled out a no-nonsense revolver. Taking a wide
stance, the man established his presence, then stepped
slowly over to the passenger side of the cab and
eased open the door.

"Thank you." Amy lifted both hands to her heart
and took a deep breath.

A few seconds more and Maury Steinberg would
have escaped, vanishing into the throngs of New
York and the safety of his hidden bank accounts.

But just like that and it was over. She had done it. She'd finally taken a risk, and the risk had paid off. She allowed herself to feel proud, but not too proud.

She couldn't allow herself to feel too proud—since the gun-toting passenger just happened to be Lieutenant Rory Rawlings.

CHAPTER 44

*B*eing kidnapped anywhere in the world is no fun. TrippyGirl should know. So far, in the history of this humble blog, I've been kidnapped in Dubai and Cleveland and shanghaied in Shanghai. Given all that, I guess I shouldn't have been surprised when my Mongolian veterinarian heartthrob dropped me off in the capital city of Ulaanbaatar, and within hours, I once again found myself being kidnapped.

It all started yesterday, after Arban had dropped me off at my hotel. I had grown quite fond of Arban during our few days together—and even fonder of Elvis, the baby yak that I had helped him deliver and give a name to. In my funk of sudden loneliness, I went out to a bar that night and got myself a little tipsy—sick on fermented mare's milk. When I finally stumbled back to my hotel, I was surprised to find a middle-aged, gray-haired burglar with gorgeous eyeglasses ransacking my five-star suite.

The saga devolved from there, until yours truly escaped and was forced to run across the hotel court-

yard and take refuge with an Asian businessman named Douglas, whose door just happened to be unlocked and who grew to be quite upset by what unfolded in the next hour or so. It all ended—happily, I'm glad to say—when my sexy travel companion Mark broke in and cut us free from the four-hundred-count percale sheets that Douglas and I had been forced to cut up and use to tie each other up with. Woo, what a bunch of information and run-on sentences! So let me start at the beginning. Again.

Fanny glanced up from the laptop on her kitchen table and sighed, not at all pleased with the flow of her latest piece of fiction/nonfiction. "I feel like a prisoner of this thing," she announced. "Two blogs a week and everybody wants more. And I keep getting demands to do videos, which is not going to happen."

"Videos would be hard," Amy agreed.

From over the top of her reading glasses, Fanny shot her daughter a bemused grin. Amy returned the grin and held a gaze directly into her mother's eyes for a few seconds longer than seemed comfortable, at least for Fanny. "What? Do I have something in my teeth?"

"No. I'm just glad you're alive. Can't I be glad you're alive?"

"And I'm glad you're glad, dear. But you don't have to make such a fuss. He was never going to kill me."

"Well, I didn't know that. You had me worried sick."

Fanny turned from Amy's uncomfortable stare to the garden window just in time to see her neighbor Douglas walking by on the path, puffing on an e-cigarette and scowling in the direction of her kitchen. "I think he blames me, like it's my fault. I already reimbursed him for the sheets. What more does the man want?"

"I believe he wants us to move. To another state."

"Well, that's not going to happen."

"It just might," said Amy. She was at the other end of the kitchen table, combing through a raft of overdue invoices, bank statements, and threatening-looking "final notices" laid out in front of her. She'd barely gotten through a third of her mother's pile of neglected mail. If people were serious about final notices, she wondered, why did they always send out a dozen of them?

"Is it that bad?" asked Fanny, leaning across and looking suitably contrite.

Amy sipped her lukewarm coffee, wondering if it was time to put on another pot. "Not if we sell to Peter. He'll take over our debts and our lease. And with his cash, we can arrange to consolidate our home mortgage and our second mortgage. I'm just sorry you had to go through all of this alone, without telling me." There was a note of reprimand in her voice.

"Oh, it wasn't hard, dear. I just ignored it. And your little murders helped keep my mind off it."

Amy knew what she meant. As long as she'd had some life-and-death drama to be involved in, she had also put their financial woes out of sight, out of mind. "It'll all work out," she said without mustering much enthusiasm.

"But we'll just be part of Peter's company, without even the name Abel. You don't suppose you can find another investor, dear? Someone who can give us money and leave us alone? That would be preferable."

Amy scrunched her mouth, forming almost a pout. "We're not even going to find anyone to buy our assets, especially not the kind of deal Peter's offering. I don't know why he's doing it."

"You don't?" Fanny regarded her with a skeptical tilt of the head.

"Okay, maybe I do."

Amy was grateful when this suddenly uncomfortable conversation was interrupted by the ringing buzz of the new doorbell. "It's the security guy," Fanny guessed. She pushed herself up to go answer the intercom by the door. "He's been tinkering and testing it all morning." She pressed a button and spoke into the speaker. "Hello, Paulie. Yes, I can hear you."

"Good morning, Fanny," replied a familiar voice.

"Oh, Lieutenant. What a surprise. Paulie, let him in."

Less than a minute later Rory Rawlings was sitting down in their kitchen, accepting a cup of ancient, warmed-up coffee fresh from the microwave. "New doors," he said, blowing across the brown liquid. "Paulie says they're top of the line."

"Insurance is paying for them," said Fanny. "And as long as we're in the murder business, we thought we might as well add a video system."

"Mom's kidding."

Rawlings sipped and grimaced, then smiled. "No need to apologize. In fact, that's why I'm here, to bring you up to date on the murder business."

Fanny had been waiting for this moment. "Did

Maury confess? I knew he would. The man is such a bumbler. Couldn't even do a good kidnapping."

"After five hours of interrogation, with a lawyer present, yes, he confessed. We may have implied a few things about the crime scene in India, which the lawyer didn't have the resources to check up on. But we got an ironclad admission to both murders."

"I don't want to tell you your job, but isn't it against the law for cops to lie to a suspect in order to get a confession?" asked Amy.

"Whose side are you on? No, it's not against the law."

"So it's really over?" Amy couldn't quite believe it.

Rawlings nodded. "The DA is arguing with the attorney general's office in India, but in all likelihood we'll get first crack. It's the international concept of finders keepers."

Really over. Amy wasn't sure how she felt. It was what she'd wanted, of course, what everyone had risked their lives for, but . . . "What about his wife, Laila? Have you been in touch with her?"

"We have," said Rawlings. "We told her Mr. Steinberg had to stay in New York for a few days to help the police with their investigation. I believe that's a well-known euphemism for being a suspect. We haven't yet told her about the confession. I thought you should be the first to know."

"Thank you," said Amy. "If you don't mind, I'd like to be with you when you make that call. Laila and Maury have a rocky marriage, but I don't think it would be easy for any woman to hear that kind of news about her husband."

"No problem." Rawlings took another sip of the

coffee and seemed to be getting used to the taste. "I have to say, I was pretty livid after our little excursion, until Marcus sent me that text. I was just sitting down with a cold beer, complaining to my wife about these goddamn amateurs. **Emergency. Marry kidnapped funny.** Being a police professional with some knowledge of AutoCorrect, it took me just a few seconds to figure it out."

The lieutenant sat at the kitchen table for ten more minutes, chatting easily about AutoCorrect and families and gardens, and finally exchanging his coffee for a tall glass of ice water.

He wasn't such a bad guy, Amy concluded reluctantly as she stood to shake his hand and as Fanny gave a hearty hug good-bye to the man who had put her in jail. Not that they would ever need to deal with him again, Amy thought. Most people went through an entire lifetime without ever having to deal with a homicide detective.

By 12:15 p.m., Amy and Fanny were walking out the new front door themselves, inspecting Paulie's workmanship along the way. By 12:30, they were sitting down at the Cindilu Dairy, a neighborhood institution with weathered shingles, cats lounging in the window, and the best blueberry muffins in Greenwich Village.

Of the three messages left on Amy's voice mail last night, two had been from Barbara Corns, asking to get together sometime soon. Amy had called her this morning and had arranged for a quick lunch.

Barbara had never heard of the Cindilu. Few people outside the West Village had. But the modest eatery had been Amy's second home since childhood. It was a safe haven, perhaps not the perfect place to sit down with the widow of one of her clients, but better than any alternatives she could think of. Amy had brought along her mother for backup.

Barbara was in a back booth, the same one where Amy and her first real boyfriend had carved their initials in the tabletop fifteen years ago. Fanny slid in beside the waiting woman, just like an old friend.

"I'm so glad you came," said Barbara, more to the mother than the daughter. Amy had long ago ceased to be amazed at Fanny's gravitational pull.

The Abels had agreed not to bring up their late-night adventures. At some point everyone on the tour would find out about Maury Steinberg's arrest. When that happened, they would pretend to be as clueless and as astonished as the others.

"How is the music box, dear?" asked Fanny, with a squeeze of Barbara's hand. "It must be comforting, having it back."

"Yes," said Barbara. "It was a lifesaver. Emotionally, I mean. Evan always regretted that we gave it away."

"Has there been any news?" asked Amy. "About Evan?" She felt she had to ask.

Barbara waited until Lou Halpern, the establishment's co-owner, the "lu" of Cindilu, delivered the menus and glasses of water and walked away. Lou was an old friend, but he had a sixth sense about when to speak up and when to shut up. And there was something about the Abel women and their solemn-looking guest. . . .

"As a matter of fact," Barbara whispered as Lou vanished into the kitchen. "Almost all of yesterday I was going back and forth with the National Park Service and the Hawaii Police." Taking a deep breath, she turned over the smartphone lying facedown on the wooden table, next to her menu. She pressed the screen a few times, used her fingers to enlarge whatever she'd just called up, and passed the phone across to Amy.

It was a photo of a dark brown object, almost completely burned. But judging from the general shape . . . a shoe, perhaps? A man's shoe? It was on a metal table, posing ominously under the glare of operating room–quality lights. Amy had never paid much attention to Evan Corns's choices in footwear, but . . .

"Where did they find it?" she asked.

"Some student researchers from some organization . . . the Volcano Observatory, I think." Barbara spoke calmly, enunciating each word, doing her best to keep her feelings in check. "They were collecting samples from inside the lip of the crater. Rappelling on ropes, something like rappelling. I'm fuzzy on the details. My mind at that moment . . . You can imagine."

"A burned shoe," said Fanny, with a reassuring shrug. "So what? I lose shoes all the time. That doesn't mean there was a foot in it."

"There was a foot in it," said Barbara, enunciating even more. "At least part of a foot. They ran the DNA from that sample they took from Evan's toothbrush." Her expression finished the rest of the thought.

"Oh, Barbara," Amy whispered. "I'm so sorry."

"Oh, no. It's good. It's good to have some confirmation. Better than not." She let out a little burp of a sad chuckle, then covered her mouth. "You're the first people I've told. When I break it to Evan's family, it'll become all too real. Too final. I think I'm going to miss having the hope."

Mother and daughter nodded in unison. "At least you know he didn't run away," said Fanny, which seemed to Amy to be an odd thing to point out, rather insensitive, but hardly atypical for her mother.

"Yes, I have that," said Barbara, taking no offense whatsoever. "And it wasn't suicide, thank God. That's what the forensic investigators told me. The scuff marks. Their photos of the rock slide. The placement and calculating the distance. I don't know how they would know, but they're calling it accidental."

"Suicide would have been so much worse," Fanny said. "Especially since there was no reason for him to commit suicide now—now that everything is working out. That would have been pointless. Such a waste."

"Suicide is usually pointless," said Amy.

"Yes, it is working out," said Barbara, responding to Fanny and ignoring Amy. "And I'm so grateful to you."

"Grateful for what?" Amy looked back and forth, from her mother's face to Barbara's, then back to her mother's. "What aren't you telling me?"

"Nothing," Fanny said, perhaps a little too quickly.

"I mean, you've both been so nice to me," explained Barbara, "throughout this whole ordeal."

"That's not what you meant." The only thing Amy could guess was that Barbara's gratitude had something to do with Paisley MacGregor's apartment and the few minutes when Barbara and her mother had been alone together, before she'd walked in. Just a few minutes, and yet . . .

"Mother?" No response from anyone. "I'm never going to get the whole story, am I?"

"No dear." Fanny and her newfound conspirator exchanged quick glances. "I don't think you ever will."

CHAPTER 45

"**W**as it something in the music box?"

"Better you don't know. For your own good."

"Mother, you're not the CIA. Was it illegal? Is that why you won't tell me?"

"Just a smidge."

"How big a smidge?"

"If this was Twenty Questions, your turn would be over."

They'd been on this topic ever since they said good-bye to Barbara and walked out of the Cindilu. Now they were three blocks away and arriving at their new front door. Fanny pulled an envelope of keys out of her purse and handed a set to her daughter.

"That's the outside key, the vestibule key, my front door, your front door. Don't go handing out any copies to killers, okay?"

"I didn't hand out copies to a killer," said Amy.

"I didn't say you did. Just don't. No one needs a key but us."

They both tried their keys on the front door and the vestibule door. The fits were perfect, snug and exact. Once inside, Amy fingered the key for her mother's door, but it was already unlocked and open.

Fanny saw her reaction and waved it away. "Oh, don't worry. It's just Marcus. Marcus!" she called into the darkened house. "Yoo-hoo."

"You gave him a key? Already? I thought it was just us."

"And he's one of us. Get that look off your face."

"Fanny?" It was Marcus's voice. "Hello. I'm back here."

They found him in the kitchen, sitting at Amy's end of the table, continuing to work on the piles of neglected mail.

"What are you doing?" Amy was annoyed. "I had a system."

"I'm not interfering with your system, just trying to help." He puckered and leaned up. Amy leaned down, meeting his lips more than halfway. "Did you read any of these letters from TravelWeb.com?"

"I hadn't gotten that deep. Mom?"

Fanny shrugged her stubby shoulders. "Anything that looked legal or official, I threw in the drawer. TravelWeb?" She took one of the letters from Marcus. "I got a ton of e-mails from them, too. They're just trying to sell me ad space. We don't have the money to buy ad space."

"Actually," said Marcus, "I think they're trying to buy ad space from you."

"From me?"

"That's what it seems like. Do you carry any ads on TrippyGirl?"

"I don't think so," said Fanny. "It's just a blog that clicks through to our Web site."

"Can you do me a favor?" asked Marcus. He got up and pulled out the chair in front of Fanny's laptop. "Can you go to your blog's management page and check exactly how many followers you have?"

"I don't know offhand," said Fanny as she lowered herself into the kitchen chair and nudged her machine out of hibernation. "All I know is they're very insistent and chatty, which I don't have the time or the inclination to deal with. I suppose if I was nicer and encouraged them, I'd have more fans. But to be honest, I'm not sure what it gets me, except a little traffic going to Amy's Travel." A few more screens flipped by. "Oh, here's the number." Her drawn-on eyebrows furrowed together. "Hmm, not as much as I thought." She gave up trying to find her reading glasses and just squinted. "Five hundred and eighty-nine views of yesterday's post. A small but loyal following."

Marcus leaned in over her shoulder. "Five hundred and eighty-nine thousand."

"What? Are you serious?" Amy was peering at the screen herself now, hovering over Fanny's other shoulder. "I had no idea." The comma and three zeros were clearly visible on the counter. "Mother?"

"Well, that's more like it," said Fanny, sitting up a little straighter in her chair. "Half a million? Half a million is pretty good, no?"

"With no publicity or support or tie-ins?" Marcus had to laugh. "Yes, I think that's very good."

Amy was not looking forward to her meeting with Peter Borg. Any kind of confrontation was unsettling for her, even though she knew it was often a good thing. Today's confrontation, for instance, could be a very good thing, the two of them going over the details of his proposed buyout of Amy's Travel. A good confrontation and a memorable moment in her life. It was certainly a necessary moment.

Taking the subway was not an exact science, Amy found. On this occasion, the F train pulled into the West Fourth Street station just as she was coming down the stairs to the platform. It deposited her at the Sixty-Third and Lexington stop in what seemed like record time. Eleven ten, according to her phone. Even with dawdling, she would be early for the eleven-thirty meeting, which Peter was probably hoping would spill over into a romantic lunch at an expensive bistro, something she was determined would not happen. Not today.

When Amy rounded the corner onto Sixty-Fourth, she was surprised to see Peter out on the curb in front of his polished storefront, hand raised as he tried to hail a cab. It wasn't for him, she noted. It was for Herb Sands and David Pepper. The Pepper-Sands were a yard or so behind him on the sidewalk, in the midst of some sort of heated domestic tussle.

Amy ducked into the entryway shelter of the flower boutique on the corner and turned her back. Using the angled window as a makeshift mirror, she waited until a taxi slowed and stopped and the Pepper-Sands were safely inside the vehicle, before venturing back out onto the sidewalk. Peter saw her a few seconds later, and his expression turned from harried to happy.

"You're early," he said, making it sound not like an accusation but like she'd just given him a present.

"I warned you about the Pepper-Sands," she said, crinkling her mouth.

"No you didn't. You, in fact, encouraged me." He leaned forward into an air-kiss, aimed first at one cheek, then the other. "We should get this merger done ASAP. Then I can turn their whole gala anniversary excursion over to you."

"You try that, and it's a deal breaker," said Amy. "I'll write it into our contract."

"They have me doing their invitations," moaned Peter. "They wanted them to be handwritten in gold ink on black envelopes. But I checked with the post office, and that's a no-no. Their computerized sorters can't read gold on black. So it's back to the drawing board. Or should I call it the bloody, acrimonious, name-calling fight board?"

"And that's just the invitations."

"Exactly."

The two travel agents continued their banter back into the airy confines of Peter Borg Travel. Peter led the way past Claire, his young, smiling, and imposingly perfect assistant, and back into his private office. Amy wondered if she could somehow get a young, smiling, and imposingly perfect male assistant for her own storefront. *Instead of Fanny? Hmm. That would take some doing.*

"Here it is." Peter was pointing to his mahogany desktop and the two manila folders, the one centered in front of his chair and the other in front of the client chair, both chairs in brown leather. He pulled out the client chair, and Amy accepted. "We'll go through the details as much as you want. But, of course, you should have your own lawyer look things over. I want you to be comfortable with this, Amy. I really do." His sincerity seemed genuine, which Amy found more than slightly annoying.

The document in Amy's folder looked tightly spaced, with small print. Fairly daunting, although it was probably less than twenty pages long. She had been prepared to go through it line by line with Peter, saving her question, her big question, for the appropriate moment. But suddenly she felt she didn't have the heart or the patience. She barely waited until Peter had settled in and opened his own folder.

"Is TrippyGirl part of the deal? The reason I'm asking . . ." She rolled her eyes. "Mom says she's getting tired of it, so I'm thinking we may just discontinue. There doesn't seem to be much point."

Peter frowned. "Oh, that's too bad. I love Trippy-Girl."

Amy adopted a helpless smile. "You know Mom. A woman of enthusiasms. Once her enthusiasm cools . . ."

"Are you sure? You should talk to her. Seriously. I think the fans . . ." Peter stopped and took a breath. "I mean, it doesn't completely fit the Peter Borg image, but with some work, we can totally make TrippyGirl a part of the brand. Let's keep it in there for now."

"Even if Mom doesn't want to write it?"

"Well, we can't force her, I suppose." He said this with some reluctance. "But if worse comes to worst, we'll hire a ghostwriter. Continue with the TrippyGirl style, which, like your lovely mother, is totally unique. After all, TrippyGirl is part of your company, and we're merging. Right?"

"Peter, it's just a blog."

"I know, but I'm going to have to insist."

"Insist?"

"Yes." His gaze was level and serious. "We need to merge everything, even her little blog."

"So that's it." Amy pulled her lips tight and nodded slowly. "Marcus was right. It's all about Trippy-Girl, isn't it?"

Peter cocked his head, all innocence. "I don't know what you mean."

"Marcus kept saying there had to be something else, something other than my business sense and incredible good looks."

"You're an incredible-looking woman." Peter extended a hand across his desk. Amy didn't move. "Don't be like that. We'll make a great team, you and me. And let's face it. You need me."

"No, I don't," she countered, keeping her voice low and calm. "The online travel segment is huge. Businesses are looking for all kinds of click-throughs and Facebook content. Not to mention ads. Trippy-Girl has six hundred thousand fans without even trying, all word of mouth. Did you know that? Of course you did. Marcus and I made a few calls, one of them to a literary agent who's been trying to get in touch with us for two weeks. Fanny could have a book deal."

"I thought she was tired of writing."

"Peter!"

"What?"

"You knew it all the time. All the time I thought you were after me, you were really after my mother. It would be funny if it weren't quite so weird."

"No," he protested, then leaned forward, doubling down on his sincerity. "The merger was Fanny's idea. She approached me, right here in this office. It was a chance for us to work together. I love working with you. Sure, I did a little independent checking. I'd be stupid not to."

"And when were you going to tell me we were sitting on a gold mine?"

"I wouldn't call it a gold mine. Maybe silver. I figured you already knew." He tried staring her down but gave in first. "Okay, that's a lie. In my defense, I do think I valued it fairly."

"Then why didn't you tell me? You were prepared to let me sign away my company without letting me know about our biggest asset."

"I wasn't going to cheat you. We can still work together. You keep your name on the downtown office. Amy's Travel." He punctuated the name with air quotes. "I know how important that is."

She had expected this moment to be more satisfying. To confront the great Peter Borg, to let him know that she was on to him, and that no, she would not be signing any papers. She could, in fact, succeed on her own.

Ms. Amy Abel would not be joining forces with anyone—except her unpredictable and interfering mother and maybe her boyfriend, the one she actually respected, despite everything, and who was definitely not and would never be Peter Borg. . . . But when the moment came, it wasn't very satisfying at all.

No matter what Fanny and Marcus thought, Peter was not a bad guy. He had taken her around the world and had let her make a few bucks. He had let himself be dragged into a forest above the Taj Mahal to discover a bloody corpse, and while he hadn't exactly proven himself to be Superman, at least he hadn't gone screaming for the hills.

At the end of their meeting, they stepped around

the mahogany desk, hugged awkwardly, and thanked each other for the memories. Peter hoped they would be seeing each other soon, and Amy didn't contradict him.

On her way back to her own office, Amy opted for the M2 bus instead of the subway. She managed to find an empty window seat toward the back and spent the long, slow trip downtown staring out at the maddening Fifth Avenue traffic and wondering what TrippyGirl would have done in her place. How would her mother's creation—that mythical, intrepid, adventure-loving explorer—have handled the situation? Not just here and now with Peter, but with everything? This brave, thrill-seeking avatar, which her mother obviously wanted her to be, instead of an indecisive girl who would prefer to ignore the world and pull the covers up over her head . . . what would she have done?

By the time Amy got off the bus on Eighth Street and started walking south toward Washington Square Park, she had her answer. TrippyGirl might have jumped a little faster into life, she thought. Trippy might not have second-guessed herself at every bend of the road. She might have shown a little more enthusiasm all along the way.

But she would have done exactly the same.

Turn the page for a preview of the
next Amy's Travel Mystery,
MURDER ON THE PATAGONIAN EXPRESS

PROLOGUE

TrippyGirl was not prepared to die in Patagonia.
The first fall had broken my left leg. The second fall wasn't technically a fall. It was a deliberate, painful jump from the cliff onto my saddle, which Milly, the horse underneath the saddle, didn't seem to appreciate. As I lay on the hard, dusty ground and touched my side, I could feel the freshly broken ribs from where Milly had landed a kick right before abandoning me here on the windy, arid plain. Enough adrenaline was coursing through my system, keeping much of the agony at bay. But it would come. The worst pain I felt at the moment, more than from the ribs and the broken leg, was from looking at my black Lafonts, my favorite frames, which had been all but destroyed in my attempt to escape this cold-blooded killer.

Fanny pushed herself back from the keyboard, picked up the earthenware gourd, and sipped through the metallic straw. She refused to acknowledge the presence of the woman right behind her, who was reading over her shoulder.

"Mom, that's not how it happened."

Fanny mashed the herbal mixture, took one more sip, then turned to face her. "Your leg is in a cast," she said, pointing to the cast. "You have two broken ribs. Your left eye is all black. You have more cuts and scrapes than a creature in a horror film. . . ."

Amy's hand went to her face. "Is it that bad?"

"Not quite. The sunburn gives you a nice healthy glow. But . . ." She pointed to a pair of black Lafont frames on the kitchen counter, the two sides loosely held together with electrical tape. "Those *were* your favorite glasses, if I'm not mistaken."

"Yes, but I can get them repaired."

"Okay, I'll change it. Not destroyed."

"That's not what I meant. Everything you write is an exaggeration."

"Excuse me for trying to liven up the truth."

"It doesn't need livening up."

An impartial observer, someone just walking into the living room of the Greenwich Village town house, would probably have sided with the younger Ms. Abel. Amy was in her early thirties; relatively tall at five-ten; with brown, shoulder-length hair; brown eyes; and pleasant, unremarkable features. She was indeed decked out in a leg cast, with bandages holding her ribs in place, and various bruises decorating the rest of her body, including a sunburned face. The truth, whatever it was, probably didn't need livening up.

Her mother's appearance was tamer by comparison. Fanny was a good eight inches shorter than Amy, shaped like a curvy fireplug crowned in a henna-dyed pageboy. At the moment, the pageboy was covered by a Peruvian wool cap with a red pompom on top and a silver Batman insignia, like a mirror, adorning the front.

"Everything needs livening up," said Fanny. And she punctuated this statement with a long slurp from the earthenware gourd.

CHAPTER 1

Two months earlier . . .

Amy gazed out at the lazy, uncommitted snow-flakes, then reluctantly returned her focus to the overheated confines of the Village Gastropub.

For as long as she could remember, since her kindergarten days, when she'd first learned to order from a menu, this space had belonged to Tony & Bill's, a dusty Italian eatery revered for its unchallenging menu and unchanging prices. Now it had been turned into a trendy, faux casual café, with burnished redbrick walls and a polished bar and featuring Kobe beef burgers and white truffle mac and cheese.

She was sitting alone at a window table for three—not physically alone, since her mother was seated just opposite her. But for all practical purposes. "You're like a teenager," she complained and got no reaction. "Hello?"

Fanny readjusted her reading glasses but did not

look up from her phone. "Just doing some tweeting. My public expects it of me."

"Since when do you have a public?"

"Aren't you being a tad jealous of Trippy? You
shouldn't. I love both my girls equally."

It was a joke. But Amy couldn't help seeing the
truth underneath.

She had never been impetuous, unlike Trippy.
She had always thought too much about what could
go wrong. She had just begun to overcome this
trait, one that she'd inherited from her calm and
passive father, when the violent death of her fiancé,
Eddie, plunged her back into her quiet, unadven-
turous existence.

This had been three years ago, and Fanny had
tried everything to bring her daughter back into
the world of the living. The eventual solution was to
start a business together, a travel agency focusing on
exotic, action-filled vacations. Amy would be forced
to face people and problems again and would be rewarded by going around the world. Travel had been
her and Eddie's mutual passion. And Amy's Travel,
a cute little storefront on Hudson Street, was
founded as a living tribute to their life together, the
life they'd almost had together.

In retrospect, it wasn't the best business plan.
The Internet had nearly destroyed the brick-and-
mortar agencies. And the fact that Amy's Travel pe-
riodically showed up in the news in conjunction
with murders and arrests worldwide didn't make
things any easier.

The saving grace had turned out to be *TrippyGirl*,
a modest blog that Fanny had come up with on her
own, featuring the fun-loving, carefree girl that Amy
wasn't. Almost without knowing it, the Abels had a

viral smash, allowing them to sell ad space and drive traffic to a myriad of other travel sites. In some ways, Trippy had become an alter ego, the fearless daughter that Fanny could approve of without hesitation. Without the daily fights over everything that actual mothers and daughters fought about.

Fanny returned to her tweets, thumbs flying. Amy retaliated by taking out her own phone and pressing the Facebook icon. She scrolled down through the array of cat videos and political calls to action and selfies featuring people she barely knew. "Oh, my!" she exclaimed a few seconds later. Her tone was shocked and sad and genuine enough to make Fanny look up.

"Oh, your what?"

"You remember Danny D'Angelo from high school?"

"Of course. Danny Angel. You had a crush on him."

"No, Mother, you had a crush on him."

"Well, the boy was adorable, and he knew it. A very high opinion of himself. What's he doing? Starring in a movie?"

"Danny D'Angelo died," Amy said, scrolling farther, trying to piece together more information from the Facebook comment section.

"Oh, that's horrible," said Fanny, hand to her heart. "The poor family."

"He was on a vacation somewhere." Amy read the next part twice and even then paused before saying it. "Apparently, Danny was killed by a mirror."

"By a mirror? That's ironic. Mirrors were always his friends."

"Must be an AutoCorrect error."

"Did he like younger women? Maybe he was killed by a minor."

Amy was still scrolling when the last person in their party arrived. "Sorry I'm late," she said. "So great to finally meet you." What looked like a sixteen-year-old girl stood there, smiling anxiously as she whipped off her plaid Eskimo parka and her knit winter cap. She was dark and short, rather waiflike, with curly hair and shining teeth that seemed a size too big.

"Great to finally meet you," echoed Amy. Both Abels rose for the obligatory hugs and air kisses and general assurances that everyone looked wonderful. During all of this, Amy slipped her phone off the table and glared until Fanny did the same with hers.

It was odd that they'd never met Sabrina before. But that was the way it was. You could communicate a dozen times a day, gush over their children or fiancés, and donate money to their next 5K run without ever physically meeting. You could find out how they reacted to a midnight e-mail sent after you'd had one too many glasses of chardonnay. As far as Amy had been able to tell, Sabrina Marx was quite a nice person—energetic, personable, willing to share, even by Fanny's intrusive standards. But, surprisingly, just a kid.

Book editors were getting younger, Amy knew, a result of low pay and the changing dynamics of publishing. But still. It was hard to look at this youngster and not ask what subject she was majoring in.

"Banyan Press is so excited about *TrippyGirl's World*," Sabrina assured them. "We've got contracts lined up with Audible and the Literary Guild. We even have some top-notch travel writers wanting to review it. The crossover potential is going to be super."

"Real travel writers?" Amy asked, trying to sound more excited than frightened at the prospect.

"For real. Todd Drucker from *TD Travel*."

"You mean the magazine's owner and editor? That Todd Drucker?" Amy knew of him, of course. This was the man who had, in the past decade, taken the world of travel writing up a good five notches, the single biggest force in making exotic travel part of the mainstream. And, according to all reports, not a very nice or forgiving guy.

Sabrina grinned at her coup. "Uh-huh. As soon as we did our first press release, he was all over us about a review copy." She dumped her coat into a nearby chair, settled in, and raised a hand to catch the waiter's eye.

"Imagine that," Fanny gushed. "A big-time writer reviewing a book made of my little blogs."

The personal pronoun (singular) hung in the air as their waiter stepped up, introduced himself (Bradley), and took their orders for three iced teas, passion fruit and mango. Amy tried to secure a plain iced tea, but passion fruit and mango was as close as the Village Gastropub was willing to go.

Last year, when the publishers first started calling, Amy had emphasized that the *TrippyGirl* blogs were a collaboration, with her mother taking Amy's real-life escapades and embellishing them. They had labeled the work faction, like a nonfiction novel, which in hindsight was probably being generous. For example, the blogs about the Taj Majal murder were largely true, while the ones sent from the Trans-Siberian Express were entirely made up. The editors had to understand that TrippyGirl was not Amy Abel, and this was not a memoir. After hearing this disclaimer, several publishers had lost interest, but not Banyan. Or maybe Banyan just hadn't wanted to hear. All they'd heard was that Amy and Fanny had a blog with an avid readership of over a million and growing.

Sabrina waited until the waiter had recited the lunch specials and retreated. "You write the blogs together?" she said, phrasing it as a question.

"Of course," said Fanny.

"Actually, no," Amy said, clarifying. "I read the drafts and make suggestions, but Mom does the writing. It's her style that everybody loves."

"I understand," said Sabrina in a tone that said she didn't. "But photos of you are on the site, Amy. That leads people to believe you're at least a coauthor."

"But I'm not TrippyGirl. No one is."

"I understand," Sabrina repeated. "But when you post a photo of yourself on a train in the snow . . ."

"That was a PATH train in New Jersey during that December blizzard."

"That was some blizzard," Fanny recalled. "I couldn't get out of the house."

"But you used it to illustrate a blog set in Siberia, if I'm not mistaken." Sabrina stopped a moment to think. "Why didn't you use a photo from your trip to Siberia?"

"Her camera was stolen," said Fanny.

"I was never in Siberia," Amy said, clarifying some more. "That part of the book is more fiction than the rest. Again, we don't claim that the blog is real, and everyone seems fine with it."

"I understand, too. But when you show yourself in these settings, that's what people imagine. What I imagine. No one wants to find out that Trippy is—

no offense—some older, stay-at-home mom who's making it all up. That's not your image."

"Ooh, boy," muttered Amy.

Sabrina must have heard. "No offense," she repeated with an anxious smile. "I mean, if it was Amy exaggerating the facts . . . well, that's one thing. Kind of an irreverent, young thing."

"Upper end of young," Fanny pointed out.

"And," continued Sabrina, "Amy is this world traveler who's known for getting into weird scrapes."

"Right. So what am I?" demanded Fanny. She kept her gaze steady, straight in the eyes, and her voice low. "Some troll under a bridge? Some deformed, old Rumplestiltskin who sits in a dark corner and spins the worthless straw into gold?"

"No, no, no." The editor almost physically backtracked, holding out her hands as if to brake Fanny's momentum. "I'm so sorry. Please. Fanny, you're wonderful. I love your style. And you're not a rumple . . . whatever." She made a helpless, childlike face. "What is that, exactly?"

"Rumplestiltskin?" Amy couldn't believe it. "A fairy-tale character. You never heard of Rumplestiltskin?"

"I don't see many Disney movies," Sabrina admitted.

"Not all fairy tales are made into Disney movies," Amy said. "Didn't your parents ever read to you?"

"Not about Rumplestiltskins."

"It's a classic. How could you not know . . ."

"I think you're missing the bigger picture," snarled Fanny through clenched teeth. "The bigger picture is that you're embarrassed by me, aren't you? You are. I'm the real TrippyGirl, and my own editor is embarrassed."

"Amy and I are not embarrassed," pleaded Sabrina. "But public perception is everything."

"I'm not embarrassed at all," said Amy. Sabrina didn't have to go home and live with this. "Let's change the subject, okay?"

Somehow, they made their way through their hour plus at the gastropub intact. Amy, Fanny, and Sabrina all managed to call a truce and order their salads from Bradley. Like a mother at a bedside, Fanny informed their child editor of the whole *Rumplestiltskin* fable, and they all could agree that (a) the king was a jerk for wanting a wife who could spin straw into gold, (b) the peasant girl was irresponsible for agreeing to give up her firstborn child to some trollish dwarf named Rumplestiltskin, and (c) being saddled with that last name alone would wreak havoc on any child's self-esteem, not to mention being given up by your mother and raised by a dwarf in a cave, which luckily never happened. And if the peasant girl hadn't lucked out and guessed the dwarf's name, how the hell was she planning to explain the whole thing to the baby's father, the king? All in all, a very unsatisfying, un-Disney tale.

The lazy snowflakes had stopped by the time mother and daughter stepped out onto Bank Street and headed toward the Barrow Street house. Neither said anything during the six-block walk, and Fanny did not do any *TrippyGirl* tweeting along the way, which was probably a good idea, Amy thought, given her almost combustible state of mind.

Their silence lasted until they got into their separate apartments, Fanny on the lower two floors of the Abel brownstone and Amy on the upper two. Amy went immediately to her greenhouse office on the top floor rear and brought her computer out of its sleep mode. A few minutes later she came down the three flights and found her mother in the rear garden, in a corner next to the wall, out of sight of the upper-floor windows.

"I'm not even going to mention the fact that you're smoking."

"Too late," said Fanny. She took one long, last inhalation, then dropped her stub onto the gray slate tile and ground it under her heel. "The dwarf in the dark corner smokes. What can I say?"

Amy took a deep, sighing breath. The smoking argument could be left for another day. "Mom, you know I'm on your side. You created Trippy. She's you."

Fanny blew out the smoke in an even stream. "The me I wanted to be forty years ago maybe, before I settled into being this old stay-at-home mom. Not that I'm blaming you for putting me in that position."

Amy lowered herself onto one of the metal garden chairs. It was still wet from the melted snow, but she hardly noticed. "First of all, what does Sabrina know? She's a teenager. And second, that's still you. I don't joyfully run into the face of danger, not on purpose. But Sabrina was right. We do have to start being careful about Trippy. That's what she meant."

"I know what she meant," said Fanny. "Your adventures are exaggerated and fun. Mine are made up and desperate and sad."

"Now you're being maudlin."

"Desperate and sad and maudlin, right." She tapped her skull. "Duh. How could I have left out maudlin?"

"Okay. Changing the subject now." Amy stood, the wet chair finally beginning to annoy her.

"That's right. Change the subject."

"I'll do my best." She paused dramatically. "I found out how Danny D'Angelo died."

"Oh?" Despite herself, Fanny was curious. "Was it a full-length mirror? They can be dangerous."

"Apparently, he was on a motor scooter in Old San Juan, in Puerto Rico."

"Was he checking his hair in the rearview mirror? Because you have a tendency to do that, too."

"No. He was riding down a very narrow street, trying to pass a bus. He got clipped by the bus's rearview mirror and landed on his head on the cobblestones."

"Poor Danny." Fanny stared off into the distance as the news of the tragic, random accident slowly sank in. Then she brightened. "You know, I think I can use this. Change Danny's name and make him Trippy's old high school flame." Her excitement grew as she spoke. "He's riding down an old narrow street, on his way to see her for the first time since graduation. Meanwhile, Trippy's in that same fateful bus, looking casually in the rearview mirror, when she sees Danny in the mirror. Her heart leaps. Danny! He comes closer and closer to the mirror. And then *bam* . . . What a scene! Is that near enough to the truth for you?"

Amy didn't know what to say. "Fine."